# A VILLAGE UNDER
# THE STREETLIGHT

# A Village Under the Streetlight

A novel
by

## THOMAS PALAYOOR

Adelaide Books
New York/Lisbon
2020

A VILLAGE UNDER THE STREETLIGHT
A novel
By Thomas Palayoor

Copyright © by Thomas Palayoor
Cover design © 2020 Adelaide Books

Published by Adelaide Books, New York / Lisbon
adelaidebooks.org

Editor-in-Chief
Stevan V. Nikolic

For any information, please address Adelaide Books
at info@adelaidebooks.org
or write to:
Adelaide Books
244 Fifth Ave. Suite D27
New York, NY, 10001

ISBN-10: 1-949180-39-5
ISBN-13: 978-1-949180-39-8

Printed in the United States of America

*My parents, Devassykutty and Kunjamma Palayoor.*

*Sanjeewani.*

*Vinoo.*

# Contents

# Introduction

Dr. Harte Weiner Ph.D. (Stanford)
Formerly, Department of English
Harvard University.

This rich, first novel by Thomas Palayoor takes place over the course of several generations, during which the world and the village in the title change cataclysmically. These changes are, however, cumulative. They emanate from a small set of characters who make their appearance early on. Identified and characterized by custom of the day, this handful of villagers and their neighbors—who appear at first glance to occupy recognizable types—move inexorably (if not in unison) toward the complexities and contradictions of modernity.

Yet, an unthinkable, stumbled upon phenomenon at the Streetlight almost immediately signals the onslaught of the new. This one event importunes a whole array of changes; many are at first gradual, involving accommodation but not really challenging the village fabric. For a time, changes are mentioned by the narrator almost in asides. Despite this, small offshoots come to portend a trend. Moreover, not infrequently as the novel moves in a forward direction, a seemingly large number of aberrant instances from the past are, likewise re-

vealed. As readers, we find ourselves in the company of characters only vaguely aware, from their small perch, of the departure of the colonizing British, and of the forces of change
and conflict larger than any one village—grand collisions of
philosophies, religions, ethnicities, and ambitions. Palayoor's
narrator contributes by filling in stories from characters' pasts
that contradict who they appear to be when first encountered.
At long last, perhaps three fourths of the way into the tale of
interacting lives and places within the greater village life, when
aberrations seem to overwhelm the number of givens, some of
those whose lives are poised to change dramatically join this
or that countervailing movement from within, even as historical forces press in from without. Colonial rule, leaving an
indelible mark on a Village and its inhabitants, sets the stage
for India's ensuing partition. When the colonial British depart,
the privileged classes succor within themselves a deep memory
of cultural icons the likes of Shakespeare; furthermore, as we
are to learn, changes that the West leaves by no means stop
here. Meanwhile, the historical linchpins of the era, include
waves of migrants headed off, now in the grasp of world-his-
torical mechanisms, grand collisions of philosophies, religions,
races, and peoples.

What had begun on village terms as predominantly gen-
erational rifts within families about the place of women in
society, or the obligations of sons, progresses into the great
events reconstituting the world's stage. Thus, what happens
within this or that family, infidelities and resulting insanity
of the jilted; women off to work, men disappearing on longer
and longer ventures before returning; strangers showing up,
staples changing jobs, the fading of the old community customs or their expansion to include far flung and seemingly
contradictory elements—all allude to the widening gyre–towards what ultimate vision no one particularly knows. Since a

certain amount of information is only as good as the one who recounts it, this novel's presiding narration exemplifies it.

It has been expressed that each character's past is as dogged as his shadow. Stories retrieved from the past, relevant to a given incident or character, abound. Curiously, these sometimes accompany or appear shortly after the relevant event in the characters' life or the villages', and at other times, so much later on that they cause us to completely rethink much of what we've read in a new light. Time is a toy of sorts in the narrator's hands—this he is aware of, but does immediately divulge everything. In so doing, this author's proxy withholds information, at key instances, not only from us but from characters themselves, who are left to learn their own histories after a great deal of time passes, here and there, from another who appears on the stage. Storytelling is a deliciously favored means of conveying biographical information. Almost never merely summarized, new information about the past of a certain character very often involves a scene until itself, with its own set of characters who have played a part in the forming the former of a character first met as an adult. Often flashbacks occur when the narrator, relating a current story, wishes to disclose its relevant origins—whether based in the terms of prior relationships or prior happenings. As a result of this delightful narrative bent, we are almost never told, and almost always *see*. The inset stories within this novel often live on in our imaginations, placing an emphasis on them alongside the forward motion.

Since I am a reader acculturated in the West, my first point of reference upon entering this rich tableau was George Eliot's *Middlemarch*. In Eliot's 19th Century British novel of character, manners, and custom. Old paradigms coexist as a new era encroaches. As here, what happens among these occupants of a certain place and time projects well beyond the borders of the book. In such enormously capacious novels, the reader accompanies a period of confusion, marked by the threat and the temptation of the new. Turning points in history affect individuals, and vice versa.

Entering *The Streetlight*, we tread a path toward the village center accompanying a minor character, Kunjayi, who comes upon an accosting spectacle, a beef carcass hangs for sale, although the day is midweek, rather than Sunday—a new butcher set up shop in town. Historically, only one man has sold meat—and his father too before him. News quickly reaches the infuriated Varu, a knife-swinger, who is accompanied by his son, Varunny, and the brother – the novel's enigmatic, central character, Muthoma. As Varu waxes violent, brandishing the tool of his trade, the characteristically passive Muthoma seizes on the chance to emancipate himself from one of the denigrating roles that have been his life's lot, a half-way expelled family member whose nightly embodiment of externality is to bed on the porch hammock. Marked an outsider early, as we are to learn: for Muthoma, grade school was made torturous by his school-mates mocking and the "sadistic" canings by the school master. In significant part, a whiter than normal complexion and plumper shape set up the outsider for his reception. The canings, in turn, foreshadow a scene much later on, during which Muthoma will come to the rescue of a young woman, undergoing the same, sexually-tinged humiliation, a similar form of humility by the very butcher who had become his own boss.

The numerous instances in the course of *A Streetlight* in which Muthoma—fairly inconspicuous otherwise—arrives to save the day, point to his identification with the persecuted, into which category women, and the poor, and the diseased often find themselves. For these acts he seeks neither recognition nor heraldry. Unlike two modern Western paradigms,

Marvel comic heroes and John Wayne, this character arrives and vanishes quietly. At a time when native customs are falling asunder, and foreign ideologies invade to fight for the soul of India, Muthoma once again dodges the seeking of an historical role. Nonetheless, he is found representing a formidable spirituality opposing the doings of large and small-scale narcissists alike. He arrives at 'the right thing to do' and simply does it, human adjectives like "good" or "unselfish" don't seem to fit either.

In A Streetlight, where the question of ambiguity overhangs both the presents and the past, though, one retrospective anecdote seems bent on exposing the outright unflattering nature of the human condition where material terms are concerned: in this instance, someone from the "untouchable" caste gains the favor of a British official, prostrating himself before the glittering whiteness of the uniformed spectacle, and is at that moment proclaimed a village power, and this position continues to be handed down during the successive decades that the novel covers, such that along the way the 'marrying up' and taking on a class exalted name, the family itself becomes among those in a position to oppress.

By dint of his enduring incorruptibility, alongside his existence as exception to firm, partisan, cultural, national, and gender-bound distinctions, the unlikely Muthoma truly seems to rise above the fray. Who is this mysterious being? Why does he not marry? Why is he considered a safe bet when left with a young woman to chaperon? How does his native passivity give him power? Read the book and find out.

# One

The hamlet of Manoor wakes up late, at its own slow pace. The main thoroughfare running through the village lays desolate, silent; nothing stirs before the early sun is well above the distant hills. Until then, the only movement on the unpaved road could be an occasional stray cat running across and rarely, an emaciated mongrel in hot pursuit. The singular exception was Kunjayi walking to his work. Kunjayi was on the road even before the palms of the coconut trees start glistening in the rays of the rising sun. He used to be the village rickshaw puller. His usual fare was mainly the elderly, heading for the ferry across the shallow river at the end of the road, a short distance away. Often, his passengers were the children of the well-to-do of the village, going to their school run by the nuns. It was a grueling hard work, pulling his rickshaw and its occupants on the uneven road, in torrential rain or under a scorching sun. For some inexplicable reason, however, Kunjayi loved his job. He took enormous pride in reaching his passengers to their destinations in time and alleviating their monotony by engaging them in pleasant and often humorous conversation. Frequently, while galloping with the rickshaw behind him, he had to shout so that his passenger in the canopied seat could hear him. His rates were modest, nonetheless, a steady income for him.

Then, one day, the local government, the Panchayat, declared rickshaw pulling illegal. On the part of the elected officials, it was a courageous and humane act, upholding human dignity. For Kunjayi, nevertheless, it was too hard a blow to bear; he was shut out from the only work he knew. He curled up in his thatched house for weeks on end, dejected and depressed, drinking toddy, the local coconut brew, to bury his pain. His only daughter, Chamy, working as a maidservant at a couple of upper class homes, saved the family from starvation. One morning, as he emerged from the stupor of the previous night's drinking, Kunjayi had a lightening idea: why not seek a job at the ferry. For him, it was a logical thought; with years of experience in rickshaw pulling, Kunjayi considered transportation his forte.

When Kunjayi arrived at the ferry, Lona, the owner and chief oarsman of the ferryboat, was at its helm. With the oar in one hand, he stood there silent and motionless, sniffing the air, taking in the surroundings. Against the sizzling sunny sky and the expanse of calm silvery waves of the river, his dark figure etched a silhouette. The boat, carved out of a log and painted black in tar, was anchored a few feet away from the riverbank, it was swaying gently with the waves of the river. Under Lona's watchful eyes, the passengers were wading through the stretch of shallow water, climbing into the boat, taking care not to get their clothes wet. Kunjayi followed the small stream of passengers to the boat but did not step into it. He stood there in knee-deep water looking at Lona. To answer Lona's stare in askance, Kunjayi asked him:

"Do you need some help with the ferry boat? I am looking for a job."

"Get in and row when the boat is full"

Lona's answer came swiftly in a short sentence. Kunjayi was hired on the spot. Kunjayi and his current circumstances were not unfamiliar to Lona. In the past, many of the riders in his boat were also passengers in Kunjayi's rickshaw. He has seen them alighting from the rickshaw with Kunjayi's help, walking towards the ferry: always a satisfied group of customers. It was only a few weeks since Kunjayi and his rickshaw disappeared from the scene when the Panchayat banned rickshaw pulling.

Rowing was an entirely new line of work for Kunjayi. The first few hours were tough and strenuous; blisters appeared on his palms. In spite of the needling pain on the palms, he struggled on to keep the boat steady and build a rhythm into his rowing. The stern stare and directions from Lona manning the rudder, made him a bit nervous. Nevertheless, by the end of the day, Kunjayi had gained a degree of confidence in his new job and himself.

When Lona handed him the day's wages at the end of the last ferry, Kunjayi was so overjoyed that he did not even bother to count it. He just wanted to get home and share the happiness with Chamy; however, not before having a couple of glasses of fermented coconut sap at the toddy shop on the way. Late in the evening, when he reached home moderately drunk, he had a smile on his lips and two tiny packages in his hand. One of the packages contained soda bicarbonate powder for his stomach ulcer and the other, two **laddoos**[1]. Chamy emerged from the kitchen with a glass of water for mixing the bicarbonate powder in.

"Chamy, I got a job at the ferry."

Kunjayi said while handing the package of laddoo to his daughter.

"Appa, now you don't have to sit at home all day brooding, I wish Amma was here with us."

---

[1] *A sugary sweet*

Chamy said lifting her eyes heavenward.

Rothu, her mama, had passed away after a brief illness when Chamy was only twelve. Though nine years have passed since, Rothu was still a breathing, ever-living presence in Chamy's life. Amma was always with her, she felt; during her loneliness waiting for Kunjayi late in the evenings or while quickening her pace to dodge the hungry eyes of the young street miscreants. For her, it was, a comforting, reassuring thought.

Kunjayi left home for work much before Chamy woke up in the morning. When he is on the lonely road to the ferry, it was still dark, the first sunrays would not hit Manoor for another two hours. Kunjayi wore only a **mundu**[2], a length of white cloth wrapped around the waist, it was folded at the knee and tied again just below the waist according to the local custom. A shirt was not called for, the air was hot and humid in the coastal village even during the early morning hours. He walked, hearing his own footsteps, head bent, shoulders drooping, still self-pitying at having to surrender his old job where he was his own master. It was only at the ferry he emerged from the morning melancholy. He brightened up and energized himself by being with the boat riders, some of them his old customers who exchanged pleasantries with him. Kunjayi returned home every evening with the euphoria of the time spent at the toddy shop, always with the bicarbonate powder, the antidote for the accompanying acidity and the tiny packet of sweets or snacks for Chamy. Every day, as he gave the snacks to her, Kunjayi felt Chamy was still a six-year-old, the capricious and lively girl, snatching the sweets from his hand, climbing on to his lap claiming her rightful perch. With Rothu at the kitchen door, smiling at the father and daughter, the picture was

[2] *It is worn by men and woman, but in different ways.*

alive and complete. Kunjayi loved to retrieve and relive those moments every so often.

It was not yet daybreak, a sultry morning. Kunjayi was on his way to his work at the ferry; still his head bowed, eyes planted on the ground, lifting his head only occasionally. He was not paying much attention to anything around and appeared to be lost in his own thoughts. Kunjayi was approaching a three-way junction on his way to the ferry. The intersection and the roads leading to it appeared desolate, deserted. The singular streetlight of Manoor was at the junction. Though it was lit, the light from the flickering oil lamp was so faint, it hardly illuminated even its immediate surroundings. During the day, the junction was the business hub of Manoor. The villagers shopped there for their daily needs and services. In the afternoons, street vendors on the roadside displayed their wares of fish, vegetables and baskets made of bamboo strips. On either side of the street, there were a few stores; there was a grocery store and a bicycle repair shop almost side by side; the grocery invariably crowded. A short distance down the street was a tea and coffee stall run by Bhanu Nair. The joint came alive at the first rays of dawn. The customers at that hour were Bhanu's regulars coming for their early breakfast of hot *idlis*[3] with coconut chutney and sweet tea. An added attraction for the customers was the three newspapers Bhanu subscribed to. Soon after the breakfast, some of the customers poured over the newspapers while others discussed politics or current happenings at Manoor. Occasionally, the discussions broke into clamorous arguments, turning the tea stall into an island of sound and fury in the morning calm and tranquility of the village. Sitting near the cash box was Bhanu Nair, appearing dispassionate, skillfully moderating the discussions. It seemed

---

[3] *A steamed bread of rice and lentils*

there were no political parties or ideologies he did not like, he just wanted everyone to stay longer, have the good time flow, let second orders for idlis and tea come in steadily. Apart from the daily sales tactics, he held strong political views. At one time, he prompted himself to compete for one of the open seats in the Panchayat committee and to everyone's surprise, won it handily.

The barbershop of the village was only a few feet away from the coffee shop. Kelan, the barber, kept a close watch on the road as he was shearing and clipping his customer's hair; he was watching for women, especially the pretty ones, passing by. The customers on the chair noticed Kelan's eyes, were elsewhere most of the time, and not on their head he was working on. In a mirror in front, they anxiously followed every movement of his scissors with great trepidation. Kelan, nevertheless, was generous to share his roadside observations with his customers, restrained in the chair, unable to make their own surveillance of the road. He gave them an eloquent description of the women that took his fancy, with proper emphasis on their physical plentitudes that titillated and tickled him. The younger clients considered it a welcome bonus from Kelan. When the elderly was in his chair, nonetheless, he kept his street side observations discreetly to himself.

The narrow pathway merging with the main thoroughfare at the junction could hardly be described as a road; rather, it was a ditch running all the way to the seashore through coconut palm groves, bamboo thickets and banana plantations. From the nearby houses nestled among the coconut trees and the majestic jackfruit trees, the passersby on the pathway could hardly be seen, they seemed to sink in the depth of the ditch. So were the occasional elephants being marched for the temple procession on the other side of the village, their voluminous bodies vanishing in the ditch road, only the mahout with their festive headgear was seen at the ground level. From the embankment of the ditch, the village children watched the elephants marching along heavily. For them, it was a thrill to see the mahout at their own eye level. They also avoided looking directly into the elephant's eyes; they have heard many horror stories of those who did.

During the monsoon rains, the ditch was flooded with ankle deep water; children waded through it to their school. For some of them, there were enough on-the-road attractions in the ditch to make them habitually tardy at the school: they were delighted to pursue the darting tadpoles in the water; splash after the tiny silvery fish with a black dot on their heads. During the rainy season, the youngsters excitedly searched the slanting banks of the ditch for something they considered precious: monsoon weeds bearing glittering crystal trinkets on their external roots. They collected those heavy droplets of the weed sap in tiny bottles. When wetted and wiped with the rare collection, their slate boards, they believed, would darken as night, their struggled letters on them shimmer.

Kunjayi walked past the tea stall, dark and silent, its doors closed and its signboard, "Bhanu's Tea Shop" gently moving in the wind. When he was approaching the flickering streetlight at the junction, he was arrested in his path by a peculiar sight: carcass of a freshly butchered bull. Blood still dripping, it was hung from a bamboo beam tied to a coconut tree at one end and a young mango tree at the other. Nobody was around and nothing stirred around the slaughtered animal except the dancing flame of a kerosene lamp on a wooden plank placed just beneath the carcass. Hoisted on the raised ground at the corner of the side road and the main road, the carcass commanded attention from every angle.

Kunjayi was puzzled by what he saw in the auburn light of the kerosene lamp, accentuated by the predawn skylight. He scratched his head wondering who might have killed the bull and selling beef on a Wednesday. Varu was the sole butcher of Manoor, he slaughtered bulls at his shop further down the road, only on Sundays. Varu's Sunday customers were mainly the Christian community of the village. They flocked to the butcher after the Sunday service at the local church, went home with chunks of beef wrapped in teak tree leaves. Served at lunch and dinner, that was the meat for the week at most households, it was mainly fish and vegetables, rest of the week. The Christians were the strict adherents of their distinctive customs and traditions. They claimed to be the descendants of Brahmins chased away, generations ago, from the temple village of Palladi several miles away. Their expulsion and exodus to Manoor were the subjects of folksongs and lore. At dusk, melancholic strains of these songs can be heard from many homes, like a wail wafting into the air. The ballads narrated the story of a foreign sage arriving at the tranquil and Vedic Palladi village of many temples. He came from across the seas along with the Middle Eastern spice traders, their sail ships visiting the ports of Kerala. The religious scholars of the village welcomed and engaged him in several active discourses. However, the high priests were enraged when some of their own deserted them to embrace the foreigner and what he preached. They declared the renegades dead to the community, conducting the rituals for the dead and throwing them out of the village boundaries. Cursed and ostracized, the outcasts moved south seeking friendlier pastures and they found them in Manoor. They flourished through generations and became landowners and prominent citizens of the village. The property where the bull was slaughtered and hung for sale belonged to one of the landlords, Devassy. Being the singular college graduate of Manoor and principal of the local high school, he commanded great respect and adulation among the villagers. Kunjayi wondered if Devassy knew about the butchered animal and who did the killing. He had no doubt, Varu, the butcher, should be informed of his new competition just sprang up at Devassy's compound, mysteriously, overnight. Occasionally on Sundays, Kunjayi helped at Varu's shop, developing a degree of loyalty to the butcher. When he reached Varu's house in the rear of his shop, the butcher was still asleep.

Kunjayi called out from the road. His voice reverberated in the silence of the early morning stillness, but no response, nothing moved. He called out again and again:

"Pooo.....hooo.....eee"

Kunjayi was about to give up and move on when Varu's face showed up faintly, at the only window of his house facing the road.

"Go and see what a curse has come up at the junction" Kunjayi said

"What are you saying? Why don't you say plainly whatever you want to say, Kunjayi"

"Someone is selling beef at Devassy's compound at the junction. The bull is killed and everything ready"

"Who? On a Wednesday?"

"I don't know. You go find out. I am getting late for work"

Gratified he has done his part, Kunjayi walked on.

At the first crack of daylight, Varu woke up his only son, Varunny. He came out to the verandah to wake up his brother, Muthoma. Muthoma was sleeping on the verandah, his body covered head to toe with a sheet, like a corpse, snoring heavily. Varu kicked his brother with his bare foot. Muthoma pushed the sheet off his face with a loud moan, sat up, half-awake. Varu told the men of their early morning mission: find out what heathen has violated the 'slaughter only on Sunday' tradition or rather, who has intruded into his business territory.

They strutted towards the junction: Varu, son and the brother. Varu, salt and pepper hair, thick mustache, slightly protruding front teeth and a six-inch knife dangling from his waist. He was in a checkered *mundu* and a thin folded towel tied around his head. Rarely anyone quarreled or disagreed with Varu; those who did, received a threat from him, stern and startling:

"I will cut your throat, you dirty pig"

For someone who slits the throats of goats, bulls and pigs for a living, it would not be too difficult to extend the routine to the member of another species: people of Manoor had the chilling logic; they were a bit edgy at the butchery. Varunny, far from being an imposing figure, always pumped his chest forward and wore a smile on his lips, scornful and challenging at the same time. Varunny can easily be persuaded to do anything, if one sing praises of his physical prowess; no matter if it was to beat up someone, climb a tree or march in front of a political rally. Muthoma, docile and resigned, always wore only a **mundu**, off white and often not so clean. Unusually fair complexioned, his bare torso and legs were totally hairless. Historians of Manoor assert he had never shaved in his life. On his chin, nearly denuded, there were four or five strands of hair grown long and curled up against his pale skin. His thick lips were crimson, like those of a habitual [4]**pan** eater. Muthoma, however, never ate *pan*. He was busy on Sundays helping his brother at the butcher shop. Rest of the week, he spent on the steps of Bhanu's tea stall, waiting for someone to hire him to do odd jobs.

As the breakfast customers at Bhanu's Tea Stall saw the Varu clan marching menacingly towards the junction, they saw trouble in the horizon. They strained their necks to have a better view and one of them queried:

"What happened, Varu, this early in the morning?"

---

[4] *A mixture of tobacco, lime and cracked areca nuts wrapped in betel leaf.*

"Haven't you heard? Come and see at the junction", boomed Varu.

Whatever Varu is up to can't be pretty, have not been in the past, they mused. No one was inclined to get involved, nonetheless. The breakfasters went back to their *idlis* and chutney. The junction, clad in the pale morning sun, remained still and silent. The dead animal hung at the corner in its nakedness, ready for sale; the kerosene lamp beneath it had been blown off.

"What son of a pig did this on a Wednesday?"

Roared Varu, addressing none in particular, staring at the suspended carcass, his eyes burning.

No one answered.

"Didn't you hear me? Who did this? I want to know" Varu repeated.

Something stirred a few feet behind the carcass. The door of a thatched hut opened. From the darkness of the hut, a pair of piercing eyes of a man crouched on the floor stared at the Varu clan. A total stranger, Varu has never seen him before. He emerged from the hut unhurriedly, straightened and supported himself with a cane. Tall and wiry, he was limping slightly. Hair cropped closely, his face angular, accentuated by a prominent nose and wide lips, thick and sensual. There was something distinctive about his eyes, maybe it was the shimmering whiteness of the white of his eyes, maybe it was the crystalline darkness of his irises. Under his stare, people felt broiled and smarted, rabbits caught in the glare of a hunters' light. That was what Varunny and, to a lesser extent, Varu felt when they faced the stranger. In spite of the apprehension stinging inside, Varu asked sternly:

"Who are you to slaughter a bull on a Wednesday? That is not the village tradition"

"It is a new convenience for the people of Manoor. By the way, I am Anthrayos. Do you like to buy some beef?"

"Sell it to your blasted mama. You, son of a dirty pig"

Varu fondled the knife hanging at his waist. Anthrayos was unmoved, his eyes were fixated on Varu, scorching him.

Varunny murmured something in Varu's ears. Realizing the evolving situation, he was trying to calm his father. Anthrayos seemed to ignore Varu's angry protestations.

"I need some help at the meat stall. Would any of you be interested? I pay well."

"Pha…! Even my dog wouldn't come for your job"

Varu fumed at the slight. However, Muthoma saw the silver line of a job opportunity presenting itself and jumped at it without hesitation. No sooner than Varu finished his sentence, Muthoma climbed up the elevated ground where Anthrayos was standing and presented himself for the job.

"I can help you," he said to Anthrayos.

Anthrayos smiled faintly; he went inside the hut, came back with a brand-new meat cleaver. Giving it to Muthoma, he said:

"Five Rupees per pound. Hump, leg, liver: all one price."

Varu could not believe what he was witnessing: his own brother bolting the ranks and joining the enemy! He was brimming with rage mixed with sadness and frustration. He felt losing grip.

"This is a cursed dump; the lame bastard is a blockhead. Let us get out of here"

Varu started walking towards his butchery, seething. Varunny followed silently. Anthrayos kept the trace of his smile. He had his first conquest in Manoor.

# Two

Muthoma sat on a tiny wooden stool next to the suspended carcass, waiting for customers. The stool was so short, he appeared crouching. The main road remained desolate and deserted. Occasionally there were old women going for the morning mass at the church, shrouded head to knee in their muslin veils. Muthoma idly shifted his gaze from the road to the carcass and back, keenly aware of Anthrayos in the hut, measuring him, watching him and the sale. Whenever he turned towards the hut, he met Anthrayos's penetrating pair of eyes, the stare made him uneasy.

Manoor was fully awake. The music and rhythm of the morning was in the air: women drawing water from a well nearby; the squeaky noise of the unoiled water pulley; distant baying of cows and buffalos eager to be milked and fed; a lonely bicyclist ringing his bell incessantly warning no one on a vacant road; clang and clatter of a cook at the tea stall, vigorously whipping up a lather in a fresh mixture of coffee, cream and sugar.

Veeran, the fish hawker, came along the ditch road, bathed in sweat, a heavy load on his shoulder.

"Poo-oo-oo-o-o"

He gave out the fish hawker's trademark shrill hoot every few feet, announcing himself. At both ends of the crossbar on his shoulder were large baskets hanging heavily with the day's catch, glistening in the sun. With each pace, he took, the crossbar flexed rhythmically and the baskets creaked. As if propelled by the heavy load and in his effort to balance himself, Veeran's paces were very rapid, almost like running. Seeing Muthoma and the slaughtered bull, he slackened his steps a little. He wondered why Muthoma was not at his brother's butchery, who might be selling meat on a Wednesday. He had no time to investigate, however, he had a load of fish to sell before it goes stale in the summer heat. Veeran resumed his labored speed, moved on hooting,

"Poo-oo-oo-o-o"

Muthoma did not have a customer so far; the meat cleaver remained clean and shiny as it was given to him, unstained by blood. Perhaps, the villagers were yet to know of a meat stall open for business on a Wednesday, Muthoma tried to reason. Nonetheless, he was not particularly concerned about the slow business or no business at all. He was merely happy and grati- fied that he was the one in charge of the meat stall. He smiled at the thought that he might even be able to reward his favorite customers and friends with the choice cut of the meat. At his brother's butchery, only Varu had that privilege. Muthoma's role there was restricted to wrapping the meat in large teak tree leaves and handing the package to the buyers; he was not allowed anywhere near the cash box. It pained Muthoma that his elder brother did not trust him and gave him a better role in the family business. Then again, Muthoma has been sub- jected to neglect and ridicule from his childhood; he has gotten benumbed to the slight and disrespect of the adulthood as a natural progression.

As a little boy, Muthoma was chubby, plump, and much fairer than now. With straight, bristling porcupine hair, he had a persistent vacant smile on his large face. He did not last long at the school, tumbling out of it by third grade. Even that short stint at the school was a parade of bitter, painful, humiliating experiences for little Muthoma. What culminated in his final exit from the school was the harrowingly raw treatment he suffered at the hands of his classmates and Desu master, his sadistic third grade teacher. Desu master, short and stumpy, curly dark hair, prematurely wrinkled face marked by bushy eyebrows, had a stingingly sarcastic smile. Whenever he met one of his wards in the school corridor or on the street, his smile astonishingly squeezed in and out, the lips quivered a little - a strange way of expressing recognition. He walked around the school with a checkered shawl folded and characteristically thrown on his right shoulder, his worn-out sandals scraping the floor. Many a generation of Manoor have suffered at the hands of Desu master as children. Their collective wrath and gripe crystallized in coining a nickname for their not-so-beloved teacher, mercilessly emphasizing his short stature: "Kooran", the stunted! Behind his back, everyone, including grownups, referred to him only by that name, tasting sweet revenge every time they uttered it.

Muthoma was promoted and finally arrived at the third grade after failing and staying back in the second grade for two consecutive years. By the time he made it to the classroom on the first day of school, most of his new mates were already in their seats, Desu master was yet to appear. No sooner than Muthoma entered the classroom, someone called out from a corner of the room:

*"Vellana"* – white elephant.

*"Vellana" "Vellana"*

Many tiny voices repeated the chant; there were a lot of laughter and giggling. Silence fell only when Desu master came in. From that day on Muthoma abhorred school, constantly warding off pranks and teasing form his classmates. He was slow in the classroom just as he was on the playground. His teacher was merciless at his academic failings. No one willingly accepted him as partner in games. Muthoma hated dictation tests; one wrong answer in the test, one flogging on the palm, that was the rule in Desu master's third grade class. Muthoma consistently got many answers wrong on his tests, his teacher meted out the punishment with elated pleasure. Many afternoons he went home with his palms burning red.

In spite of being the butt of jokes and the target of everyone's pranks, Muthoma did have occasional escapades of his own. Once, he was caught red handed looking up the skirt of the girl sitting next to him, as he pretended to be picking up his pencil from the floor. When reported to Desu master, the teacher, frenzied and fuming, charged at Muthoma, caught the little boy by his shirt collar. He lifted him off the floor, carried him to his chair in the middle of the classroom like a tiger clutching the prey between its teeth, dragging it to the den. The teacher sat on his chair, placed Muthoma on his lap with his stomach down on Desu master's lap, his hands and legs dangling on both sides. Adjusting Muthoma to a convenient position, Desu master started caning him repeatedly on the buttocks. The boy wriggled in pain and screamed aloud, it only made the teacher more enraged. That afternoon Muthoma went home with his classmates milling around, poking fun at him and calling him names. At home, he refused to eat and went to sleep sobbing. Muthoma never set foot in the school again.

Muthoma soon realized spending time and growing up at home was not easy either. The domestic tormentor was none other than his elder brother, Varu. With better physique and agility, he dominated Muthoma everywhere. He pestered and harassed him at every chance he got: while eating, while playing, while doing chores. They fought at the least of provocations, Muthoma, invariably, ending up the aggrieved, bruised, having received most of the blows. His only source of solace and consolation was his Amma. She always had a soft corner for Muthoma being the younger and weaker of her two sons. She was there unfailingly to shield Muthoma against Varu's onslaughts: his taunts, nudging and insults. Muthoma was devastated, felt orphaned when she died after a prolonged illness when he was eighteen. He refused to leave her gravesite for hours until Varu took him home by force. He unabashedly wept aloud all the way home.

The brothers, Varu and Muthoma, though lived under the same roof, kept their distance. Varu continued his dominance over his younger brother, always treating him in a despotic and often demeaning vein. Muthoma resented the treatment, however, endured his brother helplessly. The rift came to a head on the day Varu married a woman from the neighboring village. The wedding celebrations had wound down, the bustle and din abated, guests departed. The bride and bridegroom had retired to their bedroom for the first night. Though Varu had extinguished the kerosene lamp, the room was awash in moonlight streaming in through the sole window of the room. Varu was coaxing his young bride intimately, she coyly resisting his entreaties. All of a sudden, even in his state of excitement, Varu could not help noticing the shadow of a head appearing in the window. He instantly recognized Muthoma, a faint silhouette, peeping in. To the utter confusion of the bride, Varu bolted from the room in a murderous rage, trying to chase down his brother. Muthoma, however, had already disappeared into the dark shadows in the yard. Frustrated, Varu returned to his bride, sitting at the edge of the bed, puzzled and embarrassed. After the wedding night incident, Muthoma was never allowed inside the house to sleep. Raining or chilly, he slept on the verandah, ate alone on a tiny porch adjacent to the kitchen.

When Muthoma accepted the job offered by Anthrayos, he, indeed, was jumping at an opportunity. At the same time, it was also a revolt, a challenge.

When Muthoma heard an approaching bicycle bell, ringing frequently and at regular intervals, he turned his eyes towards the main road. He could see a looming figure peddling unhurriedly forward. Soon he recognized it was Varkey on his way to open his bicycle repair shop. Seeing Varkey, Muthoma cringed a little, he owed him money. Muthoma did not know how to ride a bike. The local boys learn the art by the time they are ten or twelve. Though Muthoma was well past his youth and cruising around the fringes of middle age, he decided to master the technique, a couple of years ago. He rented an old bicycle from Varkey and took it to the playground in the rear of his old school. Every time he tried to mount the bike, he hit the ground even before his backside touched the bicycle seat. After several attempts, he was finally able to ride the bike a few feet before collapsing again to the ground in a heap. Encouraged, he got on the bike determined to go even farther; this time, however, no sooner than he peddled a few feet, Muthoma catastrophically crashed into a coconut tree stump, the splinters on the stump bruised him all over and the bike was badly damaged. When the wreckage of the mangled bike was returned, Varkey was furious, demanded the full price of the bike. After prolonged pleading and haggling, Varkey relented to accept the price agreed upon in installments from Muthoma. He had not made the installment this month or the last.

Noticing the newly appeared meat stall and Muthoma at its helm, Varkey applied the break and got off the bike. Approaching Muthoma and the gutted carcass, he said partly to himself and partly to Muthoma:

"Manoor is making progress; beef on a Wednesday!"

"Yes, yes" Muthoma smiled. "Shall I pack a couple of kilos for you?"

"Why not. This does not happen often"

"I am packing you the choice cut"

Muthoma was trying subtly to appease his creditor. Finally, the first customer, he was happy.

While Muthoma was cutting and wrapping the meat, Varkey looked around aimlessly and met the eyes of the figure in the hut watching the scene, motionless. In a flash, Varkey identified his younger brother. Anthrayos had changed a little: his face is more angular, his eyes more piercing, his hair cut short. The recognition, however, was instantaneous. Their eyes were locked several moments. Neither of them betrayed any signs of recognition nor uttered a word. Varkey picked up the meat package Muthoma had placed on the wooden plank, mounted his bike and left for his repair shop, peddling very slowly.

While peddling strenuously to propel his bike on the unpaved road, Varkey was pensive. When did Anthrayos come into the village? When did he set up his hut and the meat stall? None of these were there last evening. He came back to the village just as he left it, unannounced, stealthily. Anthrayos had left Manoor fifteen years ago; no one had heard from him ever since. As a bolt from the blue, now he was back and set up a business overnight. Why did he return to the village? His presence in this sleepy village, certainly, would open old wounds, provide fodder for rumors and gossip. Manoor has forgotten the gruesome details of the events preceding his departure from the village. It had taken a long while for the village to do so: removing them from the collective memory.

# *Three*

Varkey, Anthrayos and their only sister, Ammini, grew up in a comfortable house. Their father, Tharu, had built the house in the interior part of Manoor, away from the main thoroughfare, among tall coconut palms, green paddy fields in the background. The pathway to the house was a ditch road, dug in a few feet from the level ground, thickets and shrubbery on the raised ground on both sides. During monsoon, the road had ankle deep water and occasional pools, two to three feet deep; people trod along the shallow banks of the little ponds, holding tree branches, ever careful of their clothes not getting wet.

When Ammini was going to Mathiri, there was no water on the road, not entirely dry, but a little mushy and slushy. Mathiri was Ammini's maternal aunt, unmarried, living alone in a small house at the northern part of Manoor. She was very fond of Ammini, always looked forward to her niece's visits, at least once a week. Ammini too, enjoyed spending time with Mathiri, helping her elderly aunt with household chores, chatting with her, having the sweet dishes her aunt specially made for her. Normally, Ammini did not spend more than one or two hours with her aunt; on that stormy day, however, she could not return home for several hours because of incessant monsoon downpours. No one dared to step out into the horizontal rain, howling wind, occasional thunder. When the storm finally abated, Ammini set out for home. The ditch road to her home was flooded, the water reached well above her ankles, she hardly could know where the deeper pools of water were. Ammini plodded on through the water; the branches of trees above swayed in the wind, with every flutter of breeze, heavy water drops from the soaked leaves dripped on her, drenching her. Half way through her walk home, Ammini slipped and fell into one of the little ponds on the road. Afraid of water even from childhood, she was terrified, desperately struggled to reach the shallow bank of the pool, finally reaching and grabbing a branch of a tree leaning into the pool. As she wrestled to heave herself out of the ditch, the branch broke and gave way, plopping her back into the water. Though the pool was not very deep, there was enough water to drown Ammini. She fought and tussled to stay afloat, doggedly trying to reach the bank, only to drown again and again. From far away, Chacko happened to see someone in the water struggling, about to drown. Chacko was one of Ammini's distant cousins. Young and swift, he rushed to the scene not knowing who it was in the water. He jumped into the pool, lifted Ammini from the water, putting her on his shoulder and clambered out of the pond. He walked towards Tharu's house with Ammini on his shoulder. She was limp, languid and seemingly unconscious. Water squirted from her partly open mouth as Chacko strode on weightily. Her drenched clothes clung to her body contours.

Ammini was still unconscious when Chacko reached her house. He laid her on a wooden bench on the verandah. She appeared lifeless and enervated. Thick tresses of wet hair framed her face, morose and sullen. The bench was rough and narrow, hardly enough to hold Ammini, her left arm dangling down listlessly, her palm touching the cement floor. There was a small cut on her upper arm bleeding slightly. Chacko tried to lift and place her arm on the bench, but the arm slipped to the floor lifelessly.

Alarmed and anxious, Rosa, Ammini's mother, came running to her daughter's side, but rushed back to the kitchen, retuned with a bowl of water. She sprinkled the water on Ammini's face forcefully to wake her up, but in vain. Holding Ammini's shoulders, Rosa shook her daughter vigorously, calling her name aloud, pleading her to wake up. Ammini opened her eyes slowly, looked around seeking and asked incoherently, "Chacko, Chacko?"

"I am here, Ammini"

Chacko replied reassuringly, straining to position himself so as to be seen by Ammini. Ammini extended her hand in the direction of Chacko, felt her way to hold on to his hand and would not let it go. Rosa looked on disapprovingly. Since Ammini regained her conscience only moments back, was it appropriate for these two youngsters locking palms so passionately and openly. As the mother of three children, Rosa was guarded and vigilant.

Rosa was slender, petite and pretty when she and Tharu were banished from their village, years ago. Now she was slightly well padded with a few white streaks in her otherwise jet-black hair, all apt and befitting for a middle age mother. The lady of a well-to-do household, she carried herself well with dignity, self-assured and commanding, a stark contrast from her days when she toiled in the fields with her husband, struggling to feed and care for her growing family. Tharu, meanwhile, devoted himself to expand his land holdings and overall wealth. He remained very much close to his days of stress and strain, plainly dressed in a characteristic thin towel tied around his head, turban like. Often, he could be seen toiling in the fields along with his hired hands. Though owner of sizable land and property, class and status were irrelevant to him; a few hours in mud and water in the paddy field was worthwhile if it all amount to saving a few hours of labor cost. Rosa, on the other hand, was acutely conscious of her social status as the wife of one of the richest landowners in Manoor. She was achingly ambitious of appending even more facets to her family's standing in the community, there were many more steps to be climbed on the social ladder. Upper most in her dreams was to have a doctor from her own family. Manoor had no hospital or doctor; the hospital was forty miles away. Men had to carry patients in their terminal stages, all the way to the hospital. The only doctor was Namby, an Ayurvedic [5] ***Vaidya***, a practitioner of native medicine. Being an upper-class Hindu, patients were never allowed in his house, they were seen in one of his out houses. He never touched the patients, diagnosis made and treatments dictated by observation and listening, all from a distance, a few feet away. Patients in need of treatments for diseases including, not so uncommon snake bites, were many in Manoor and surrounding areas. Left to the nature's mercy, many of them succumbed. Rosa imagined all of them flocking to her house seeking care from one of her sons, the doctor. Indeed, a dizzying thought for her. Varkey, however, innately knew he neither had the intelligence nor the ability to go through the rigors of prolonged medical training. In spite of that, Rosa convinced herself that Varkey, her eldest son, had all what it takes to be a doctor. Nevertheless, Rosa's dreams crumbled and collapsed when Varkey at age twenty, seriously threw himself headlong into bodybuilding.

Varkey's fascination for bulging biceps and a protuberant chest was ignited when, from a faraway state, Balram appeared

---

[5] *Physician*

in Manoor, unexpectedly, unannounced. He did not know the local language nor knew anyone, not even an acquaintance, in the village. Unfazed, he set up his camp in the shade of a big *banyan* tree in front of the village temple. The ancient tree had a crowd of external roots scaffolding its large, expansive branches; the needle tipped leaves shivering in the morning breeze. Shedding his traditional attire and the oversized headgear conforming to a distant culture, Balram slipped into a scant red brief, started working out with a massive dumbbell shaped wooden weight, periodically switching to a circular granite weight at the end of a rope. Oversized and bulbous, every muscle mass of his anatomy stood out distinctly, glistening in the morning rays, rhythmically moving up and down, tightening and relaxing along with his measured moves. From his body, smeared with medicinal oils, channels of sweat slipped, fell and meld into the ground.

This has never happened in Manoor: an unforeseen event, a strange individual and even stranger activity he was engaged in. Manoor wakes up only to what was yesterday or days before, an unaltered cycle of existence and rituals played out by monotonously familiar characters.

Curious and inquisitive, wide eyed villagers trickled around Balram, gradually growing into a thin crowd, keeping a cautious, awed distance from him, leaving him in the middle of a circular clearing. Unfettered, oblivious of the onlookers, Balram went on with his grueling exercise, occasionally flashing a toothy smile directed at no one, almost as a part of his workout routine. Balram's performance with the weights was not to build up and strengthen his already impressive musculature any further; it was self-promotion, a solicitation for students and followers. Not knowing the local language, that was the only way he could communicate with the gathered people, the virtues and desirability of his pursuit.

Balram continued his body building exercises the next day and day after, the number of onlookers, however, had thinned down. From the villagers, no exercise enthusiasts came forward to greet him or ask questions, they kept a safe distance with apprehension. Varkey, however, was among the spectators every day, marveling at Balram's sculpted body physique, his prowess with the weights. Imagining himself in Balram's body was excitingly invigorating for him, the power, the self-confidence. On the third day of Balram's appearance on the scene, when he called it a day from his performance, as the scant bystanders departed, Varkey gathering all the courage he could muster, gingerly approached Balram and fell at his feet: a total submission to his prospective guru, a humble request to be accepted as a *shishya*, a novice. Balram helped him rise, affectionately holding his shoulders with both of his hands muttering inaudibly something in Sanskrit. They did not exchange a word as they could not: but they understood each other in silence. Balram pulled out a bottle of oil from among his personal belongings in a cloth bundle, poured the oil on Varkey's head, an initiation of some sort. The green colored oil ran down his neck, on to his shoulders and down his torso soaking his white shirt in green. The guru signed him to remove his shirt and *mundu*- the long waist wrap- leaving only his under short. Looking and gauging Varkey's not so prominent chest and biceps, Balram smiled, his slightly protruding incisors showing between his thick lips.

"*Aplyala pushkal kam karayala pahije*" – we have much work to do, he said partly to himself and to his nascent student. He began demonstrating the first of exercises he wanted Varkey to practice; weights were way down in his coaching plans for Varkey, now only a few body exercises.

Varkey started to practice right in earnest looking occasionally to the teacher for approval. He presented himself every morning before the guru under the banyan tree, enthusiastically working on prescribed exercises. As the days went by, Balram gave him new exercises to practice, making them a little more difficult each time. Varkey was happy that he was making steady progress, the guru pleased. He even thought that his biceps are developing steadily.

Then, one day, Balram disappeared.

That early morning, when Varkey came for his lessons, there was no trace of Balram. Under the banyan tree, gone were his cloth bundle containing the medicinal oils, his other possessions and most prominently, the weights, the wooden and granite ones. Varkey went everywhere looking for his guru, in and around the temple, among the thickets of aerial roots surrounding the banyan tree; he even searched the small forest behind the temple where snakes are fostered and worshiped among the towering trees heavy with dangling creepers. Frustrated, he scaled the large trunk of the banyan tree, reaching the highest point with much effort. He wanted to scan the whole village from the top of the tree. He looked as far as his eyes could reach. He saw the Enamu River, a serpentine, luminous line of blue, the Vilangan hills, billowing clouds and a foggy horizon beyond. But no sign of Balram, not even as a dot moving away. Exasperated and discouraged, Varkey was climbing down; all of a sudden, he felt piercing stings all over his body; inadvertently he had hit a nest of red ants on one of the branches, the ants were swarming and stinging the intruder. Varkey was squirming with pain, trying to sweep and wipe off the ants. As he was wriggling with the ants crawling on him, Varkey lost his grip on a tree branch he was holding on to and was crashing perilously to the ground. In exasperation, he managed to get hold of another tree branch while flashing down, hung on to it to exhaustion. Finally, he had to let go of the branch, before he smashed down to the mud and dirt below. During the fall, Varkey broke the tibia of his left leg, he could not walk without help and had to be under Nambi *vaidya's* treatment for months. When he was on his feet again, he walked with a slight limb, hardly noticeable. His bodybuilding efforts, however, ended abruptly.

Ammini remained home for several days, nursed by her mother, helping her to come out of the mental shock of drowning, and healing herself of the bruises and sprains from the mishap. Chacko visited her every day, they spent time holding hands, not saying much, looking into each other's eyes. They were falling for each other. Rosa was reproachful of the development, as the time went by, however, her resentment gradually blunted.

Ammini and Chacko started making it into a practice to go to church every day, together. Each morning, Chacko was at Ammini's house gate awaiting her to walk to the church. It made a stir of some sort in Manoor; it was exceedingly unusual and scandalous in the village for a young unmarried couple seen walking together. Many a morning, the villagers peered at the spectacle through their house windows gulping and gasping. Chacko and Ammini were unaffected, they were engrossed in exchanging their own thoughts and sentiments. As the time went by, they were planning a life together. Ammini felt safe and secure in a life with Chacko, he was drawn to her by her sheer passion for him. Though Rosa's displeasure of their relationship had abated in some measure, she secretly wished her daughter to break up with Chacko. As the days and months rolled by, however, their love for each other only grew in intensity. Then one day, unforeseen, out of the blue, Ammini's world collapsed around her.

Ammini and Chacko were stepping out of the church on that cloudy warm day, ready to walk back home as usual. Chacko asked Ammini to sit and rest a few minutes on the low parapet on one side of the church's main gate. Surprised and askance she complied, looking at Chacko anxiously.

"I want to make my life more meaningful, fulfilling." Chacko said abruptly.

"How you are going to do it"

"Serving the poor and serving God"

"I don't understand Chacko"

"I am going to be a missionary priest, working among the people in the northern part of our country"

Ammini stared at Chacko in disbelief, she froze as she could not comprehend and sort out the thoughts and emotions rushed and welled up in her. She stood up and started walking in silence, Chacko followed. Walking home, Chacko continued talking about his decision to become a priest, Ammini did not hear anything; she was lost in herself, devastated by the overwhelming impact of Chacko's unexpected announcement. When reached her house gate, she ignored Chacko, dashed to her home and shut herself in her room. Rosa came and knocked at her door, the response, however, was only a long silence. When the mother persisted, Ammini came out. Her face drawn and taut, she seemed to be oblivious of her surroundings, even her mother standing in front of her, puzzled and concerned. She sat on a chair for a while, silent, not answering any frantic queries, then retreated into her room, slamming the door after her.

During the days followed, Ammini spent most of the time withdrawn into her room, quiet and still. She rarely came out except for dining with her family, becoming, however, increasingly less communicative with them. Though it was agonizingly painful for her to retrace the pathway to the church and back, she continued the practice every day.

More than two years passed since Chacko left for the seminary, neither Ammini nor anyone in her family ever heard from him. It was nothing atypical for a seminarian. In their almost cloistered life, communications with the external world was considerably restricted. Since she left him in a rage at her house gate, Ammini never even attempted to contact him. He had already exited her consciousness, leaving only a few pleasant memories, shrouded in pain and deprivation.

It was rather an unusual day, the locals call it the crows' wedding day: sun and rain at the same time, thin threads of rain drenching the sunlight. Tharu heard the creaking of the iron gate of his house. He saw a couple entering his front yard, he could not recognize Chacko until he came closer. Chacko looked different, modern attire: pants, striped blue shirt; the woman with him tall and fair complexioned, wearing a colorful dress distinctly alien to Manoor. Surprised and puzzled, Tharu welcomed them in. As soon as he entered the house, Chacko was scanning the interior with some haste and urgency, impatiently looking for someone.

"Where is Ammini?" eventually, he asked Tharu.

"She is in her room, I will go get her"

Within moments, Ammini was at the opened door of her room, she walked hastily towards Chacko and halted a few feet from him, staring steely eyed.

"Ammini, this is Sukanya, my wife,"

Chacko said gently touching his wife's right shoulder.

Even before he finished his sentence, Ammini lunged at him and clawed his face, cat like, leaving red scratch marks on his cheek. She took a few steps walking back, but abruptly turned around and slapped Chacko, stormed back to her room banging the door behind her. All were startled to hear an unearthly scream from her room, along with some shouted sentences crammed together, hard to decipher and understand.

Why Ammini was so furious, Chacko did not have to think too hard to figure it out. Everyone was shocked by what just had taken place, all beyond themselves to react. Chacko was more embarrassed than smarting from Ammini's transgressions. Sukanya's face pale with terror.

Ammini never came out of her room that day, next day or thereafter. She confined herself to the four walls of her room, occasionally talking to herself in loud voice. She refused to open the door for anyone including her mother. Those knocking at her door had to hear only abuses and curses.

Every day, Rosa had to be patiently persistent, spend considerable time to persuade Ammini to open the door, give her daughter food.

It was harvest time; Rosa was busy supervising the workers. She asked Thresia, one of her maidservants, to take the lunch for Ammini. Thresia, balancing the food tray in one hand, knocked at Ammini's door. Ammini recognized that it was not her mother at the door. Unlike her usual response, she opened the door. As soon as the maid was in, Ammini grabbed the tray from her, emptied the whole tray on Thresia's head. Lumps of rice stuck in her hair, curry and chunks of vegetable streaked onto her face, wetted and colored her clothing and plopped to the floor. Ammini caught Thresia by her hair and beat her repeatedly, kicked her out of the room and closed the door. Frightened, hysterical and crying aloud, Thresia dashed to the kitchen, alarming everyone in the household.

Only Rosa dared to go to Ammini's room with food and water. In the room, not many words were exchanged between them, Ammini gave single word answers to Rosa's persistent questions. She was always disheveled, her room untidy and filthy. She looked forlorn and incandescent at the same time; Rosa had the strange feeling that Ammini was not seeing her, she was beyond her, she was past the walls of her room, she was not there.

Rosa continued to take food and care for the other needs of her daughter. Gradually she was aware her daughter no longer recognized her, there was an eerie fire in her eyes; was it hostility? Rosa became more and more apprehensive and nervous about going to Ammini's room. Then, one day, as she was entering the room with the tray of food, Ammini pushed her aside and darted out of the room screaming at the top of her voice. She ran to the front gate guarded by two terracotta lions on both sides, climbed the short masonry wall next to the gate and settled down on it. She was constantly talking to herself, shrieking in between. A small crowd of concerned neighbors gathered on the road in front. Tharu and Anthrayos rushed to the scene, brought Ammini from her perch by force, took her to her room against her noisy protestations and latched the room from outside. Tharu made a small window in one of the walls of her room to provide food and water through. Rosa was in tears saddened by what has befallen on her only daughter.

Ammini was to spend months and years locked up in her room. Her intermittent squeals reverberated in the house day and night, casting an uncanny pall upon the house.

# *Four*

Enamu River flows between two different states with contrasting drinking laws: alcohol was freely available in the state bordering its southern bank, in the state on the northern bank, strict prohibition laws were in force. Between a good time and sobriety runs a river. Those from the northern state seeking a drink or two had to ferry across to the south. Many from Manoor including Muthoma frequently indulged in this escapade from the enforced abstinence.

Alighting from his ferry, Muthoma invariably headed for a toddy shop not far from the harbor's edge, almost as if lead by a homing instinct. He loved the sap from the coconut inflorescence, it is affordable and there is nothing to match its flavor, he believed. As much as he liked his drink, Muthoma enjoyed the steamed tapioca root and fish curry served at the small food stall at a corner of the shop. The hot, spicy fish curry and the split-opened tapioca are known to go down well with toddy. The stall, a favorite of regulars at the toddy joint was run by Kochumariam. In her forties, chatty and friendly, men enjoyed her chit chats peppered with slangy jokes, often raunchy and risqué. She considered Muthoma a special friend, he relished a tete-a-tete with her over his drink.

On that night, Muthoma was rather late when he finished his drink. Though a bit unsteady in his steps, he rushed to reach the ferry before it closed; however, it was when he got there. Kunjayi had gone home, Lona, the chief oarsman might have been asleep in his small mud house on the other bank; Muthoma could see a faint light from a flickering kerosene lamp in Lona's house. He repeatedly called out as loud as he could to wake up Lona. Finally, he saw some movements in Lona's house. Soon he saw a tiny light on the surface of the water moving towards him. Lona's boat was approaching.

When Muthoma got off the boat, it was rather late at night. There was no streetlight in the narrow road he had to take home, Manoor had only one streetlight, it was far away up the road. It was a moonlit night and there was enough light to walk home, Muthoma thought. Otherwise he would have bought a torch from Lona. These torches of dried coconut palm leaves were made by Lona's wife and sold at the ferry. He could have swung it as he walked to fan the flame at its tip and light up the road in front. However, there was no need for it that night, Manoor was calm and veiled in the cool comfort of moonlight.

As Muthoma was walking home, he heard a heart-rending scream when he was approaching Tharu's house; threads of deep melancholy and insanity woven into it. It did not take too long for him to discern where that wail was emanating from. He grew curious, felt an intense urge to investigate.

There was no compound wall fencing the backside of Tharu's property, only a shallow open gutter running along the periphery. Muthoma hopped across the gutter, started walking in the direction of the house where the screams were coming from. The backyard of the house was awash in moonlight. No light in any windows of the house except the faint light coming from a single window at the far end of the house. His curiosity aroused, Muthoma walked towards the window. What he saw at the window arrested him in his steps. Ammini was howling like a wolf crouching on the windowsill, clutching the iron bars of the window. She had peeled off her clothes, rolled them into balls and thrown at the mutts barking at her from the vacant courtyard. The iron bars pressed against her breasts furrowing them into ugly segments. Her light brown body smeared with her own feces appeared strangely mottled. Her long hair, dark, luxuriant and in a tangled, unruly cascade, blanketed her entire backside. Ammini noticed Muthoma in the courtyard. She stared at him with wild and bewildered eyes. Her howling instantly stopped. She got off from the window-sill, pressed her face against the bars of the window,

"Open the door"

"Open the door"

Impatient and insistent, she begged.

The only door of Ammini's room faced a long verandah, Muthoma climbed the short flight of steps to the verandah and walked towards the door, the door was latched but not locked. He lifted the latch taking care not to make any jarring noise and wake up anyone in the house. Even before Muthoma opened the door Ammini pushed it open from inside; she dashed out of her room in a wild fury, completely ignoring or not seeing Muthoma. She bolted to the yard and soon disappeared into the dark shadows of the shrubs and trees.

Muthoma went home; the house was dark and silent, Varu and family asleep. He pulled his mat from the hanger, unrolled and spread it in his usual corner of the porch and stretched himself. The image of Ammini at her window lingered in front of his closed eyes for a short while, then faded and disappeared as he fell asleep.

Ammini emerged from the darkness of the thickets, climbed down the gutter and came up on to the deserted road - a narrow ribbon of moonlight, sporadically interrupted by grey shadows of tall trees. Suddenly in a flash, she became conscious of her nakedness. Withdrawing into the bushes, she ran back to the yard outside her room. Two black dogs in the yard growled at her, she drove them away throwing stones at them. She picked up one of the balls of clothing she had thrown out of her room days back, unfurled it and wore it on: a thin *kurta*, a one-piece dress covering her up to the knees. She sprinted back to the country road, dashed northward talking to herself, cursing and howling intermittently. She was retracing her way to the church, insentient, as if being led. She had trodden this road back and forth several times with Chacko and alone; today, however, there were neither.

Ammini entered the church compound and ran to the cemetery in the back of the church, a ground bordered by five-feet masonry walls with a massive metal door of corrugated iron. The door was closed; she pushed it open, setting off a loud metallic rattling din. Frightened night birds fluttered away. In the cemetery, the tombs and headstones were not laid out in any particular order, tombs interspersed with simple gravestones. A white tomb stood out among them with elaborate Gothic tracery and two angels guarding: a wealthy man's final resting place. Ammini wandered among the graves for a while, finally stopping at a tomb with granite slab on top with inscriptions about the dead. It was Tharu's grave. Because of the mysterious circumstances of his death, there were gossips and rumors prevalent in Manoor if his whole remains were ever found and buried in his grave. Ammini sat on her father's tomb for a while muttering to herself. Had she assiduously sought and found her father's tomb? Had she consciously run all the way from her home to the church and the cemetery? She was escorted, perhaps, by a few abiding memories imprinted in her subconscious, still intact.

Ammini left the cemetery leaving its door open, walked to the ditch road leading to the main thoroughfare of Manoor.

At the fork where the two streets met was the tile roofed village temple. A low, unassuming structure, so low, it appeared to dissolve into the ground it stood on. Arrays of granite oil lamps on its exterior walls, unlit. What stood out more than the temple was an expansive pond in front of it, a thin sheen of moonlight stretched out over the water, shimmering white dots of water lilies on isolated pads strewn around the pond. There were flights of long stone steps leading down to the water. Ammini sat for a while on one of the steps close to the water mumbling, gesticulating. Abruptly, by impulse, she started moving into the water, feet first, finally immersing herself in the pond. She emerged from the water, climbed up the stairs drenched. Initially, water pouring down from her *kurta,* then in drips, drawing a trace in the alluvial soil of Manoor as she walked towards the main road. As she reached the deserted road, walking further northward, Ammini started to sing to herself softly first, then at the top of her voice. Neighborhood dogs barked. Mournful and lamenting, those songs she had had learned from Rosa during her childhood. She used to recite them with her mother even after growing up, a daily twilight ritual.

Ammini had ceased her frequent squeals. Frenzied, she walked aimlessly, her loose *kurta* clinging to her, her soaked, matted hair sticking to her back. She had been locked up in her room for a few years then; this was the first time since she came out of her internment. She was impervious to once familiar landmarks along the street: the dirt road to aunt Mathiri's house; a tiny shrine with a black cross on a white pedestal. She was unaware her favorite aunt had passed away two years ago, buried in the same cemetery she just had been to. She passed in front of Kelan's barber shop, a tiny sign board with crudely drawn pictures of a partly open scissors and a mechanical clipper, dangling above the front door. (To every customer, Kelan used to ask if they prefer scissor cut or clipper cut; he exacted more money for the clipper cut) As Ammini hastily walked past Varkey's bike shop, she did not recognize that it was her brother's, she did not notice the prominent sign: "Bicycles Rented Repaired". Not far from the bike shop was a small house roofed with red tiles, a fence along the roadside with a gate painted blue in the middle. The house belonged to the retired army man, Anthony. As a little girl, Ammini along with her friends used to hang around the fence ogling Anthony's pet monkey, Rhemo. The monkey chained to a T-shaped perch in Anthony's kitchen yard, restlessly moved up and down the pole, sometimes took a break from his restive aerobics to sit on the horizontal bar of the T, looking at the girls with a twinkle in his tiny eyes. Occasionally, Anthony, a tall middle-aged man with greying mustache used to come out of his house to chat with the girls: he explained to them that Rhemo belonged to the species Rhesus, "mo" for monkey and hence the name Rhemo. He told them he had brought the monkey all the way from the Garden of Eden which he visited when he was posted in Iraq during the World War II. Ammini and friends listened to his stories with wide eyed fascination and respect for the former soldier. Ammini was unaware of her childhood allure, as she walked past Anthony's home. She was in a rush.

As Ammini made it to the area of Bhanu's Tea & Coffee Shop, everything was in total darkness, silent and still, even the narrow signboard hardly noticeable. Adjacent to the teashop was a tobacco store run by Chakunny, a middle-aged man with a kind smile, walking habitually with a right-hand tilt. Every morning he walked to his store from the nearby village of Thokav, an oddly large lunch bag in his right hand, a folded umbrella hung on his left shoulder by its curved handle. He was a voracious reader as he had to, his customers were few and far between. When not reading, he hummed old tunes to entertain himself or as a habit while his mind was busy otherwise. Chakunny arrived at his store late in the mornings as most of his customers were seniors and not normally early shoppers. His merchandise was tobacco leaves cured and dried to the shape of flexible sticks, an essential ingredient of *pan,* an admixture of pieces of tobacco sticks, lime and cracked areca nut, all wrapped in green betel leaves. The old folks chewed it after each meal or when they are merely bored.

Chakunny's was a modest store consisting of an inner room and a raised platform in front of it; all the sales took place on the platform. Chakunny squatted on a lightly cushioned mat on the platform, a short cash box beside him, a pan balance hung from the ceiling with the gradation of weights underneath. Before he closed the store by sundown, he locked up the cash box and everything else in the inner room; the platform remained open and vacant.

After her dip in the pond, Ammini has been walking continuously without stopping anywhere. As she just took a few steps past Bhanu's Teashop, she abruptly turned around and climbed up the three small steps to the teashop. It was the open area of the shop; a few desks and benches crowded the floor. As she was negotiating through the furniture, she hit the leg of one of the desks and tumbled down to the floor. Getting up quickly and cursing aloud, she walked up a small corridor linking the coffee shop and the tobacco store. Seeing Chakunny's sale counter, the platform, at the end of the corridor, she hopped and stretched out flat on it. She was unaware of another soul sleeping on the platform, a few feet away. Covered head to toe under a sheet, it was Apputan, a cook at the teashop. Sensing a stranger at arm's length, startled and frightened by Ammini's appearance, he jumped off the platform, tried to drive her away by shouting at her,

"You stinking street walker! Get away from here, go away, go away"

Ammini was unmoved, kept on murmuring to herself, paid no attention to Apputan. Apputan went to his kitchen, returned with a big wooden stick. He menacingly moved closer to Ammini brandishing the stake at her:

"Go away! I would break your leg, otherwise"

Ammini jumped down the platform in haste, gave out a blood-curdling cry, waking up the dogs in the neighborhood, their discordant barking interspersed with extended howling. She ran down the corridor cursing Apputan, hurried through the benches and desks of the coffee house. She climbed down the steps and went on to the road. In moments, she disappeared into the darkness.

Early morning, it was Thresia who darted to Rosa's room to deliver the disconcerting news.

"She is gone"

"Gone?"

"Yes, Ammini is not in her room!"

Thresia, as her daily routine, had gone to bring a jug of water and a towel for Ammini, though everyone knew that neither would be used and most likely, both would be misused. As always, she strained to push the jug and towel through the small rectangular feeding hole in the wall, craftily place them on a table right beneath the opening on the other side. She casually peeped into the room through the hole. Ammini was nowhere to be seen. As most of the time, she was not at the window talking to herself or scolding and chastising the dogs in the yard.

Rosa was saying her morning prayers when Thresia burst into her room. Aghast, she rushed to Varkey asleep in his room, knocked at the door; Varkey came out disheveled, hardly awake.

"Ammini ran away. Go find her"

Exited, panicking, Rosa was almost shouting. Varkey changed into whatever clothes he could grab and hurried to the front yard, no one knew where he was headed. He scurried to the well just outside their kitchen, anxiously looked into the depth of the well for his sister, the water was calm and still, no sign of Ammini. Varkey was remembering his aunt, Annamma walking around her house sad faced, doing chores, but talking to no one for years. One day she disappeared only to be discovered floating in the family well.

Varkey went to search his neighbor, Gopan's well. Gopan's wife, Lakshmi, was drawing water from the well, she has not seen anything unusual in or around the well, she told him. Gopan came out of his house and hearing Ammini had been missing, volunteered to join Varkey in the search. The two neighbors first went to the temple pond as if Varkey had a premonition that his sister had drowned somewhere. The pond was serene and quiet; a thin haze of morning mist rose from the water and hovered above the surface. Far away at the other end of the pond there were three priests bathing in preparation for the morning prayers at the temple. Varkey called out to them and asked if they have seen anything out of the ordinary in the pond that day. They hollered back to say that they had not.

Varkey and Gopan entered the main road, searched everywhere along the road. They were impatiently looking for someone on the road to enquire about Ammini. There was no one on the road, it was too early in the morning. Desperate and desolate, they continued their search. Unexpectedly, far away, they saw an unrecognizable figure moving towards them. As the person came closer, in the dim morning light they could make out who it was: Philomi, a white muslin head wrap covering her down to the knee, a bunch of scarlet red hibiscus flowers in one hand, a thick binder in the other. Philomi was a fixture in the church, invariably she was the first to arrive at the church, the flowers are her daily offering at the altar. As her wont, she stopped any one she came across on her way to the church to engage in short conversations, asking them what their troubles were, what their unmet needs were on that day. Arriving at the church, she would settle on one of the steps, and open her binder. On separate sheets of paper, Philomi wrote the names of the individuals she met on the way with their needs and troubles listed underneath. The sheaf of paper was then hidden in one of the crevices on one side of the altar. Knowing about Philomi's rather eccentric routine, Varkey was certain, she could not have missed Ammini if she was on the road that morning, she could give some clues about Ammini's whereabouts.

"Philomi, did you see Ammini anywhere today?"

"Ammini! Isn't she locked up in her room?"

"Yes, but she escaped and ran away last night."

"May God have mercy, I would be praying for her"

Philomi moved on. Varkey grew more perturbed and feared the worst for his sister. However, he with Gopan persisted in their forage along the road. Further down the road, Bhanu's Coffee Shop was awake. Two kerosene lamps lighted up the shop, the rattle of someone whipping up coffee and cream in a metal tumbler disrupted the morning tranquility. Three or four customers were already on the benches for their early breakfast. Gopan told the patrons at the café that Ammini was missing, their efforts to find her so far had been futile. Hearing the account, two of the customers did not even wait for their breakfast order to arrive at their desk; they eagerly joined Varkey and Gopan in the search.

Not far from the coffee shop, Varkey and friends saw the solitary street light of Manoor, still lit. As they moved in closer, on the cement base of the lamp post, they noticed a human figure overlaid with small branches of shrubs, fresh, leaves still green. The figure hardly moved, the leaves covering the body heaved up and down as the person breathed. Could that be Ammini, a thought flashed through Varkey's mind. He was amazed and relieved at the possibility; however, he could not imagine her at rest and not agitated. He moved in haste, quickly removed the boughs to unveil Ammini in a deep slumber, curled up in fetal position. He tried to wake her shaking her by the shoulder and loudly calling her name. Ammini lazily stirred, opened her eyes in a daze, vacantly stared at Varkey.

"Why on earth are you here? Come, let us go home"

Ammini did not respond. Holding her by the arm, Varkey helped her rise, escorted her walking towards their home. Ammini began murmuring in low voice, almost obediently followed her brother unconsciously. By that time, a small crowd had gathered, everyone looked on in curious disbelief.

Muthoma was standing on the embankment, across from the street light at the junction. Aloof and detached, he viewed what was taking place below with an impassive smile.

When Ammini, Varkey and his friends entered the house gate, Rosa came running to embrace her daughter. Ammini was passive, did not betray any sign of recognition of her mother, she started to mumble loudly. Varkey led her to her room, closed the door and secured the latch. Thresia came with a tray with [6]***puttu,*** Ammini's favorite food and two yellow bananas on the side. The maid pushed the tray through the feeding window to place it on the table in the room. As usual, she bent and lowered her head to survey the room through the wall opening: Ammini was fast asleep in one corner of the room, snoring.

---

[6] *Rice flour and grated coconut steamed into a segmented cylindrical shape.*

# Five

When Mary, the daughter of Vareed and Kochammu, grew into a young woman, the whole Manoor stood up and took notice. With sculpted figure, large darting eyes and full lips, she commanded attention from the eligible young men and sometimes, not so eligible grownups as well. As she strutted along the main road on errands, the menfolk felt edgy looking at her, a challenge brewing up in them, in spite of themselves. Intimidated, few dared to make a move, however. At the barbershop, Kelan intuitively stopped snipping the hair of his customer in the chair, froze to ogle Mary as she passed by. As he met her eyes, with one piercing gaze, Mary set him ablaze; he reflexively withdrew and got busy again with the scissors.

Among the three children of Vareed and Kochammu, Mary was the youngest: Poulo and Iyyapu her older brothers. The family, given to wild behavior nearly all the time, Poulo was the most equable and controlled. Vareed's house was always alive and noisy, mainly, because of Kochammu. She was incapable of speaking in a normal voice; whether calling her family for meals or admonishing her children, she was habitually loud. Her everyday domestic language was always laced with curses and profanities. Her blaring outbursts reverberated in the community. Unsolicited and helplessly, the neighbors shared and endured every detail of what went on in Vareed's household. Kochammu even yelled and screamed at night birds, especially **Strix Ocelleta,** a species known among the villagers as the bird of death. Its rumbling, resonant mating calls in the dead of night, frightened and maddened Kochammu. She thought it a bad omen. Coming out of the house, planting herself in the front yard, brandishing both her arms up, she clamored abuses and expletives at the bird, to drive it away.

Kochammu came to Manoor along with Devassy's new bride, Anna, as her maidservant. Anna was from a faraway village, down south. Marriage alliance from a distant, unfamiliar community was unusual for anyone from Manoor. Devassy being one of the richest and the most educated in the village, dared to break with some traditions, the village went along with it, unquestioned. Anna and her maid spoke with an accent alien to the people of Manoor, they heard them speaking with some degree of fascination, amusement. Like a shadow, Kochammu followed her mistress everywhere, tending to her needs. Devassy too had someone at his beck and call: Vareed, a short young man, slightly bent, unruly hair, big downcast eyes. Whether he had some work to do or not, Vareed was at Devassy's house dawn to dusk, lingering or circling around the house in a slow pace, awaiting a call from Devassy. At times, he was seen crouching on the front yard plucking the occasional grass patch sprouting on the sandy yard. Years ago, the white sand was brought from the beach a few miles away by bullock cart to spread and beautify the yard. Vareed made sure the burgeoning grass shoots does not mar its snowy splendor. Vareed seldom went inside Devassy's house; inside or out, however, he considered himself to be part of the household. That sense of belonging gave him great contentment. He thought a call from Devassy for any service to be a testament of his master's closeness and trust in him; indeed, a reward in itself. Vareed's servility was not foisted upon him; rather it was self-imposed for his own satisfaction. Devassy, in turn, deemed him his trusted valet and a dependable scout.

The thought came to Devassy's mind first, Anna wholeheartedly supporting it: it is time for Vareed to find a bride and start a family. Anna was concerned about Kochammu remaining unattached, considering the vulnerability of her age. Vareed's world was very constricted and confined, Devassy's house and his own. Being aware of it, Devassy thought the marriage would give another dimension to his dreary life. He did not have to engage a marriage broker to arrange the marriage as was the common practice, he only had to look into his own household for a suitable bride for his loyal minion. Kochammu was young and trustworthy, she would make a good wife for Vareed, he thought. One late morning with a cup of coffee in hand, Devassy beckoned Vareed, introduced the proposal for his marriage. Wide eyed, Vareed looked at him earnestly, anxious to oblige just as he takes any other instructions from his master. Devassy did not have much convincing to do with Vareed; obedient as he was, Vareed was most willing to carry out anything his boss wished, even getting married. He was innocent of the privileges and responsibilities of matrimony, he agreed to the proposal solely because it came from Devassy, another command from his master.

The wedding was to take place at the bride's parish church several miles away. As the groom's wedding party was all ready to depart for Kochammu's village, Vareed nervously came to Devassy, looked at him as if he wanted to tell him something, but hesitant to express himself. Devassy prompted him to speak.

"Do I *have* to go for the wedding? Won't it be enough Sankaran go and stand in for me at the wedding?"

Vareed wanted a proxy wedding! Sankaran was his good friend from the neighborhood. Amused, looking at Anna, Devassy only laughed in disagreement.

Though Vareed remained bemused and vacillating, marriage did take place as planned. Devassy and Anna were happy and content: two of their favorite wards are now a couple.

Mary was ten years old and her teenage brothers on the cusp of adulthood when Manoor was in the grip of a raging epidemic, smallpox. Like a wildfire, the disease was spreading from house to house. People panicked and stricken with fright; an eerie, ghastly air enveloped the village. By dusk, doors and windows of the houses were closed shut, everyone inside. The nights were macabre and spectral. With an uncanny silence in the background, even the innocuous nocturnal sounds and rustles of nature perturbed and alarmed villagers. When dogs howled in the distance, some conjured up the image of a gruesome goddess of annihilation stomping along the alleyways of the village. Only dogs could perceive her, they believed. In the summer nights, as migratory wild ducks flew and whooshed over houses, children huddled to their mothers, scared. Mothers crossed themselves, with their thumbs made the sign of cross on the foreheads of the little ones too.

Weak and faint wails of the afflicted with the malady could be heard from some houses. Febrile, covered with blisters all over their bodies, itching mad, the patients were gently flapped with leafy twigs of *Neem* tree, a prescription from Nambi, the *vaidya*. People thronged in front of the country medic's house, seeking any tenable remedy for their loved ones. The *vaidya* gave the same medication for everyone: a gunk of macerated **Neem** leaves laced with herbs, all wrapped in green banana leaves.

Many in the village believed the outbreak was some way rooted in the supernatural. On Fridays, the village temple was decorated with streamers and garlands of yellowish tender coconut palm leaves split into thin strands. At variance to the usual practice, the tracks of oil lamps on the temple walls remained lit even after the evening service, the *pooja*. The foliage of the trees surrounding the temple glimmered with the light from the oil lamps. Announcing the conclusion of **pooja**, the ringing of the hand bells ended in the temple. Shangoo, the oracle, emerged from the door of the temple. The door was so short and narrow, he had to bend to exit. Yelling and roaring incomprehensibly, he rushed to the small crowd of devotees assembled at the temple courtyard. The believers withdrew forming a ring, awe and reverence in their eyes. The oracle's face was covered with vermilion with streaks of turmeric, wide eyes aflame with rage, the long unruly hair smeared with the red powder; a belt of shiny brass rattles he wore on top of his scarlet red waist wrap, jingled rhythmically as he walked, so did his metallic ankle ornament. In his right hand, he carried a large sword, curved at the end like a sickle. The oracle worked himself into a frenzy, walked around in the circular space ringed by spectators, shouting unintelligible cries. The belief was that he assumed the persona and divinity of the deity enshrined in the temple when he was in a trance, feigned or otherwise. As his screams were rising to a crescendo, he was crying out a litany of reasons for the deity's wrath, the scourge: the community was neglecting the temple, not conducting festive rituals to please the gods. In a fury he raised the sword, hit his forehead with it; blood gushed from the cut rolling down his eyes, cheek and dripping to his bare chest. Then a vociferous threat:

"Want me to curse and throw more seeds on the village? Want more deaths?"

Alarmed and terrorized by the thought of more seeds of smallpox befalling on them, the villagers fell to the ground, prostrated themselves imploring and begging the deity for mercy.

The church of Manoor was dedicated to St. Thomas, the apostle who came to the Western shores of India trailing the Middle Eastern spice traders, spreading the messages of a new religion among the natives. However, when calamitous plagues struck, it was St. Sebastian, the believers flocked to, seeking relief and protection. They likened the pustules encrusted bodies of the smallpox victims to the torso of the saint riddled with arrows as depicted on the statue at the church. There was a tiny chapel on the side of the church gate, dedicated to the martyr saint. During the seasons of epidemics, the villagers inundated the chapel with votive offerings. At harvest time, grains fresh from the field, more frequently a few coins, at times live chicken, their legs tied up, the birds noisily struggling to free themselves.

Manoor was reeling with the unrelenting bane of smallpox. Every evening a small cortege of believers, starting from the church, moved along the main road and small lanes of the village reciting prayers, stopping in front of every house they passed by, sprinkling holy water in the directions of the houses. Walking in front of the procession was one of the elders of the village carrying a framed picture of the saint under a large colorful umbrella, silvery filigree sparkling at its edges, a golden finial at the top. Two young men holding burning candles on each side escorted the elder, flaming torches lighting the path forward.

When the prayer group arrived in front of Vareed's house, they stood there some more time than they usually do at other houses, said a special prayer ending in a song before sprinkling holy water and moving on. Vareed was stricken with the dreaded disease, has been enduring harrowing pain and sufferings for more than two months, His house had gone dark and silent, even Kochammu was not heard any more. He was afflicted with a particularly virulent strain of the disease. All over his body, the pustules had coalesced and turned into gaping, oozing wounds. The vaidya's *Neem* leaf treatment had no effect on the overwhelming infection of the wounds. No one went near the house to steer clear of infection, overcome with an unexplainable fear. Folks avoided walking along the pathway in front of Vareed's house, they chose other routes.

Most of the smallpox patients recovered within a few weeks, the disease leaving unsightly poke marks on their face and trunk; deaths, however, were infrequent. When death did happen, the family of the deceased was left in a terrible quandary. Besides enduring the loss of a loved one, they had to struggle and scramble to arrange the burial of the dead. Most people, even the relatives, were reluctant to handle or take the body to the cemetery: besides a mortal scare of infection, many mysterious myths and lore associated with the disease struck terror into the villagers. There was, however, a small group in the village, ready and willing to do the grim job for a hefty price and a generous supply of alcohol: a gang of daredevils toughened by their previous experiences. They preferred to do their somber work in the dark, in the middle of night. In a fully drunken state, they stealthily slid into bereaving household avoiding any attention from the neighbors. Ignoring the grieving family, they wrapped the dead body in a mat of braided and dried pineapple leaves, lifted it to their shoulders and unceremoniously marched into the darkness, towards the burial grounds.

In the predawn stillness of a sultry night, a sudden mournful wail was heard from Vareed's house, the neighborhood woke up, startled. The neighbors knew then, what they have been anxious about for some time, has finally taken place.

Vareed had died.

Kochammu's moaning whines gradually faded into silence, an uncanny hush.

The family did not have much time to mourn, they were immediately confronted with the formidable challenge of making funeral arrangements. Under normal circumstances, it would not have been such a daunting task. Friends and relatives gather at the home of the deceased, take over all that was needed for the burial, leaving the immediate kith and kin to grieve. They bathed and prepared the body to be placed in the coffin, decorated it with flowers: red hibiscus from a neighbor's yard, wild flowerets from the bushes fencing compounds. A floral circlet was placed on the head of the deceased. The coffin usually was black, frequently with a dire inscription in white on the side: ***"Today me, tomorrow you"*** Four men closely related to the dead, carried the coffin on their shoulders, marching to the cemetery. Often, a small brass band wailing funeral tunes accompanied the mourners, a coterie of friends and neighbors moved along in slow pace. On either side of the procession, hired hands carried giant black umbrellas, silver filigree glittering at the edges, a tiny golden globe crowning the top. Men in dark attire walked on both side of the coffin, carrying two large crosses, silver or golden denoting the social status of the dead, golden for the rich, silver for the less rich.

In Vareed's case, everything was entirely atypical. Everyone in the neighborhood knew the family's loss and their uneasy predicament, but no one dared to came in to condole, to offer help; all strived to be distant and detached. When alive, discrimination hurt and pain the one discriminated against, when a corpse was deemed untouchable, it is the kindred who suffered and tormented.

Being the eldest in the family, Paulo was to make all the funeral arrangements somehow, single handedly. His younger brother Iyyapu had not been seen in Manoor for many months, no one knew his whereabouts, there were only a few rumors and gossips about his disappearance. Realizing it would be impossible to arrange a normal funeral for his father, Paulo decided to seek the services of the gang usually do the job of burying smallpox victims. They were a mysterious lot, none really knew who their leader was, nor where they lived; their whereabouts were known only by the word of mouth. With intense probing among the villagers and help from Devassy, Paulo extracted the name of the gang head, Porinjoo. He lived on the Kannoth hill. Paulo scouted the hill and came across an isolated house, thatched and in a desolate part of the hill. A narrow footpath leading to the house was lined by thickets of tall grass. He approached the house cautiously hoping that it was the house he was searching for. As soon as Paulo reached the edge of the narrow courtyard of the house, a man appeared on the verandah, a short, wiry man, full head of salt and pepper hair, a droopy mustache. He looked straight at Paulo with an uncanny air of recognition,

"Son, I can't do it"

A hint of sympathy and helplessness in his voice.

He already knew what Paulo had come for, the news of Vareed's death has reached his ears, he was anticipating someone to show up at his house any time.

"I am sent by Devassy; please help me; I have no one to turn to" Paulo pleaded.

"I would explain to Devassy. None in my group is willing to do this job"

"My father is dead; I am begging in his name, don't turn me down"

"Son, it is because of the terrible type of smallpox your father died of; I am helpless"

Porinjoo abruptly withdrew into his house leaving Paulo dismayed and disappointed. He trekked down Kannoth hill, walked along the road and bylines of Manoor aimlessly, not knowing what to do next; wondering which door to knock at for help. In the dire situation he was in, he expected a solution to appear in front of him miraculously. Irrational, as it was, such a hope was necessary for him to move forward. When he was passing in front of the shrine of St. Sebastian, he sat on the steps of the chapel to rest.

By the time Paulo reached his home, it was late in the evening. Nothing stirred, complete silence in the house, Kochammu and Mary might had fallen asleep in their pain and agony. It was the second day of his father's death, the air at home had become unbearable; a pall of gloom hung over everywhere. Paulo settled in one corner of the house, frustrated and exhausted; he sat on the floor leaning on to a bare wall. He was continuously mulling over all workable solutions for the problem at hand. Each scenario, however, ended up in a dead end. Fatigued and hungry as he was, Paulo did not know when he fell into an all effacingly deep sleep.

Paulo woke up startled, hearing footsteps on the verandah and a knock at the door. He opened the door to find the silhouette of a man standing in front of him; hardly recognizable in the darkness of the night.

"Don't be scared. It is me, came to help bury your father"

From the voice, Paulo instantly knew who it was: Muthoma. He had a roll of pineapple leaf mat in one hand and a shovel in the other. Paulo was choked up with a mixture of emotions: relief that a solution for the agonizing problem he had been wrestling with for the last several hours has finally materialized, suddenly, surprisingly. His father is about to depart from him and his family forever. Ever since his father's death, he did not have had much time to feel and experience his loss with all the sentiments of a son. He was immersed in finding a way to lay to rest his father's body, under strange and unusual circumstances.

"Where is your father, we must hurry and get everything done before daybreak, before the village wakes up"

Paulo led Muthoma to a tiny room in the back of the house where Vareed lay dead. As the door of the room creaked open, the stench of death overwhelmed them. Muthoma unrolled the mat and slid it under the dead body, wrapped it around the cold corpse and secured everything with ropes. With Paulo helping, Muthoma lifted the emaciated body, placed it on his shoulders and moved on to the front door of the house. Kochammu and Mary were heard sobbing in an adjoining room. As he stepped down to the tiny front yard, Paulo came with a lighted torch of dried coconut leaves.

"Put it out, we don't want anyone to notice us," Muthoma said in a hushed voice

He stepped into the darkness of the narrow road, heaved forward, towards the cemetery.

Paulo, shovel in hand, followed in silence.

# Six

Butchers of Manoor and the surrounding villages had a long tradition: they slaughtered only bulls, never the cows. It was in deference to the religious sentiments of the Hindu community of the region; the cow was sacred to them, in reverence they addressed the animal, "Cow the Mother"

Sunday: that was the busiest day at Muthoma's meat counter. At Varu's butchery down the road too the sale was brisk on Sundays. Beef was available in Manoor, only on Sundays.

The villagers flocked to the two meat stalls after the Sunday services at the church, almost a weekend routine for most. The church was closer to the butchery of Anthrayos, the proximity gave him an edge in the sales, the worshipers exiting the church encountered his stall first. Varu's regular and loyal customers, however, walked the extra distance and made their purchases there.

On that Sunday, Muthoma was sitting on his short stool in front of the meat counter. The animal slaughtered on the day was mostly sold out, only some remnants remained on the wooden plank. The road in front was bare and desolate, the Sunday worshipers already have gone home, occasionally old ladies were seen slowly treading their way home. Surveying the road in front, Muthoma saw Mary coming along, may be on one of her daily errands. She came near, stopped at the meat counter, greeted Muthoma. She needed to buy half a kilo of beef. Muthoma knew her and everyone in her family from her pre-teen years. He selected a few good pieces of meat from the remnants for her. As he was wrapping the meat in teak leaves, he engaged Mary in conversation, enquiring about everyone in her family: Kochammu is all right except her persistent dry cough; Paulo spends most of the days working at Devassy's house; is it true what is being talked about: Paulo has an affair going on with the eldest daughter of his master; absolutely untrue, he used to carry her on his shoulder all the way to her school when she was tiny and young; lazy people fabricate and propagate stories to entertain themselves. When the conversation turned to Iyyapu, Mary's face fell, sadness in her voice. He had not come home for months, no one knows his whereabouts. Sometime back he had come, knocking at the door in the middle of the night, having said only a few words, he went to sleep. Before daybreak, he was gone with Varuthu. Some say they are into politics, working against the government; then again, it was just gossip.

Muthoma was not aware when Anthrayos came out of his hut. Noticing a sudden change in Mary's facial expression, he turned back to look; Anthrayos was walking towards them, a cane in the right hand, limping.

"Do you know cooking?"

Looking straight at her, Anthrayos asked Mary abruptly, a glint in his eyes, a faint smile on the face.

"Yes"

"Do you know how to cook hot and spicy beef curry?"

"Yes"

"Would you make my meals? Every day"

Mary hesitated to answer.

"I would pay you well"

"I have to ask my Amma"

Mary said after a brief pondering silence.

As Mary walked away with the package of beef, Muthoma felt perturbed about the prospect of Mary being employed by Anthrayos, he was very skeptical.

Kochammu was overjoyed that her daughter was going to be gainfully employed. The family was eking out a living by the meager income from Paulo's job at Devassy's house, any additional earning, however small it might be, could mitigate the dire family circumstances.

The next morning, Muthoma was sitting behind the meat counter. In front of him, a freshly slaughtered goat hung from a wooden beam. Mutton was a new item being offered at Anthrayos's butchery, available every day of the week. It was in direct competition with Varu, mutton was sold at his butchery too. Their rivalry, however, was not expressed in loud, vociferous skirmishes as in the past; they had come to an implicit understanding to co-exist, reluctantly giving room for each other. Nevertheless, beneath the calmness of the surface, there was simmering rivalry, each one plotting and conspiring to outsmart the other. For Muthoma, mutton sale every day at the butchery was a stroke of luck: steady employment for him, the whole week.

Muthoma's meat counter was very quiet. Though sitting with his back to the hut, he was feeling Anthrayos watching him, sternly prodding him to better the sale. Unlike Sundays, week days are not very busy at the butchery. The high-priced goat meat was exclusively the privilege of the well to do of Manoor, they were not that many in numbers. Muthoma hardly could do much to change the situation. He lazily sat on his short stool waiting for the next customer to show up, feeling uncomfortable by the stinging stare from the hut.

The following day, when Mary walked past him towards the hut, Muthoma knew she had accepted the job offer, with her Amma's approval. He tried to smile,

"Go meet your boss; watch out and be careful" he threw a gentile warning after her.

Expressionless, Anthrayos watched Mary walking towards him,

"It is almost lunch time, get to work, make my lunch," he said; no pleasantries or formalities, just a rude command. Mary stared at him blankly, then she looked around: the hut had walls of corrugated metal sheets, the bottom of the walls had rusted, brown patches in places; the roof was thatched with dried coconut palm leaves. Daylight seeped in through a small solitary window with criss crossed bamboo bars. With Anthrayos sitting at the door and blocking the view, Mary could see only parts of the hut's interior: his cane was hung from the frame of the window, a narrow cot with a checkered sheet and a flattened pillow, all ruffled and slackly thrown on.

There was no semblance of a kitchen anywhere. Mary walked around the hut, came back and looked at Anthrayos askance,

"Where do I cook, are there any pots or pans?"

Anthrayos smiled wryly and remained silent for a moment,

"I don't have any of those"

He pulled out a sheaf of notes from his pocket and handed some to Mary.

"Go buy all that you need from Apputy's store"

Apputy's was the only grocery store in Manoor. The store was lively and busy all times of the day, especially during evening hours. The storefront was not very wide, behind a wooden bar some of the consumer items of daily use were displayed in gunny bags: rice, varieties of lentils, cotton seed as animal feed. A plethora of other items like spices and sugar were tightly stacked up, ceiling high in the inner part of the store. Next to the item display, a large pan-balance hung from the ceiling with cast iron weights on the floor. In a small floor space among the crammed grocery items, Subu, the store clerk tried to move around, taking orders from the buyers, often two or three layers thick. They elbowed and arduously clamored to draw Subu's attention. Once he established eye contact with one of the shoppers, he took the order and called it out, item by item, to Para, the store helper. Para assembled the ordered grocery in a wicker basket, handed them to Subu, he hollered the items with their weights and measures to Apputty, the store owner and cashier. Apputty with thick black framed spectacles tabulated and calculated the total bill for the customer.

The grocery store was crowded as usual when Mary came to shop for Anthrayos. She stood behind the milling crowd, waiting to be noticed by Subu. He, in fact, did more than just notice her, his face brightened up looking at her over the heads of others,

"Please move to one side" he requested the shoppers in front.

"Make way for my friend to come forward, come Mary, what do you need?"

Mary stepped ahead with an inscrutable face, recited her shopping list in one long breadth.

"Oh My! From A to Z, there is everything for starting a new kitchen! Are you starting a new family, Mary? When did *that* happen? Hum, we never heard anything about it"

Subu was trying to humor and tease Mary a little. Resentful, she did not like any of it, the unwanted attention, the subtle overtures.

"Get on with it, Subu, I have to leave, have work to do"

Mary was curt and piqued. Subu's face, riddled with pimples, turned a bit crimson. He silently got busy again, scrutinizing the items in the basket Para just brought out.

Mary carried the provisions and a couple of essential utensils in a large basket, effortlessly balancing it on her head as she walked back to the butchery. Closing his counter, Muthoma had left already; Anthrayos was still sitting at the doorsteps of his hut, a package of fresh goat meat beside him.

"Let it be mutton curry today" he said pointing the meat pack near him.

"Did you get all what you need? I am already hungry"

Mary nodded her head affirmatively; but she was immediately confronted by a problem: she did not know where to cook. She peeped into the hut wondering if there is a cooking place somewhere in there. Sensing what she was searching for, Anthrayos pointed to the small yard outside, directing her to cook there. The yard was covered with wild grass and weed. Uprooting them one by one, Mary cleared a small space just enough for her to try cooking. She walked around, found three large pieces of stone, arranged them in tripod fashion. She collected dried twigs and tree branches as firewood, lighted a fire in the middle of the stone tripod. Twigs crackled and flamed as she fed them into the fire. Mary fetched the newly purchased aluminum pan, placed it on the tripod to burn off the film of water still remaining in the pan after washing. She poured four spoons of coconut oil into the heated pan and waited before adding a few pieces of cinnamon bark, cardamom, peppercorns, cloves and black cumin seeds. As the spices got roasted in oil, she added pieces of fresh ginger and a cup of thinly sliced onion. The mixture fizzled and hissed in the pan sending an appetizing aroma into the air. As the onion turned golden brown, Mary added two spoons of turmeric powder turning the pan into a bright yellow palette, as she quickly followed it with a few spoons of red chili powder and stirred, the blend assumed an orange hue, sizzling and luminous. The brilliance, however, was soon subdued as she sprinkled two measures of dark brown curry powder into the mix. She emptied a plate of mutton pieces into the pan, poured a cup of cold water into it, the blend of spices cooled and stopped frizzling. Feeding more twigs, Mary whipped up the fire, waited to see the mix gradually heat up and simmer. The chunks of meat bobbed in the spicy mix, aroma arising in steamy whirls from the succulent surface. She placed an aluminum lid on the pan, steam quickly built up within the pan and spewed out, gently lifting and rattling the lid.

Leaving the mutton pieces to be cooked to softness and the sauce to thicken, Mary set out to boil some rice to go with the meat dish. She laid out another stone tripod, kindled a fire to cook the rice. Though she has done it multiple times, she felt a little tenuous about the volume of water to be added to rice, too much water would result in damp, soggy rice, too little would burn it. Finally, Mary trusted her hunch about the water, and proved to be right. The rice came out crisp, moist, jasmine white. She thought the mutton curry was done, she lifted the lid to peep into the pan, she liked the meaty, spicy flavor of the rising mist. She put out the fire under the pan.

Mary mounded up the boiled rice on a plate, a generous helping of the steaming mutton curry on the side. The fluffy grains on the periphery of the rice heap, soaked up the curry juice, turned yellowish brown. She took the plate into the hut, the aroma of freshly cooked food followed her. Anthrayos was sitting on the edge of his cot, a bottle of liquor on a short stool in front of him. As Mary came in, his face brightened up with a smile. Mary has never seen a hearty smile on his stern face before, her angst and trepidation slackened a bit. She placed the plate on the stool,

"It is a late lunch" she said apologetically.

"Does not matter, your food smells good,"

Mary went out, brought in the remaining rice and the curry, placed them in one corner of the hut; a left-over dinner for Anthrayos.

Anthrayos pulled out a few notes and handed them to Mary. He did not count them, perhaps he had counted them already, placing them aside for Mary. She too did not count them, she was just happy to hold and feel the paper in her palm.

"Come early tomorrow, I want you to make my breakfast".

As she was getting ready to go home she was surprised to see Muthoma still busy at the stall. He was picking up fish from a basket and arranging them according to their variety and size on the wooden plank in front of him, a display for the evening market. A fish stall was the newest addition to the expanding business ventures of Anthrayos. Once the mutton sale winds up in the mornings, Muthoma was asked to go to the sea shore a couple of miles away, haggle and bargain with the fishermen, buy and haul the catch to the stall. The meat stall doubled up as fish stall every evening. Veeran was the sole fish hawker for Manoor, Muthoma's fish stall appeared to be in direct competition with the hawker. Nevertheless, Veeran delivered fish to individual homes; women folk bargained with him, engaged in few minutes of gossip. His sale and hawking were all over by late morning. Anthrayos fish stall catered mainly to the evening shoppers, the people of Manoor welcomed the convenience.

Kochammu was very happy her daughter came home with some money in her hand. She had a number of needs to use the money for: the rice container in the kitchen is practically empty, it had to be replenished for the week along with a supply of lentils and other grocery. Mary was happily enthusiastic going to her new job the next day.

Anthrayos feasted on the left over for dinner, washed them down with a local brew from cashew fruits. The village moonshiner, Shanguroo, routinely supplied the drink to the hut. Anthrayos did not care much for the fermented coconut sap, "*kallu*". The hearty dinner and the alcohol went to his head, he could not contain himself in the hot metal walled hut. He came out, stepped on to the road in front, unsteady, supporting himself with the cane, eyes bloodshot. He planted himself in the middle of the road swaying, loudly challenging everyone seen or unseen. The passersby and onlookers stared at him, surprised. They had seldom seen him outside the hut, they have only felt his presence. With his challenges unmet and limbs becoming increasingly flaccid and limp, after a while he withdrew into the hut, collapsed on to the cot, fell asleep.

# Seven

Mary regularly came for work at Anthrayos's hut every morning, each day exactly at the same time. She did not have a watch or a clock at home, somehow she kept her time, instinctively perhaps. She cleaned and swept the hut and surroundings each morning, cooked and served breakfast and lunch for Anthrayos, his dinner kept ready in the hut before she left for the day. Anthrayos liked her cooking. In a strange way, he also was pleased her being around. He paid her well, not a fixed salary, it differed each day, assuredly generous all the same. Mary was happy with herself for having a job, being able to help her family in dire financial straits.

It was not long since Anthrayos arrived at Manoor. Though defiant and brazen by nature, it was not all smooth sailing for him to set up his business in the village. There was stiff resistance from the established merchants, local people viewed him warily. They had not forgotten how he mysteriously disappeared from Manoor. Rumors and whispered speculations abounded about his departure, about his whereabouts and exploits during the years of his absence. He was well aware of the angst and apprehension of the villagers, it made him consistently cautious and guarded. Essentially a recluse, he seldom moved out beyond his hut and its periphery. He conducted all his business from the hut, perched on the narrow door step of his pad. At his strict command and prompting, Muthoma managed the meat and fish stall and lately, Mary took care of his household, if it can be called as such. He was surprised at himself when he started feeling happy and content inexplicably, even sensing an urge to stir out a little. After his dinner and a couple of drinks Anthrayos began venturing on to the road, walking along, leaning on his cane, unsteady in his steps, occasionally muttering to himself. Before going too far, he usually returned to his hut, went to sleep.

It was late evening on a sultry Sunday. Anthrayos had his dinner, it was fried chicken and rice. After finishing his drinks, he started walking north on the road, an oversized chicken leg in his hand, burying his teeth into it time to time, still relishing it awkwardly. He had a little too much of the cashew drink that day. Forgetting to stop and walk back to his hut as usual, he kept on going, almost as in a reverie. After a while he stopped in front of a wrought iron gate for no particular reason. He stared at two ferocious lions in terracotta on either flank of the gate, the artistic grill of the gate. It was not bolted. Anthrayos pushed it open, walked wobbly toward a large, well-lit house. A short flight of steps led to the closed front door; he sat on the uppermost step, murmuring. He needed to rest.

In his drunken stupor, Anthrayos did not realize he happened to have arrived at the home of Devassy. Sensing someone stirring outside his door, Devassy opened the door. Seeing Anthrayos, he was a bit taken aback. He recognized the figure sitting at his doorstep, they did not know each other, however. He had heard about the new butchery down the road and its owner. Canards and titbits encircling him had reached his ears as well.

"Why are you sitting outside, come in if you wish"

Devassy invited Anthrayos, he mumbled something ramblingly in reply.

"I shall get you a glass of water, come on in" Devassy insisted.

Anthrayos stood up, walked in unsteadily, sat on the nearest bench he found.

"What brings you here today, is there anything you need?"

"She was a beauty, she was a bitch, hell with her"

His words were severely slurred, hardly comprehensible. He was trying to speak aloud, but words stuck in his mouth half way.

"She was a beast, hell with her"

"Who? Whom are you talking about?"

Anthrayos mumbled again, not a discernible reply.

"You were away for a long time, when did you get back?"

Not responding, Anthrayos kept looking down, then raised his head, vacantly stared at Devassy

"Where were you all these years, tell me" Devassy persisted, Anthrayos went on gazing at him glassy eyed.

"Where were you all these years, tell me" Devassy repeated his question in a much louder voice, almost as if he wanted to rouse Anthrayos from his stupor.

Even in his drunkenness, Anthrayos was anxiously awaiting someone to ask him this question, it seemed.

"It is a long story" he spluttered.

"It is a long story" he said again, stumbling over his words.

Devassy's second son, sixteen year old Anto, was in an adjoining room. A fledgling writer, he has already published a short story in a small magazine. For him every event in the village was seed for a story. He wrote prolifically but most did not make to print, he kept on writing, nevertheless. Sensing an unusual conversation taking place in the living room, Anto came and joined his father. Anthrayos was still struggling to narrate a story, often his words jumbled up and was left half spoken, his sentences fragmented and muddled. Anto, just as his father, was attentive to the strangely vague but nonetheless colorful tale being unfurled. They were captivated by the narrative, the elements of adventure, the romance, the exotic landscapes and incidental humor. As Anthrayos enthusiastically labored through his account, Anto and Devassy tried to knit together a tale from his incoherent, often disjointed sentences:

Strangely, Anthrayos's journey to nowhere did not start from Manoor; for some mysterious reasons, he drew a veil over that segment of the story. For him everything started from the port city of Kochi, a coastal city soaked by backwaters, airbrushed with coconut palms and verdant rice paddies in the suburbs. Anthrayos was sipping tea at a two-bench stall at the corner of a forlorn beach. Two weather- beaten, middle aged men were sitting at the other bench pensively gazing at the sea. One of them with a droopy mustache turned to Anthrayos and casually asked him,

"Do you want to go to Dubai? We can reach you to a [7]*dhow* leaving this evening"

"We won't charge you much" said the other.

Anthrayos did not have any idea where he wanted to head; he undoubtedly needed to leave the land, go far away, as far as he could. Hearing the name, Dubai, instantly gave him a possible destination. Beyond the seas, he had heard only about two countries, one of them was Dubai and the other Ceylon. For him, Dubai was the whole Middle East, he was unaware of the other countries and sultanates the geographic area comprised of. After the customary bargaining about the fare, Anthrayos followed the men to the edge of water. The men's dinghy tied to a wooden post was swaying and bobbing in the water. Soon, the three boarded the dinghy and they were on their way to the dhow claimed to be anchored far out

---

[7] *A sailing boat with narrow thin hull*

in the sea. After an hour of rowing, a hazy silhouette of a craft came into the view at a distance. Coming closer, Anthrayos saw a rickety vessel in disrepair, rusty hull, paint peeled off in many places. The crew of the dhow came to the edge of the deck, conversed with the dinghy owners in a language foreign to Anthrayos. They unfolded a rope ladder, slid it down on the side of the dhow, signed Anthrayos to climb up and come aboard. As soon as Anthrayos clambered up to the deck, the crew members demanded he handover all the cash he had with him. He was reluctant at first, but acquiesced and surrendered the money, he had no other way, he was surrounded by a band of tough looking wayward sailors. They kept most of the money as his fare, the rest was given back to him.

Anthrayos was the only passenger on the cargo vessel; that distinction soon vanished as he was asked to do menial jobs on the boat just as the other low-ranking staff. Rain or shine, he spent most of his time on the open upper deck, cleaning and sweeping. Occasionally, he was ordered to the lower deck to move and stack up crates of merchandises. He slept among the heap of tarpaulin sheets in a shack on the deck. During the bitter cold nights, he crawled and shivered under the tarp sheets. The boat was well stocked with food, it was mainly dried fish and flat bread. What was in short supply was water. Anthrayos was given three quarts of a liter per day. Being exposed to sun on the open deck, he needed much more than that, his ration was exhausted by late mornings; if he needed more, he had to pay for it from the meagre cash left with him. Following four days of sailing, the same crew who exacted the fare from Anthrayos at the beginning of his journey, turned up again, this time to demand more money from him for the onward travel to Dubai. Anthrayos's argument that he had already paid his full fare up to Dubai and he owed nothing more, was flatly ignored. In exasperation, he inverted and emptied his pockets, only a few coins fell to the floor; the crew was un-moved. They pointed towards the land, Anthrayos wondered what they meant. The crew gestured something and left the scene, Anthrayos again could not figure what they were trying to communicate. After a while, Anthrayos felt the vessel listing slightly, changing direction. He had a feeling it was heading towards the land, he was left wondering about the maneuver. It was not too long before he realized the boat, indeed, was moving in the direction of land. On the far horizon, he could see a coastline laced with green at the periphery.

The dhow slowed down as it was getting closer to the shore and then anchored at about a mile from the coast. An-thrayos wondered as he saw the crew hurriedly unfolding the rope ladder and deploying it down the side of the hull. The crew members beckoned Anthrayos to the brink of the deck and gesticulated, ordering him to climb down the ladder. Enraged, Anthrayos shouted at the crew, refused to comply. One of the sailors threateningly moved towards Anthrayos, unsheathed a dagger dangling from his waistband. The crew crowded around Anthrayos and forcefully lifted him down to the first rung of the ladder. He looked down to the seething sea, a small catamaran of three logs fastened together was bobbing on the waves; it might have been tossed down from the dhow for his transport to the shore. He was cheated, his journey to Dubai rudely interrupted. Now he was on his own in the sea on a crude contraption, his only passage to an unknown land.

At the lowest step, Anthrayos hung on to the ladder strug-gling to transfer himself to the catamaran, finally he had to let go of the ladder and jump on to it. Being tossed around by the waves, the catamaran was very unsteady. Finding it hard to balance himself, Anthrayos squatted on it, held on to the ropes holding the logs together lest he plunge into the water. He saw the dhow moving away from him. He shifted himself to one side of the log assembly to paddle with his bare hands, but the catamaran began listing to one side, he swiftly moved back to the center of the float steadying it. While fretfully racking his brains, wondering how to get to the shore, he did not realize he was being propelled to shoreline by the sea waves. After a while, however, he saw the land coming closer and closer, the coconut trees and greenery becoming discernable, a ray of relief that he was not going to drown and die, after all. Anthrayos was tightly holding on to the ropes as the catamaran being lifted and dropped down by the breakers. Then suddenly, a huge swell came, hauled up the catamaran and toppled it. Anthrayos lost his grip on the ropes, and plummeted into the sea, in horror he watched his craft drifting away, very soon it disappeared from his sight. Anthrayos started to swim towards the shore, often he felt he was not going to make it to the coast. Fatigue and weariness were getting the better of him, but the merciful surfs were pushing him forward. And finally, a last wave landed him to a sandy beach along with dead fish and seaweed. He was enveloped in glistening white froth. It was early morning; the soft sun melted away the spume as he sprawled on the sand motionless. Anthrayos was tired and exhausted, he did not have the energy even to look around, take in his environs. For a while, he kept looking up, but did not see the blue sky above or the white cumulous clouds. Then, gradually, his eyes closed; without his knowing, he soon glided into a deep sleep.

Anthrayos was awakened by someone kicking him by the foot, shouting,

"Are you dead?"

A female voice, speaking a dialect of his own language. He mused and wondered if he was back at where he started. He opened his eyes and from his supine position had a sense someone towering over him. He cleared his eyes to see a full-bodied woman staring down at him. Her face fair and oval, framed by jet black hair, long and luxurious. He thought he had never seen anyone more beautiful.

As Anthrayos woke up, the woman had had disappeared. He sat up, looked around for her, she was nowhere to be seen. He saw the expanse of the sandy beach glistening in the morning rays; at the far end of the beach he saw a circle of greenery. He started to walk in the direction of the oasis. He felt that was the way the beautiful woman had gone.

Devassy and Anto were intently listening to the halting narration of Anthrayos. Devassy was pleased the riddle of the butchery owner's disappearance from the village was finally being unfolded. Anto perceived material for a story, may be a novella or even a novel. One of his favorite authors, he re-membered, wrote a full-fledged novel from the experiences of someone drowned in a pond and remained under water for a while entangled among weed and debris, encountering dead ancestors, hearing voices from hollow caverns.

As the time went by, Anthrayos was becoming sober, his speech hardly slurred, he was emerging from his drunkenness to his reticent self. He grew uncomfortable, felt exposed in the presence of Devassy and his teenage son. As images in mist, he vaguely recalled him recounting some facets of his past, only a few minutes back. He always wanted them to remain untold forever. He desperately longed to rescind every word he uttered. Nevertheless, they had left his tongue for good to permeate the ascending layers of the atmosphere, impregnate the clouds and rain down on the village, he feared. His eyes downcast, An-thrayos was painfully self-conscious, uneasy and edgy to look at Devassy and his son, he hated to be in their presence. He wanted to meld into the darkness outside, withdraw and vanish into his metal walled hut; there he would be safe, clutching every strand of his past to his bosom, not having to share them with anyone.

His eyes planted on the floor, Anthrayos got up to leave, started to move towards the front door. Devassy and Anto, the son more than the father, pressed him to stay, complete the story. He paid no attention to their entreaties. Devassy brought a torch made of dried palm ferns, lighted it and gave it to his departing visitor to help him on his way home. Anthrayos walked towards the gate with his cane in one hand and the lit torch in the other. He left the gate open as he continued on to the road. In darkness, he walked towards his hut, swinging the torch back and forth to keep it lit, the amber light from the torch cast a halo around his moving figure.

Mary's job at Anthrayos's home went on, a daily routine for her: coming for work in the morning, returning home with the day's wage. Kochammu had set aside a small portion of her daughter's salary for a specific purpose: her marriage. Only a few months back Mary' marriage was to be settled and finalized, but the groom's family tersely withdrew from the proposed marriage at the last moment. The reason: dowry not adequate. No one at Mary's family believed it as the real reason. The boy and his parents had already agreed to accept the small amount of money Paulo had offered as dowry. They suspected Mathutty's handy work behind the mishap. Middle aged and grey haired, Mathutty was wiry and diminutive; droopy eyelids and a tight-lipped smile on his face, persistent and sinister. He savored and relished every time a proposed marriage was crumpled and collapsed. He would spare no efforts, endure any hardships to achieve the negative outcome. The villagers referred his name only with an added salutation: "Proposal Buster Mathutty". He kept his eyes and ears sharpened to every nook and corner of the village. At the very instant he

got the wind of a marriage being negotiated and nearing set-
tlement, he would embark on a mission to split and rupture it
somehow, shake the desirability of the proposed matrimony.
He would stealthily go to the girl's or boy's neighborhood to
whisper and infuse fabricated and rumored moral failings of
the girl or unsavory habits of the boy. Whenever the villagers
saw Mathutty in his white three-fourth-shirt sleeves and the
customary jerry bordered shawl around his neck, they looked
at him suspiciously. If he was seen wearing a monkey cap even
in the sweltering hot weather, they were certain, he, indeed,
was on to his disruptive mischief. Everyone wondered about
the monkey cap, however; if it was part of a disguise when on
the mission, it was, assuredly, an inept and ineffective one.

Kochammu kept Mary's marriage fund, mostly coins and
bills, in an earthen pot in the kitchen, away from view, behind
the containers of lentils and spices. She counted them almost
every day, realized how slowly the saving accumulated, how
painfully afar she was from the needed amount. One morning
when she opened the pot to count the money, to her horror,
she found there was nothing to count, the pot was empty.
She remembered Iyyapu coming the previous night on one
of his nocturnal family visits, disappearing before daybreak
as usual. Kochammu figured he might have helped himself to
Mary's money. Kochammu and Mary questioned him when
he visited them next. Without a semblance of guilt or regret,
he moralized that the money was for the right cause. Neither
Kochammu nor her daughter knew what the worthy cause was.

It was late morning on a rainy Saturday. Mary had moved
the two stone tripods and her cooking routines to the thatched
shed between the meat stall and Anthrayos's hut before the
heavy rain drops started to pound the rooftops. She rushed
out and brought in all that she needed for cooking as she
heard the rain approaching from afar. Mary always felt the

monsoon rains moving from one distant end of the village to the other, usually the rain front advancing from west to east howling along the way. Hearing the approaching rain, housewives dashed out to bring in clothes drying out on the cloth lines; goats and calves grazing out bayed and ran to whatever shelter they could find. When Mary was making breakfast for Anthrayos in the morning it was sunny and bright, the weather abruptly changed, becoming dark and cloudy and finally a cloudburst. That was the day, for the first time, she had made *Appam,* the circular crepe made of fermented rice batter and cassava stew for breakfast. Anthrayos was delighted.

Mary got busy making lunch for Anthrayos; she was unfazed by the unexpected rain or having had to cook indoors in the shed. She had the innate wherewithal of swiftly adapting to circumstances, unexpected and challenging. She set up her stone tripods and made fire only a few feet away from Muthoma's meat and fish counter. He did not mind the kitchen smell of onions, ginger and garlic, the smoke bothered him a bit however, but did not show it outwardly. He had a soft corner for Mary and above all, he should not be a hindrance when she was cooking for Anthrayos, that, indeed, would not be in Muthoma's best interests. At the counter, Muthoma was busy with a customer, the eighty-year-old Ousep. He regularly came to buy fish every Saturday, bargains to the last penny every time; Muthoma never relented nonetheless, adhering to the stringent orders from above. Finally, he managed to close the deal throwing a minuscule of a fish into the old man's basket to please him, winking at him not to reveal the favor he received to anyone else.

Muthoma saw Mary taking the lunch she prepared to the hut, the tantalizing aroma of spicy beef curry wafted into his nostrils; the sheet metal door of the hut clanked shut after her. Mary's relationship with Anthrayos was formal, that of a servant and master, they consciously retained that distance for their own distinct reasons. Mary entered the hut only to take in her master's meals or clean the interior, she never lingered around and always made a quick exit. That day, however, the door remained shut and Mary did not emerge for a while. Muthoma did not notice it, he was busy with a couple of customers who had asked him to bring sword fish from the beach front. Even after the sale, he was chatting with them. All of a sudden, he heard a loud cry from the hut. He rushed to the hut, pushed open its door. What he saw unnerved and enraged him. Anthrayos was holding Mary by her hair, beating her on her buttocks with a wicker cane, Mary struggling to free herself from his grip, writhing with pain. Muthoma scurried to Anthrayos roaring,

"Leave her alone at once, you brute"

"She is enjoying it, don't you see, she is a special woman"

"Let her go, otherwise I have to kill you, bloody drunk"

"Who are you to order me; you get out of here"

"Leave her now, at this very moment before I break your other leg, and then….."

Muthoma thundered, he bared a knife from holster hanging from his waist belt. Anthrayos dropped Mary to the floor. She collected herself and ran out wailing.

Muthoma and Anthrayos were staring at each other, Muthoma with boiling wrath and rage in his eyes, Anthrayos in a drunken frenzy.

"Get the hell out of here right now, don't you ever come back for work again" Anthrayos exploded.

When Muthoma came out of the hut, no one was around. Mary might have gone home, Muthoma hoped she did not cry all the way home. Some fish remained on the wooden plank, unsold, unattended. Muthoma started to walk home.

# *Eight*

Varu habitually got up very early in the morning, he was at the butchery much before the daybreak; he had to slaughter the animals, dress and hang the carcass at the counter. His son, Varunny, joined him only later. The young man would not forgo the early morning slumber for anything in the world. When Varu closed the front door and walked out of the house in the mornings, he seldom noticed the figure snoring on the verandah: Muthoma fast asleep under a chequered bed sheet. By the time Varu returned early afternoon for lunch, Muthoma usually had had already left for work at Anthrayos's butchery. On that day when Varu returned, he was puzzled to see Muthoma sitting on the steps of the house, lazy, pensive.

"Why are you still at home? Didn't go to work?" Varu asked.

"That son of a bitch threw me out, I have no job"

"When you stabbed me in the back and went to work for him, I knew it, this is how it is going to end"

Muthoma was silent, looking afar, avoiding Varu's eyes.

"Want to come and work at our meat shop as before?"

Surprised, Muthoma looked at his brother intently.

"I would consider you a prodigal son coming home, repentant or not"

Varu continued,

"Certainly, I won't have an animal butchered to celebrate your return. All that, written only in the Good Book"

"Come and help me at the shop tomorrow, if you wish"

Muthoma turned his face towards his elder brother, smiled agreeably.

Varu was not offering Muthoma a job at his butchery, certainly not out of magnanimity, fraternal love or not even prompted by biblical forgiveness. He was in desperate need for help at the shop; Varunny was not there anymore to give him a hand, he had been in prison for the last several months.

It was not even three years since India gained independence. The citizenry was still smarting from the partition of the country, the exodus and bloodshed that followed. Mahatma Gandhi, the architect of the freedom movement, strived to steer clear the nascent nation from violence, advocating non-violent ways. It enraged some and a religious fundamentalist assassinated him, a single bullet. Nationalist fervor was at its peak. Thinking it an opportune moment, Marxists tried to thrust themselves into Indian politics. They thought the country would be a fertile ground for their movement to grow and flourish: wide disparity between the rich and poor, uneducated masses. With spirituality woven into every thread of their lives, dialectical materialism did not appeal to most of the ordinary Indians; it was even beyond their comprehension. The leftists, however, persisted to push their cause among the masses. Varunny was blissfully ignorant and innocent of these and all that was taking place around him and beyond. He had forged a relaxed and stress-free life for himself; waking up late in the morning, having breakfast of rice porridge with jackfruit or cassava curry, a quick dip in the nearby fresh water pond, then off to their butchery. Walking the short distance to the meat shop, he always wore a vacant smile on his face, expressly happy with himself, self-assured. At the stall, he jovially chatted with the customers, boastfully sharing with them some of his exploits, often imagined, starry eyed. His tranquil and placid existence started to change as Hyder crept into his life, stealthily, deviously. Hyder was the secretary of the local communist party. He did not have much of a following except a few unemployed youths, most of them, however, sitting on the fence regarding the political philosophy he espoused.

Very often, Hyder was seen standing on a crumbled down masonry wall in the middle of an open space in front of Apputty's grocery, haranguing about workers' rights, their exploitation by the rich, their miserable lives. Gaping, a few curious onlookers gathered around him, intrigued by his rancorous vitriol, rather than taking in his arguments and call to action. Hyder lambasted anyone who was willing to pay attention to his lectures. He did not have a job or practiced a trade. There were rumors that he received funds from a foreign power.

It was sundown when Varunny arrived at Gopalan's house; Gopalan's family, his wife and two children, were sitting on the footsteps of their house, silent, sad faced. A goat was tethered to a wooden post of the house, white and black patches on its coat, a tiny brass bell on its neck chimed as it moved around. The goat already had been sold to Varu. The family was deeply saddened, they could not think of parting with their pet goat. Varunny was there to fetch the animal; it was to be slaughtered the next day. Gopalan untied the goat from the post and handed its leash to Varunny. As Varunny started to walk along the ditch road, it was already dark. The goat on the leash and the peals of the brass bell followed him. As he was midway to the butchery, Varunny heard footsteps behind him, he turned back to look, it was Hyder.

"How are things Varunny, I have been thinking of meeting you for a while" he started, Varunny looked at him questioningly.

"I have a great job for you, would you be willing to take it up?"

"What type of job is it?"

"This is something only you can do; you have everything needed for this job"

Hyder waited, trying to read Varunny's facial expression, then, continued,

"Would you lead a *Jadha,* a march, along our main road on May Day, hundreds are going to follow you, you are going to be the leader holding a large flag.".

Hyder hardly had time to breath. He went on to talk about May Day, how important a day it is for workers and the poor, it is celebrated all over the world, especially in countries where working class have captured power, it would be so great to be a participant in the march, even more so if one was leading it.

Varunny instantly visualized himself treading with a huge flag in his hand, pumping his mighty chest forward, giving commands to a huge column of men following him shouting slogans. He could feel the power building up within him, his characteristic vacant smile turned into a smile, expectant, enthusiastic.

"When is the May Day?"

"Coming Monday; would you come"

"I would be there"

"Come in front of Apputty's, three O'clock sharp,"

Manoor did not wake up to May First energized or excited, for most of them it was like any other day. For Hyder, it was the day to showcase his party, make their presence felt. He was at the appointed venue way ahead of time. He was sitting on the broken-down masonry wall, a flag rolled on a pole near him, a few bamboo sticks stacked on the ground with placards, on them crudely written slogans in red. As he saw Varunny walking towards him, Hyder stood up, grandly punched the air with his clenched fist, roared up a pro-worker slogan into the air. Varunny was taken aback a bit, puzzled. Hyder unfurled the red flag, pressed the thin flagpole into Varunny's hand; Varunny broadened his smile; whatever was promised, finally is at hand, he thought. Hyder assumed a stern demeanor, his face tightened, he asked Varunny to repeat after him as he bellowed another slogan. Varunny complied and yelled the slogan, rather meekly. Hyder continued the slogans swapping from one slogan to the other, Varunny repeated after him, his shouts growing more and more powerful and louder; their raucous symphony of slogans went on, both shouting at the top of their voice, not always in unison. A small number of people came and stood around Hyder and the flag bearer, Varunny. Most of them were leftist sympathizers of Hyder, others came in out of curiosity. Irrespective of their political leanings, everyone came in was given a placard to hold. Hyder impatiently waited for more people to come, but the assembly remained thin and sparse. Hyder ordered everyone to fall in a single line, Varunny at the head proudly holding the red flag. The column moved on to the main street of Manoor, started to march in the direction of the temple, a couple of miles north. Hyder walked up and down the file of marchers, animatedly screaming slogans, urging everyone to repeat after him. Varunny turned back time to time to look at his followers; he was disheartened by the scanty number of marchers, where were the hundreds he was to be in charge, why the procession was so sullen. He saw only some of them were calling out slogans, others were least buoyant and lively, walking silently, almost as in a funeral march. Perhaps, they did not know what the parade was about. As the march progressed, Hyder was incensed to see an occasional demonstrator leaving the column, throwing his placard to the wayside. By the time the *jadha* reached the open ground near the temple, the number of the marchers had dwindled down to single digits. Hyder had plans to give a fiery speech on the temple ground at the culmination of the march; he, however, was awfully discouraged looking at the tiny group of possible listeners, squatting on the bare ground, their placards on their side. He quickly gave up the idea of an address. He did not show his disappointment at how the *jadha* turned out, he tried to keep Varunny engaged, trying to nudge him into his political organization, subtly, cleverly.

The few marchers remaining on the open ground dissipated and went their way. Hyder and Varunny started to walk back, Hyder talking incessantly about Marxist ideology, immediacy and inherent need for a revolution. Varunny listened silently with an inscrutable face, it was uncertain if he internalized any of the concepts Hyder was trying to expound, he certainly was inundated in a torrent of words, nonetheless. When they reached Bhanu's coffee shop they went in, settled themselves on a bench and desk at an isolated corner, ordered cups of coffee and lentil patties. Hyder continued his indoctrination of Varunny, his potential disciple heard him without a word, this time, however, he had something to be busy with while listening: sipping coffee, munching the lentil patty. Hyder already had recognized ego as Varunny's point of vulnerability, he took great pains to boost it during their one-way conversations, strategically sprinkling exaggerated comments on Varunny's imposing physique, his courage and self-confidence in facing anyone and anything, and indeed, his leadership qualities.

"Village council election is coming up next year, who knows, you might be our party's candidate"

Hyder declared. The quirky emptiness in Varunny's smile disappeared; a joyous self-absorption replacing it.

Varu's butchery closes by around three in the afternoon, Varunny frees himself half an hour before that, leaving his father to clean up and bring down the shutter. When he steps out of the shop, Hyder would be waiting for him to walk along, talking all the way, ending up in Bhanu's coffee shop and then more one-way conversation. This had become a routine for the party stalwart and the fledgling follower. Even after months of relentless indoctrination, it was not evident if Varunny learned even the primary tenets of Marxism-Leninism; however, he was strongly drawn into the party, mainly for self-gratification. He regularly attended night-study classes conducted by Hyder and his cohorts, not as an active participant, he just wanted to belong. He dutifully carried out all that were asked of him by Hyder.

May is the month of temple festivals. Irrespective of cast or creed, the whole village waited for the two days of the year, joyfully noisy and mirthful. Conducted on the temple grounds, the celebrations were a rare social occasion for the people of Manoor to come together in a festive atmosphere. Everyone enjoyed the open market on the ground. There were makeshift stalls of all kind, displaying everything from trinkets and handicrafts to farm animals like goats and chicken; venders with toys and colorful balloons on slender stakes moved among the milling crowd trying to make a sale. Along the din and clamor of the open market, drum beats and clangs of cymbals could be heard from the inner halls of the temple, constantly in a tumultuous rhythm. All the festivities were concentrated on the solemn event of bringing out the idol of the deity enshrined in the temple from the sanctum sanctorum, ceremoniously, majestically. It was exposed in front of the temple for every devotee to open their eyes on, to adore. The idol was held by a priest sitting on an elephant, an assistant seated behind the priest held a large decorative umbrella above the idol and the priest; the golden filigree on the peripheral rim of the umbrella glittered in the auburn light of the array of oil lamps on the temple walls. Right behind the umbrella bearer, a turbaned man stood precariously on the elephant back, rhythmically waving two white pom-poms up and down. The elephant's head was bedecked with an enormous golden mask, covering all the way down to the trunk, sparing only the animal's eyes; big and small golden bubbles sculpted on the mask sparkled in the light; tiny golden bells along the edge of the mask pealed as the elephant moved its head. In front of the elephant carrying the idol were two long lines of drummers facing each other, horn and cymbal players closely accompanying them. Immediately behind each line of drummers were arrays of large festive umbrellas in bright colors of red, yellow, green and blue. A big crowd thronged around the musicians and drummers, listening attentively, some of them nodding their heads accompanying the rhythm of the beats.

The finale of the festival was fireworks. Though the devotees and spectators were engaged in paying homage to the idol or listening to the drums, uppermost in their minds was the pyrotechnics that was yet to come. At the very first time they heard a firecracker pop, everyone strained their necks, looking up to the sky expectantly. Each and every pair of eyes in the gathering was scanning the skies in unison as one giant compound eye of a dragonfly. Every time a piece of firework exploded and blossomed into a huge celestial wild flower, a collective exclamation of joyous amazement went up from the spectators.

There was lively rivalry among the neighboring villages about the pomp and opulence of the individual temple festivals; every item was compared and evaluated, talked and boasted about for many days, even after the festivals. In order to get an upper hand in the competition, some villages added two or three elephants in the procession instead of just one; others brought well known drumming groups from far-away places or extended the fireworks from fifteen minutes to the whole half an hour. Though the pageantries were named and known after the village temples, they all were financed and conducted by the wealthy and well-known families of the community. What was at stake was their prestige and reputation, for them an opportunity to display their affluence and might. For many years now, Namby family conducted the Manoor celebrations. Besides being the sole *Ayurvedic vaidya* or physician of the village, Bhasu Namby was also one of the largest landowners of the community. He never sowed or reaped anything from his extensive land holdings, however. He leased plots to farmers to cultivate and collected part of their earnings in kind and cash as rental. Though he planned every detail of the temple celebrations and proudly sponsored it, he or his family never came down to join the festivities. Being upper cast, they were concerned that they would be tainted and made impure by coming close to or inadvertently touching lower cast members in the crowd. The family watched the revelries from the upper floors of their house, away from the commoners, having a commanding view at the same time.

The crowd was thrilled and elated by the crescendo of the fireworks, wildly applauded it as they started to leave and trek back home. Then, like wild fire, a startling news spread among the crowd: Bhasu Namby's house was broken into, the vaidya was severely beaten and locked up in one of the rooms as the burglars made off with cash, carted away several bags of rice, the thieves practically emptying the entire granary. Apparently, the heist took place as the idol on the elephant was being taken around the temple in a procession, the drummers, horn and cymbal players accompanying, the worshippers in a transcendent reverie.

It took two days before a formal complaint was lodged at the police station miles away. Two police men came to the village to investigate the crime. They close questioned two domestic servants of the vaidya, beat them up for no particular reason, except for the presumed assumption that they were withholding some details related to the offence. The police went back without obtaining any clue about the culprit; but they were after the scent of the criminals, relentlessly. More investigators under higher police officials came to the scene, the village appeared to be under a siege. At every nook and corner of Manoor, there were police men in khaki uniform and scarlet red helmets with golden serial numbers on them, officers with waxed mustaches and pistols holsters hanging from their waist belts were patrolling the village in a Jeep. The village had never witnessed anything like that before. The folks watched everything from a distance with awe, an inexplicable fright stuck in their throats.

Initially it started as a rumor, then it gathered strength: the robbery had a political perspective to it, whiff of a class struggle, rise of the oppressed. The police already have a suspect, they are hunting for him.

When Varunny finished work at the butchery, Hyder was waiting for him as usual. They walked towards Bhanu's coffee shop, Hyder seemed unusually grave and reticent. They settled down on their regular seats. Hyder did not order their usual coffee and snacks, he seemed to be in a hushed urgency, he was apprehensive, looking around, watchful of his surroundings. He pulled his stool closer to Varunny.

"We succeeded. Didn't you see what happened on the day of the festival? It was our job, yes, our handy work".

Hyder sounded victorious, zeal and vigor in his eyes.

"We can accomplish anything, if we plan and work at it; but we have to be careful; we should be willing to sacrifice anything to achieve our goal"

Varunny listened attentively, in silence.

"It was Mazu Dada and group who did it"

Hyder whispered in Varunny's ears, pulling himself even closer to him.

"The police are already suspecting him; but we just cannot lose him to the police pigs; he is a national leader; the party needs him for struggles in other parts of the country"

"I have never heard about him, where is he from" Varunny was curious.

"He is from a faraway state; in no time, he can be at anywhere in the country to organize and act upon party's orders; he oversees all of our counter revolutionary forces"

Varunny scratched his head trying to decipher "counter revolution."

"For us, revolutionaries, party is supreme, we obey them without question, we carry out whatever we are ordered to"

Hyder paused, may be for emphasis or to draw Varunny's undivided attention, then continued gravely,

"The higher ups of the party want you to confess to the police that it was you who were at Bhasu Namby's house and carried out the entire robbery. This is just to divert them from Mazu Dada's trail"

"They feel that you are the only one having the courage and valor to face the police officers, admit to the crime and challenge them"

"Anyone else would whither, whimper and break down under questioning. The party greatly value you, they are confident you are going to do it, won't you?"

Hyder gushed, almost like a soapbox preacher, trying to inspire and persuade Varunny to take up the mission.

Varunny's lips quivered a little to precipitate into a smile, a smile exuding self-gratification; another opportunity for him to satisfy his narcissistic cravings. He hardly considered the gravity and personal peril of the task he was asked to undertake as he imagined the glory awaited him.

He did not hesitate to volunteer and go along with party's plan.

The next day Varunny presented himself at the police camp to surrender and admit himself to be the perpetrator of the break in at Namby's house. Initially, his narrative puzzled the officers, but eventually they went along, as it would be a quick and satisfactory culmination to their days-long investigation. As a customary police routine, Varunny was severely beaten as soon as he owned up the crime, he was handcuffed and loaded on to a Jeep to be taken away to the police station miles away. His lips were lacerated and bleeding, he looked lost, forlorn. At the station, he was locked up in a holding cell. He did not anticipate the torment and physical abuse meted out to him. He had an instant change of heart. He desperately wanted to shout to the whole world, especially to the officers, that he was innocent, it was all a ruse by the communist party. But it was too late. When he tried to speak to one of the officers, the inspector kicked him with his baton and roared him to shut up.

After a couple of days, Hyder came to the station to see Varunny in the lock-up room; he assured him that the party would soon get him out on bail, an attorney would represent him at the court hearing.

Charging him with grand larceny, break in and entering and several other sections in the penal code, Varunny was produced in front of a magistrate to be prosecuted. There was no attorney representing him, there was no sign of Hyder anywhere in the court. After a brief perfunctory legal procedure, the magistrate promptly sentenced him to five years and three months of imprisonment.

Varunny had completed only fifteen months of his prison term. It would have been a long time before he could come out and help Varu at the butchery.

It was only a few months since Muthoma bolted to work for Anthrayos's at his meat stall. When he returned to work at Varu's butchery, he felt at home and on familiar grounds. Varu's shop was one of the five in a structure overlooking the main road with an inner storage room and a foyer in front. The meat counter occupied most of the foyer; a two feet butcher block made out of the solid cross section of a tree trunk sat next to the counter, carcasses hung by hooks on the ceiling. Muthoma's station was behind the counter on a taller stool. He knew all the three meat cleavers on the counter by their shapes and lengths. Nothing much had changed at the butchery since he left, not too long ago. Nevertheless, something had changed, Muthoma noticed: Varu's attitude towards him, he was more inclusive and warmer. Muthoma was given access to the cash box during transactions. Muthoma almost felt that he was back again with the family business.

Varu was very much affected by the imprisonment of his son. He often engaged in loud soliloquies about the circumstances of his son's detention. Sometimes he came to share his emotional outpourings with Muthoma,

"When I saw him moving around with Hyder, I warned him that he was in bad company, should avoid the Marxist, would he listen? no; he grew up like a weed, strong, handsome, but very naïve, head in the cloud. The party cheated him outright to save a thief from the north. Let me see that Hyder again, I would give him another thrashing, he would know the brawn of the butcher, the whack and thwack I gave him last month made him cry like a baby, that is not enough; I am waiting for him"

When Varu became overwhelmed by emotions, he went to the inner room of his shop to be alone, to vent to his seething rage.

Muthoma was already familiar with most of the regular customers at Varu's meat stall. They were happy to see him back at his brother's slaughterhouse. Some of them were also curious to know what made him go and work with Anthrayos to begin with and what brought him back. While others tried to snoop and get titbits about his former boss, mysterious and reclusive: was it all true what we hear about him, all those terrible canards, did he really do it. Muthoma did not know much more than what they did. Though he did spend a few months with him, none knew how remote they were from each other. However, Muthoma did have a few details he gathered from Varkey.

Anthrayos was the youngest of the three children of Tharu and Rosa, Varkey the eldest and Ammini, their only sister in between. Tharu came to Manoor as a young man, a stranger from a faraway village, several miles east. Monsoon season was at its peak. Pregnant clouds were rising at the distant mountains as airborne elephants. They thickened and darkened as they moved towards Manoor to canopy the village in a pal. With thunder and lightning, the clouds burst over Manoor in torrential rains, flooding every pond and paddy field. Late, on one of those rainy nights, Tharu knocked at the doors of Matthu chettan, Devassy's late father. Disheveled and shivering, he was completely drenched, clothes stuck to his body. Matthu chettan, tall and of ample proportions, opened the door, measured the stranger head to toe. He saw someone moving in Tharu's shadow.

"Who is that? Someone with you?"

"My wife" said Tharu hesitantly.

A woman, completely wet, dripping and visibly pregnant, moved into the light. She tried to rearrange her soaked, sticky cloths over her bulging abdomen. With her large eyes, she looked at Matthu chettan imploringly.

"Why are you here at this hour? What do you need?"

"You should help us. We need a place to rest. We are driven out of our village................"

Tharu and Rosa. They were lovers from neighboring homes. They fell in love while working at the paddy fields: planting rice seedlings, peddling the water wheels, weeding, harvesting. They eloped and got married as soon as Rosa became pregnant. When they returned, neither of their families would let them in. Their son and daughter have shamed and dishonored the families. The families of Tharu and Rosa incessantly exchanged curses and abuses across the fence, blaming each other for the mishap. They joined hands, however, to punish and chase away their offending children from the village.

Subliminally, strains of the ballads epitomizing the flight of his ancestors from Palladi, floated into Matthu chettan's conscience. He opened one of the servants' quarters at the far end of his compound for the couple.

Next morning Tharu started working with the rest of the laborers at Matthu chettan's paddy fields. It did not take long for Tharu to impress his co-workers with his energy, easygoing ways and skills at a whole range of farm tasks. When he was at the water wheel, he could generate a water rush downstream with the fury of a monsoon flood; while tilling, he could energize his oxen, as if by magic, to furrow the earth deep and wide with lightning speed; and all this, while singing folk songs, in his deep sonorous voice, to lighten the toil for himself and others. Soon, Matthu chettan recognized the desirable qualities in his new worker. He recalled Tharu, thoroughly wet and helpless, showing up at his doorsteps with his pregnant wife, only a few months back. For long, he had been looking for an efficient supervisor, **karyakaran,** for his farm. Tharu was a natural choice. Though young, Tharu's command and control over his workers was remarkable. When Matthu chettan announced his choice, Tharu bent and touched Matthu chettan's feet to express his gratitude.

As Matthu chettan's **karyakaran,** the supervisor, Tharu was quick to recognize the numerous opportunities coming his way to further and improve his own lot. When these opportunities presented themselves or when Tharu manipulated them into being, he did not hesitate to utilize them to the fullest. In rice farming, planting and harvesting are the busiest of seasons. During planting season, the workers, relatively, are not much in demand. After a period of lull and unemployment, everyone was anxious to get into one of the available planting jobs. Tharu was ready to oblige some of them if certain conditions are met. The fortunate few, called for work, were more than willing to part with a chunk of their wages to grease Tharu's palm. Harvest season invariably needed more farm workers and the laborers fiercely bargain for higher wages. Tharu promptly inflated the salaries to attract workers, only to take a cut for himself from their increased wages.

By the time his first child was born, Tharu was prospering and thriving. His rise to wealth and dominance was meteoric. It all started with a few acres of land he leased from Matthu chettan. He fertilized it with sweat and toil to abundant harvests. Soon he was acquiring more and more acres of his own. He started a money lending operation from his home. Money strapped villagers flocked at his gate, they never knew of such a helping hand before. Some of them, however, got financially ruined in the process, Tharu conveniently ignored their plight. Most Manoor natives marveled at Tharu's sudden and mysterious rise to power and fortune; nonetheless, they suspected a much darker and sinister story behind his opulence. At Bhanu's cafe and elsewhere, stories of his forays into demonic darkness were narrated and discussed in hushed tones. Some of the narratives were so realistic that they sounded as eye witness descriptions, though none knew who the witnesses were.

Faraway beyond the borders of Manoor, on the other side of the Thully hills, there was an area, densely forested, away from any human habitation. The age old wild trees were tall, their extensive branches intertwined with boughs of other trees. The overgrown tropical vegetation matted together by thick, strapping climbers, appearing like snakes strangling the trees. The jungle appeared impenetrable. However, deep in the interior, beyond the façade, there was a small temple built of rough blocks of black granite, dedicated to the devilish deity, *Chathan*. The access and the path to the temple was as mysterious and hidden as the temple itself, not known to most. In the dead of night, Tharu trekked the miles towards the temple, alone, guided only by starlight. Climbing down the hill, he walked along the periphery of the forest looking for an entry, finally locating an opening in the thicket leading to a single -foot pathway to the temple. Mysteriously, he felt being led. As Tharu entered and cautiously walked along the narrow track, he could see a faint light emanating from a narrow doorway. He could hardly discern the outline of the temple, it was shrouded in thick shrubbery, enmeshed in the secondary roots of a huge banyan tree. When he entered the doorway, he could see a figure awaiting him. He was entirely cloaked in scarlet red, his shoulder length hair matted and framing his stern face, the black beard with streaks of grey, eyes, protruding. He gestured Tharu to follow him, they walked in silence, entered an inner room, cold and lighted by two oil lamps. In the center of the room was a grotesque idol on a pedestal, grimacing frighteningly, bared fangs, flabby tongue sticking out. On the floor in front of the idol were three icons of Christian piety. Tharu was ordered to desecrate and do blasphemous acts on the religious cyphers; in return he was promised wealth, prosperity and power. According to the stories whispered around in Manoor, Tharu did, indeed, complied with what he was commanded to. The figure in red implanted a copper talisman under the skin of his left thigh, the source of guidance to his material conquests.

The virtuous and righteous of Manoor were convinced, divine retributions awaited Tharu for his sacrilegious conduct. They thought their predictions came true after some time, when Tharu's family endured a grim and dreadful tragedy: the death of Mathu, the younger brother of Anthrayos and Varkey, contracting rabies. He died barking like a dog day and night, begging for water.

The rumors and gossips about him had reached and were droning in Tharu's ears too, he was unaffected by them, however. Ignoring the buzz, he went on with his endeavors to amass more and more wealth, very careful with his money at the same time. He quickly gained the added distinction of being called 'The Miser of Manoor'

Tharu worked hard all through his life, he demanded his male children to emulate him in building up their lives. When Varkey's infatuation with bodybuilding collapsed and the young man did not know what to do next, Tharu set up a humble bicycle shop for him and sent him forth to prosper, with a stern assertion not to expect anything further in the future.

Being youngest in the family, Anthrayos was pampered, especially by his mother. He lived a carefree life, not doing anything gainful or meaningful. Waking up late in the morning, he spent most of the day in his room on the upper floor of the house. He went out in the evenings to return late at night. Every evening, he needed money before going out, Tharu stoutly refused to oblige; but he somehow extracted the money from his mother. Once Anthrayos came home very late at night and knocked at the door, it was Tharu who opened door, he was enraged seeing his son drunk and incoherent, he slapped him across the face. Anthrayos shut himself in his room, refused to come out for two days; long before, however, he returned to his unsavory behavior. His confrontations with his father grew more frequent, their relations turning increasingly strained. Anthrayos tried hard not to come in front of his father, he did his best to avoid some areas of the house his father most frequented. Even if he saw a shadow of his son moving in the house, Tharu threw admonitions and curses at him. Tharu and Anthrayos were moving away from each other as father and son, without them realizing it. Tharu was nudging his son away from his ruinous habits and conducts because he loved him. Anthrayos felt his father interfering in his life, unduly; as the youngest son of a wealthy family he had the right to a life of luxury, a generous pocket money. The one who was most perturbed and pained by the father son encounter was Rosa. Whenever she heard Tharu raising his voice at his son, she grew anxious, ran to Mother Mary's picture to pray. She pleaded with her husband not to be too hard on their son; she counselled her son to mend his ways, change his stance against his father,

"He is your father, he loves you, that is why he is after you to change your behavior, he works hard to keep our family prosperous, go help in his work, be responsible instead of spending time with your friends and drinking".

She even warned him he would not get any money from her any more, but to no avail. He still managed to get the money from her by begging childishly, appealing to her maternal weaknesses.

It was a Wednesday morning, Tharu had just finished his breakfast of steaming *putu* and banana, Anthrayos was still in bed upstairs, then, suddenly, everything crashed and collapsed in Tharu's household. A small group of people were at their house gate shouting slogans. At the center of the gathering was a young woman visibly pregnant, some were holding placards with inscriptions in red:

"Anthrayos, do justice!"

"Be a man, own up the woman and your child"

"She is not your toy, she is human"

In front of the group was Narayan, holding a red flag, leading the litany of slogans. Narayan was the community organizer of the untouchables of Manoor; he did not have any party affiliations. Hearing the commotion, Tharu came to the gate to enquire. Seeing Tharu, the slogans grew louder. Narayan moved forward to Tharu, hauling the pregnant by her arms.

"This is your son's woman, she would deliver in a couple of months, ask your son to come out"

Narayan yelled, his eyes fiery.

It did not take too long for Tharu to figure out the situation. Hearing the fracas, Rosa came out, she instantly realized the expectant woman was none other than Kurumba; she had worked in the Tharu household for a few months. It was Thresia who brought her as a domestic help, she used to draw water from the well, heat water for the family's morning bath, feed the bulls, clean their stables. Kurumba was not allowed in the house. Rosa could not believe her to have had an illicit affair with her son. Perhaps the party had fabricated the story with their own agenda and to exact money from the rich family. Real or made up, Rosa could not imagine the shame and disgrace the tale could bring upon her family. She was raging at Kurumba and more so at her own son.

Tharu was mortified and flustered by the agitating crowd at his gate; he wanted them to disappear and fade away before the neighbors took notice or drew attention from passersby.

He was enraged and chastened by the same thoughts as his wife. He signaled Narayan to come in and drew him aside,

"What you are alleging is ludicrous."

Tharu said angrily, but in lowered voice.

"You want the proof? Let us call the woman, she would name the father of her child"

Narayan did not say it softly.

"That is not necessary"

Tharu came closer to Narayan.

"How can we settle it without making too much noise"

Tharu whispered in Narayan's ears.

"Give her money for delivery expenses and childcare. And donate a good sum to our organization, for our welfare activities among the poor."

Tharu hastily went to an inner room of his house, came back with a package in his hand, he handed over the package to Narayan, stared into his eyes,

"We don't want to hear anything more about this affire."

Narayan exited the house gate, talked to the pregnant woman and the rest of the group. The gathering soon dispersed.

Tharu walked back to his home. He felt relieved for a moment, in the next, however, he was seething with rage. Sprinting, he ran up the stairs to Anthrayos's room, banged at the door shouting,

"Open the door, you scoundrel, open up."

There was no response, he kept on thumping the door more vigorously, impatiently; finally, the door creaked open; Anthrayos was scruffy and disheveled, trying to hold a sheet wrapped around his body in place; he sleepily looked at Tharu's face, flaming with wrath.

"Are you born just to destroy this family?"

Tharu roared; Anthrayos looked at his father questioningly, wondering why his father was fuming at him.

"You have shamed me and the whole family; how would I ever face people in the community after what you have done"

"I don't understand," Anthrayos mumbled.

"You don't understand? How dare you mess with Kurumba, what have you done with her, tell me"

The moment he heard the name Kurumba, Anthrayos stiffened and bristled, his eyes widened.

"What did I do?" he feigned ignorance.

"Go ask her, she is bearing your child, you imbecile."

Even before he finished his sentence, Tharu pounced on Anthrayos holding him by the neck, repeatedly punching him in the stomach. Anthrayos struggled to free himself from Tharu's grip, the sheet wrapped around him slipped to the floor leaving him in his underpants.

Hearing the tussle Rosa and Varkey came to the scene; Rosa did not come to her son's rescue, from a few feet away she just watched the father and son struggling. Varkey rushed in to extricate his younger brother from their father's clutch.

"You, shameless brute, you don't belong in this house anymore, go live with Kurumba."

Tharu was screaming at his erring son, then he turned to Rosa,

"Don't you ever give him money any more, even if he begs and cry, if you do…..." he interrupted himself, threateningly. He angrily strode down the stairs.

Anthrayos shut himself in his room for days, one of the servants brought the food and drinks to his room, he ate alone, stopped communicating with anyone in the family and no one bothered to enquire after him either. One day, Thresia came to his room with breakfast, Anthrayos was not in the room, she thought he might have been in the bathroom, waited for some time for him to come out, then she knocked at the bathroom door, no response, she hesitantly opened the door, the bathroom was empty. Puzzled, she ran down to tell Rosa that her son was missing, Rosa hurried to deliver the disturbing news to Tharu, but she could not find her husband anywhere in the house; she thought he might have stepped out of the house on an errand, she decided to wait for his return. Hours passed and there was no sign of Tharu. By sundown, Rosa started to worry. When Varkey came home from his bike shop, Rosa told him that his father and brother had disappeared, she was emotional almost at the brink of tears. Mulling over the scuffle going on between Tharu and Anthrayos, many unsettling scenarios have been swarming and milling in her mind. Varkey went upstairs to have look in Anthrayos's room; everything in the room was in disarray as always had been, something on one of the tables drew his attention: an open bottle with some fluid at the bottom. Varkey thought it might be a left over alcoholic drink his brother was addicted to. He smelled the open bottle, it was not alcohol, the repugnant, penetrating odor was all too familiar to him: the whiff of the poisonous insecticide seasonally used in their rice paddy fields and other cultivations. Suspicious thoughts started to crowd his mind. Anthrayos's personal life was unraveling with the allegation that he fathered Kurumba's unborn child, he felt unwelcome in his own house, a scab, spoiler of family name. His father had virtually disowned him, wanted him to leave the house. Have his agonizing personal miseries pushed him to the edge, has he committed something terrible to himself. Varkey shuddered looking at the bottle of poison on the table. Even remotely, he did not associate it with the disappearance of his father, he was expecting Tharu to walk in through the gate any time. Whenever he went out, Tharu invariably came home before sunset. This time too, Varkey did not foresee anything different. However, Tharu did not return even after dinnertime, leaving Rosa and Varkey disturbed and dismayed beyond words. They spent a painful and sleepless night, impatiently awaiting sunrise, Tharu to come back.

It was well into the morning, there was no trace of Tharu or Anthrayos. Varkey was panicking, it was time for him to go to his bike shop; but he could not think about anything else but his missing father and brother. He was helplessly pacing up and down the verandah. Rosa was in her bedroom, sobbing in front a small shrine with the images of Jesus, Madonna and the Holy Family.

Varkey walked over to his next-door neighbor, Gopan, to share with him his worry and anxiety, to seek advice. Gopan was doing his morning exercise; he was pulling himself up and down, hanging on to a bar, his body dripping sweat, glistening in the morning sun. Seeing Varkey, he stopped his workout, came to greet the neighbor. He was stunned hearing what Varkey had to tell him. Gopan did not take much time to figure out what was to be done: inform the police, file a complaint. He volunteered to go with Varkey to the police station miles away, offered his bullock drawn buggy for the travel. The cute little buggy was part the dowry for his wife, Lakshmi. It had an arched top, painted bluish green, the cabin upholstered in brown leather, the wheels and chassis with golden trimmings, brass bells on both ends of the yoke. Though the cart has been in Manoor for a few years then, the villagers were still fascinated by the pretty wagon, children and adult alike came to the roadside to watch it being drawn by two white oxen, the bells pealing along.

Even before the days end, Manoor was abuzz with the news of the father and son vanishing without a trace. Within the next day or two, rumors and conjunctures abounded, there were eyewitness accounts whispered about, mysterious sightings in darkened alleys: on the same night Tharu disappeared, Velu, the coconut palm climber, woke up in the middle of the night to nature's call. In his tiny house, there was no indoor toilet, he usually goes to the bushes with can of water. The bushes were on the bank of a shallow ditch pathway leading to a pond, as he was crouching in the shadow of the thickets, Velu saw the silhouette of a tall man with a heavy, listless figure on his shoulder. He careened and strained his neck to have a better view, but before he could, the shadowy figure faded into darkness ahead. On the same day, Philomi was earlier than usual on her way to the church, it was still not daybreak, there was only a faint glimmer of morning light, even the hibiscus floret in her hand was not discernible. In the layers of darkness, she hardly noticed a figure walking towards her, when the person came nearer, she was startled to see his face,

"God have mercy, Anthrayos, where are you going at this hour!"

Anthrayos did not answer; he walked past Philomi in haste.

Varkey and Rosa were much relieved to hear that Anthrayos is up and around; nonetheless, they were distressed and agonized that nothing was heard about Tharu. He seemed to have vanished into thin air. The intrigued and curious of Manoor were busy probing into the disappearance; putting together the reports, rumors and gossips into a coherent sequence of events to identify someone responsible, a perpetrator. In the end, they all collectively pointed an accusing finger at one individual: Anthrayos.

Responding to Varkey's complaint, the police came to the village to investigate; they combed Tharu's house for evidence, questioned everyone in the household. They interviewed each and every one in the village who had an eyewitness account about the case, anyone with a related story to tell, imagined, concocted or theorized. The investigators spent several hours visiting and questioning Velu, inspected every foot of the ditch pathway leading to the pond. They had difficulty locating Philomi during daytime, finally they traced her to the cemetery, deeply in prayer for the departed souls. She dryly narrated her brief encounter with Anthrayos, then went back to her whispered entreaties for the dead. Rumors and hearsay are not meaningful leads in any criminal investigation; nevertheless, they could be fodder for creative imagination for the sleuths when there is nothing to go by, sometimes an impetus for them to intensify their pursuit.

Following repeated visits to Manoor and many interrogations, the police knitted together a sequence of events that might have culminated in the vanishing of the father and son. When the inspector of police detailed the results of the police inquiry, Varkey listened intently, his distress and anguish beyond him to bear: it was most likely Anthrayos poisoned his father with the insecticide, carried the dead body on his shoulder at night to the pond a mile away, taking several hours to the destination; took a few halts on the way hiding in the shrubbery and shadows to evade any ones' notice, to rest and recuperate. The entrance to the ditch pathway was impassable and obstructed by dense growth of wild shrubberies; Anthrayos had to force himself through the bush, it was likely he had a fall there with the corpse on his shoulder. Along the ditch pathway, there was a single streak of footsteps up to the pond, at the edge of the pool there were furrows on the ground, blades of grass parted and trampled down: an indication that something heavy was hauled on to the pond. The dead body, most probably weighted with something heavy, was pushed into the pond to sink and drown to the bottom. After disposing the body of his father into the pond, Anthrayos left the village.

The inspector's narrative was, indeed, a plausible one; however, there was an essential element missing: the dead body. The detectives had a clear idea where the body could be found – at the bottom of the pond. The pond was on the private property of *Adhikari,* the village officer; he collected taxes, registered births and deaths, vaccinated newborn against smallpox; a man of considerable sway and power in the village. The womenfolk of his family bathed in the pond morning and evening, no one from a lower cast was allowed to take a dip in the pond or even touch the water, lest it make the pool contaminated and rendered impure. When the police wanted their divers to enter the pond to search for Tharu's remains, the *Adhikari* vehemently opposed the idea and threatened the police with legal action.

The police unable to produce the crucial evidence, the disappearance of Tharu was added to their list of unsolved mysteries of missing persons. The whereabouts of Anthrayos also remained a conundrum.

Varu's meat shop had just opened for business. He had brought a freshly slaughtered goat from the back, hung it on the hook; he had doused the carcass with water, it was dripping fluid tinted with blood, all the internal organs of the goat were hanging in the exposed hollow of the dead animal. Muthoma was sitting on his stool behind the counter, waiting for the first customer, instead, he saw Kochammu at a distance, coming along the road. As she came closer, he called out:

"Kochammu, where are you off to."

Kochammu steered off the road, walked towards Muthoma, stood in front of his counter; her face taut, no smile of recognition; she stared at him harshly as if she was about to hurtle something at him,

"How could he do such a thing to my child"

Without any introduction, she blurted out in her characteristic loud voice, her eyes burning with pent-up indignation. Muthoma was puzzled for a moment, then tried to calm her a bit, divert her from whatever piqued her, repeating his original query,

"Where are you off to, Kochammu?"

"I am going to Apputy's to get some rice and lentils, have you ever seen me on this roads on errands, Mary used to do all the running around, now I have to do it all, she won't come out of the house, she is scared, scared of everyone, she screams in her sleep; that son of a bitch has wrecked my child, how could he do this to her, he is a hobbling animal, he could do this and beyond, I should know, he is the one who killed his own father"

Kochammu was blaring and incessant, for all to hear and take notice. Hyder was at a nearby beedi stall talking to Pappu rolling beedis there. He heard Kochammu's torrent, sniffed an opportunity opening up. He came to the meat counter and exchanged pleasantries with Muthoma, then turned to Kochammu,

"I heard everything what happened to your daughter, it is terrible, we should fight against this atrocity, we could organize a demonstration in front of Anthrayos' butchery"

"His butchery is not open since I left, it is about to close" Muthoma interjected

"We still could fight to wrest compensation from him"

"You are trying to make some money out of this for you and your party, don't we know"

Kochammu was not persuaded. She walked away to Apputty's. Hyder lingered around Muthoma's meat counter.

"Did Anthrayos really killed Tharu?

Hyder asked Muthoma as an aside.

"That is what everybody believes; even the police think so"

"Why then, there is no evidence?"

"The evidence is at the bottom of *Adhikari's* pond; the police were not allowed to bring it up"

"The police could have brought a search warrant; they had many other legal means to force the search of the pond"

Hyder pondered for a moment, then pensively pronounced:

"There are many other nuances at play here, much more than what is apparent."

Hyder had a concocted theory. The power of money, it can conceal and uncover facts, transform and redefine truth and falsehood; the police has been bribed to keep the case of Tharu's disappearance unresolved, any related clues stashed away beyond reach, forever. Tharu's family loathed one of their own known to be accused of patricide, it would darken and ruin the stellar reputation of the family for generations. The patriarch has vanished behind the mystery, presumably dead. The good name of the clan should remain unblemished, preserved at any expense.

Hyder continued to expound his hypothesis flourishing it with details; Muthoma listened raptly. They both were convinced the evidence for Tharu's disappearance rested at the depths of the pond, below the layers of water at Adhikari's compound.

The pond was only a holler away from the Adhikari's house. Though the village officer held it strictly reserved and private, everyone at Manoor knew about it as village landmark with a checkered and colorful past, many of them referred to it as *Kozhikulam*, the Chicken Pond. No one knew how the name came about, even Alunny Master, the village historian and poet, was not in the know of the origin of the name. For a private pond, it was large, oval shaped; fringed by a belt of tropical vegetation, plants, creepers interspersed with wild flowers, tall grass, and reeds spiking up from the bank. The façade of shrubbery at the periphery gave a semblance of privacy for the bathers in the pond. A large branch of a peepal tree a few feet away canopied and shaded the pond. A flight of stone steps slid down from the bank to melt into the wate. Adhikari's family members bathed themselves daily on the lower steps. At one corner of the pond's bank, there was a thicket of bamboo, an uncommon variety, the hollow stem, golden yellow with dark green stripes, pointed pale green leaves quivering in the breeze. That was where Mangan was caught red handed. Mute and not so bright, Mangan was the only son of Kaliamma. One early evening when sun was about to set, one of Adhikari's domestics saw him sitting quietly among the bamboo observing the going on in the pond below. There were two women taking their evening bath on the steps. Hearing about Mangan's mischief, Adhikari was infuriated. He rushed to the bamboo bush with a wicker cane in his hand. He was disgusted to see Mangan masturbating. With his cane, he repeatedly struck Mangan across his back. Squirming with pain, Mangan jumped into the pond, swam or struggled across the pond, heaved himself up the other side of the bank and ran home. It was a mystery how he made it to the other side of the pond, he did not know how to swim.

Only a few feet away from the pond was the tomb of the village officer's father, Thambi. He has been dead for more than five years. Every evening, Adhikari's oldest daughter placed a lighted oil lamp on the white washed grave, returned to join the family in the *puja* worship. Peals of a hand bell were heard as symbolic offerings were made to the family deities. The bell was heard all around the neighborhood, the chimes were an essential element of the ambiance at dusk. Thambi had a peculiar skin condition and a miserable life. He was afflicted by uncontrollable itching all over his torso throughout his waking hours. Often, he was seen sitting half naked on the sandy front yard of the house, scooping sand with both hands to pour over himself and scratch his body relentlessly, sometimes blood oozing out on the skin. On a hot sultry night,

Thambi was unable to sleep, the sweat and oppressive heat exacerbated the itching, he felt it unbearable. Disabled to walk because of severe arthritis of both legs, he scuttled out of his room, crept all the way to the pond. In the predawn darkness, he could not see the steps down to the pond; he sat a few minutes at the edge of the pond's bank, then tumbled himself into the water and drowned. At sunrise, his body was floating face down in the still water of the Chicken Pond.

It was many years since Padmini vanished from Manoor. She was Adhikari's youngest sister. She had fallen in love with the village vaccinator, a young man from a neighboring village. Every morning, Padmini saw him coming to work on a rickety bicycle. Through the window of her house she watched him busy at the little village office adjacent to the Adhikari's house, inoculating infants against smallpox, the babies screaming with pain, the perplexed and anxious mothers trying to calm them. When their love affair reached the ears of the village officer, he was infuriated as the vaccinator was of a different religion and cast. He dismissed the young man from his job, locked up his sister in her room. Padmini was allowed out of the house only to go to the pond for her morning and evening bath. On a late evening, she came to the pond to bathe. She applied medicinal oil on her body, took a few dips and came out of the water. She was standing on one of the stone steps drying herself with a towel as she heard stirring among the shrubbery. Even before she could see and recognize him, the vaccinator emerged and swept her off the feet, carried her away on his shoulders, only a wet towel draped around her. They concealed themselves in an abandoned and tumbling thatched hut. They waited for the nightfall, looking for the lights in the house windows to extinguish, the villagers to go to sleep. Under the cover of darkness, they bid farewell to Manoor. No one heard from them ever since. Adhikari and his family never searched for Padmini or enquired after her. They deemed her dead to them. As a final rebuke, they performed the religious rites for the dead for her.

When Muthoma came to the Chicken Pond, Padmini's romantic escapade or other historical anecdotes surrounding the pond were far from his mind; he was on a specific and determined mission. When he arrived at the pond, it was pitch dark, devoid of even starlight. The dark contours of trees hardly contrasted against the blackened night sky. The ovoid surface of the pond laid still with a subdued glow, an enormous silver plate, dull and tarnished. A night bird swished over his head. Muthoma walked to the bank at the northern end of the pond where it was known to be the deepest. He dived into the pond, producing a thud and a splash. Watery darkness enveloped him as he sank into the pond; his feet plunged into the mud and clay at the bottom. With both of his hands, Muthoma started to grope and seek at the floor of the pool. Having found nothing, he surfaced for air, dived again to continue the search, but to no avail. On his third plunge, he sensed and felt something by his hand, he brought it up and placed it on the stone step: a femur. On repeated dives, Muthoma brought up a few more bones including a skull; he went into the water again looking for more bones. As he emerged out of the water with another skeletal fragment, he saw one of Adhikari's servants staring at the small heap of bones on the step, his eyes widened with fright and puzzlement. As the servant saw Muthoma's head popping out of the water, he gave out a frightened scream and darted towards his master's home. It was already daybreak.

Soon, the village officer with his retinue, appeared at the scene. He was outraged that Muthoma had entered the pond, contaminated, made it impure. It did not immediately occur to him something that was obvious: the water had already been tainted by Tharu's body lying in the pond, decomposing for more than a few years. He cringed and could not imagine that he and his kin had been bathing all those years in polluted unwholesome water. He was thinking about the cumbersome religious ceremonies needed to cleanse and purify the pond, the incidentals. Looking at the skull and bones, he figured the connections instantly: Tharu's disappearance, wide spread rumors, the police enquiry, his stout refusal to allow them to search the pool.

Some of the immediate neighbors came and stood around ogling at the bones with horrified amazement, they had already heard about the find from the Adhikari's servants. Meanwhile, no one noticed Muthoma, walking away uninvolved, as if nothing happened out of the way.

The bones remained on the pool steps drying in the scorching sun. No one came anywhere near the pond, everyone kept a frightened distance.

Leaving his initial indignation and bewilderment, Adhikari soon assumed his responsibility in the situation as the village officer. He informed the police through the official channels. The police were greatly encouraged, they finally got a solid lead in one of the missing persons case in their records for a long time. They arrived at the crime scene after two days. The appearance of police caused quite a stir and excitement in the normally staid atmosphere of Manoor. The police in their colorful regalia – scarlet red caps with serial numbers in gold with black tassel at the bottom, stiffly ironed trousers and shirts with golden insignia on the chest and shoulders. They scrupulously investigated in and around the pond, collected the bones, left the village for the day.

The police returned the next day; this time a small party of an inspector and two constables. They did not go to the Chicken Pond, instead, went straight to Anthrayos's butchery.

It was late in the morning; his hut was closed. The inspector clanked at the sheet metal door with his baton, no response; the door opened after some more knocks. Anthrayos appeared at the door, disheveled and sleepy, trying to hold his *mundu* from sliding down, startled to see the police at his door.

"Are you Anthrayos?"

Inspector asked. Anthrayos nodded his head in agreement.

"You are coming with us, you are under arrest"

One of the constables, handcuffed him and lead him to the Jeep at the roadside. By this time, a modest crowd of villagers had gathered around the butchery, viewing the scene in stunned silence. Muthoma was sitting on a masonry parapet beside the road, watching the police Jeep moving away, leaving a trail of smoke and dust.

# Nine

Like a few others in Manoor, Muthoma used to go across the river to have a drink or two. The other side of the river was wet; Manoor, on the other hand, a dry land, an area of prohibition. Shankuru's moonshine was available, but Muthoma preferred the clean natural sap of coconut palm, Toddy. At the jetty, Muthoma was a familiar figure, especially to Lona, the oars man. At the helm, Lona always wore a stern, steely face. When Muthoma stepped into his wooden boat to ferry himself across, the only welcoming gesture he received from Lona was a sterner stare. However, Muthoma, somehow felt the warmth behind the stare. Once he was in the boat, Muthoma almost always picked up an oar and paddled along with Lona, unlike other fares in the boat. Lona has grown old, troubled with arthritis, he needed help. In return, what Muthoma received from Lona was a grim silence; nevertheless, Muthoma knew the oarsman did welcome the help. Like every other boat riders, Muthoma tried to give his fare to Lona on disembarking, but he vehemently declined to accept it. Muthoma, however, persisted and never left for the toddy shop without pressing a few coins into Lona's palm. This scene was reenacted every time he came to the jetty to ferry across the river.

At the bar, Muthoma walked to the toddy counter presided over by Appu, a large rotund man, moon faced, half-naked in a *mundu*. Close to him, almost touching his ample body was a large vessel brimming with whitish palm toddy. The man and vessel appeared so closely cohesive, almost one with each other. Seeing Muthoma approaching, Appu filled two melon-sized earthen pots with toddy, kept them ready on the counter. Muthoma picked them up and walked towards the curry counter of Kochumary. She was sitting on a tiny three-legged stool, the seat was so short, rising not much above the floor, she virtually seemed to be crouching on it. In front of her was the day's prepared items in earthenware, displayed on a short wooden table, almost hugging the floor. As Muthoma walked towards Kochumary's food counter, the spicy whiff of freshly cooked curries enveloped him. Kochumary had arranged the day's menu items in a single array on the table: on the right end of the table was prawn cooked in coconut milk and spices; next was, again, prawn, roasted and soured with *garcinia cambognia* fruit followed by a dish of pomfret steaks curried in hot masala and coconut paste, next was a large bowl of fish preparation with sliced green mango. At the very far end were trays of deep fried mackerel and chunks of beef, dry roasted in grainy masala with fresh coconut pieces mixed in.

Kochumary was well past her prime, still an elegant woman. Wavy black hair with occasional streaks of silver, oval face slightly angular at the level of cheekbones, a pair of mischievous dimples, swirling and deepening as she smiled. She always wore a white chutta - a traditional loose-fitting blouse and a *mundu* tied around her waist with one end of the cloth pleated and fashioned like a fan, covering her rear. This clothing appendage was designed and insisted upon all Christian women by foreign missionaries. They thought the curvaceous backsides, even when fully clothed, was too much of an allure and incited impure thoughts in men, the pleated fan was an added safeguard.

Kochumary smiled heartily as she saw Muthoma walking towards her counter. She pulled a tripod stool for him. Muthoma settled on the offered seat, placed toddy pots on one side of the counter. While sipping his drink, he ordered prawn curry and fried mackerel. Kochumary filled his order in bowls and placed them in front of him. She would have preferred not to charge him for the food, she was very fond of him, nevertheless, she knew he would not accept the food gratis. She, however, gratified herself by being extra generous in the portions.

Muthoma and Kochumary liked to chitchat as he had his food and drink. He enjoyed her quips and off-color jests. They liked to watch other customers at the shop and make comments, on their back. Kochumary had a unique talent to make such remarks hilarious, often disparaging and risqué. Muthoma had a quirky nature of laughing within himself. Even at a riotous joke or observation from Kochumary, there was not even the semblance of a laughter on Muthoma's face, except a thin smile. Nevertheless, the rest of his body would be jiggling, tickled with laughter.

Kochumary knew Muthoma for many years; ever since she opened her curry counter at the shop when Paru Amma closed her counter. Eighty-year-old Paru Amma never got along with Appu, they constantly argued and shouted at each other, finally she quit and withdrew, she could not stand Appu's harassment any more. Kochumary liked Muthoma's somber but unflappable nature. A good listener than a talker, he always paid attention to what she was saying, her jokes and comments. Muthoma's contribution to these were restricted to single words of assent or his characteristic body shaking laughter keeping a straight face all the while. They, however, considered the quips and witticisms exclusively theirs, together, hand in hand.

Kochumary did not have particular entrepreneurial instincts or interests. She was not awaiting Paru Amma to quit so that she could plug herself in the old woman's cubicle nor she instigated Appu to pester and annoy the octogenarian to drive her away. In fact, she was forced to venture and open the food counter solely because of an unexpected turn of events in her life. Until then, she was a lower middle-class housewife: a small thatched house away from the main road, a hard-working husband, a ten-year-old daughter, Rosy. Her husband, Chakoru was a good provider, but severely lacked emotional generosity to express love and affection to his wife and daughter. This was not any different from the pattern of behavior among the men of Manoor; for them, taking care of the family was confined to fending for their material needs; anything beyond that betrayed weakness, ebbed and eroded their authority and gravity as heads of household.

Since age eighteen, Chakoru has been working with his older brother Pylee at his street side shop, selling plantain bananas and cassava roots. He was assigned the job of procuring the crop from all around Manoor and beyond. He visited individual homes looking for banana and cassava roots grown in their backyards, for many families that a was source of additional income. If Chakoru spotted a banana plant laden with a large bunch of fruits in one of the backyards, he assiduously bargained the price with the house owner before striking a deal; buying cassava roots was not any different, meticulous and haggling to the last penny. Cassava was usually planted on small plots at the far ends of the yards. Chakoru negotiated and bought the patch with a few heads of the plant, he dug up the roots with a shovel he always carried with him. His labor was free to the sellers and they liked it included in the bargain. By mid-day, Chakoru have had collected enough banana bunches and cassava roots for the day's load to his brother's shop. He shoved the roots into a large gunny bag and suspended it on one end of a bamboo crossbar, a few bunches of bananas on the other end to balance and he carried the crossbar on his shoulders, returning to the shop. The crossbar arched as he walked with the heavy load; by the time he reached the store he was bathed in sweat. Pylee always came to look at the produce his brother had brought in, helped him hang the banana bunches from a wooden beam above. The plump bananas were flaccidly dangling from the main stem; to better the display, Chakoru rolled the dried banana leaves he had brought along with him into small balls and shoved them between the fruits to prop them up; the bananas, then, appeared to bristle around the main stem. The dressed banana bunches were taken to a dark windowless room and left there for days to ripen until their color turned into deep yellow. When Chakoru unloaded the gunny bag of cassava, the roots were in clumps and caked with slushy mud. He took them out to the back of the store, washed them with water from a large vessel, separated them from clusters. When he brought the cassava to the front of the shop and placed the roots on a wooden plank; the bulbous tubers looked fresh with a watery sheen still on them.

Chakoru made regular forays into the nook and corners of Manoor and the neighboring villages, ferreting out the ripe and matured banana bunches and cassava. In his quest for the produce, he was tenacious and astute, there was nothing else in his mind besides the bananas and cassava roots. Strangely, however, it was these expeditions that helped to evolve the singular marriage proposal of his life, with no initiatives from him, wholly unbeknownst to him.

In the neighboring village of Padoor, there was a house in the middle of a small compound at the junction of the main road and a dirt road. A medium sized house, orange colored tile roof, a small grove of banana plants growing thickly in the back, a cassava patch touching the periphery of the compound. When Chakoru visited the house first time, he got to buy two large bunches of bananas and several pounds of cassava roots. Thereafter, whenever he was in Padoor he invariably visited the house and always found something to buy. Once the deal was finalized with the house owner, he got busy preparing the purchase before hauling them to the shop. As he was engaged in the tasks, there was a girl sitting on the verandah of the house, pretty and young, she was past her teenage years. She was watching Chakoru diligently engrossed in the work. She observed him cutting the large banana bunch with one swing of his machete while holding the bunch with the other hand lest it fall to the ground. He slit open the trunk of the banana plant to extract the ivory white core, tender and succulent, he kept it aside to be presented to the woman of the house, she could make a tasty dish out of it. At the cassava patch, she viewed him loosening the earth around the stem of each plant, uprooting them with his bare hand, shaking off the mud from the tuber crusted around the bottom end of the stem. Chakoru was unaware of the girl on the verandah watching his every move. He did not know her name, he never needed to, he was not even curious. She was Kochumary, the eldest daughter of her parents.

After a couple of months, a matchmaker came to visit Pylee at his store; the broker had a marriage proposal for Chakoru. The prospective bride was Kochumary. Pylee close questioned the matchmaker about Kochumary's family background. The broker recited the desirability of the family with flourish. Even after discounting the embellishments, Pylee liked what he heard. That evening when Chakoru came back with a load of bananas and cassava, Pylee told him about the marriage proposal. Though he was ambivalent about the idea of marriage, Chakoru instantly recognized the family from his brother's description; a faint picture of the girl on the verandah came to his mind. Pylee was the patriarch of a joint family; everyone in the family obeyed him; if he takes a decision on anyone of them, no one objected or questioned, they just followed his directions. Pylee told his brother that he and his wife were planning to go to Padoor to meet the girl and her family. Chakoru kept his silence approvingly. Chakoru grew up in Pylee's tutelage ever since their father died when he was in his late teens. He had grown to agree with anything his brother decided; he had complete trust in him.

For Chakoru, the marriage was an act of obedience, following a dictate of Pylee. He was least excited on the wedding day. His relatives were more enthusiastic than he was. After Chakoru's first night, Pylee was not even sure if the marriage was consummated. He was audacious enough to call his younger brother aside and discretely enquire about the night.

Soon after the wedding, traditions and circumstances nudged Kochumary to plunge into the chaos of Pylee's joint family. Initially, she was unnerved to find herself as a new bride among the large and curious mix of family members. There were three generations living within the walls of Pylee's medium sized house. As the wife of the second eldest male in the family, Kochumary had assumed, at least in her mind, a position of some importance in the family hierarchy. However, she was at a loss to discern a niche for herself in the household. She felt thrown among a bevy of strangers expected to become her kith and kin; she was to develop and nurture relationships with every member of her new family. Even a cursory knowledge of their individual nature would have helped her in the process. Chakoru, nevertheless, had not given her even an outline profile of his extended family members, their likes, dislikes and flaws. But, he had cautioned her to be careful around Thandamma, be respectful to her, he had told her. Thandamma was the wife of Pylee. A small, wiry woman in her late fifties – sand and pepper hair, a thick lock of snow-white hair on the right side of her brow with a propensity to migrate and constantly fall in front of her right eye, cheeks highlighted by a pair of wrinkled furrows, thin tight lips, no trace of a smile ever having played on those lips. She always attired in white; a wraparound *mundu* and chatta, a frilled fan, shaped out of one end of the *mundu* modestly shielded her rear. A couplet of gold earrings adorned her ears, the upper helix of the ear lobes bending forward with the weight of the rings. She was always at a strategic location between the kitchen and the dining area of the house. Perched on a rice chest, she could survey everything happening in her house, from one end to the other: what was cooking in the kitchen, what other members of the family were engaged in. She dis-mounted the chest only when someone had to get rice or other provisions from the chest. As the heavy lid opened, a peculiar smell of uncooked rice and an admixture of spices penetrated the nostrils everybody around. The interior of the chest was partitioned into large and smaller rectangular segments. In the largest partition was rice, pounded rice for making break-fast items in the rectangle next to it, then an array of smaller sections with a variety of spices, colors dazzling, an oversized palette. In the far corner of the chest were mangoes kept there for ripening, the fruity aroma of the mangoes further spicing up the air emanating from the box. Nothing escaped from the chest without Thandamma's consent and under her strict di-rections, often with a bit of unfounded admonitions, her face betraying displeasure with nothing or at no one in particular.

Thandamma had given birth to four children, two boys and two girls. Though they all have grown up, two of them having their own children, Thandamma kept a close tag on all of them; she knew precisely when the men stepped out of the house and when they came back. Of the girls, only Anna, Thandamma's youngest and better looking, was still living at home. She was married to a young man from an aristocratic family. When the marriage proposal had come, Pylee jumped at it, he thought a marriage alliance with an upper-class family would buoy his own social standing. However, a regrettable realization came much later: the groom had only aristocracy as his singular asset. Nevertheless, he lugged a full bag of vices of the rich but lacked the means to indulge in and cosset them. He and his family had exacted a sizeable dowry from Anna's parents; they ate, drank and feasted on it until it was all gone. He demanded more supplements to the dowry. Pylee stoutly refused. On a rainy day, he brought Anna and their first-born infant to Pylee's house and left them there; he stomped out of the house threatening his wife that she would not see him again until the additional dowry was paid. Anna's older sister, Rosily, was in a faraway city with her family; she regularly wrote home about their modern living in the bustling city, weekend parties, walks along the beach, evenings spent at the park. She came home only once in a few years. Those rare visits, however, was celebrated in a grant scale at Pylee's home. Pylee went all out to show off his high living daughter and family.

Mathayi was the oldest among Thandamma's children. He had a fabric store on the main road, somewhere between Bhanu's coffee shop and Apputty's grocery. He had Lonayi, the tailor, set up his operation on the front foyer of the shop: Lonayi's cutting table in the middle with his scissors, measuring tape and other paraphernalia of his trade, haphazardly laid on it. On both side of the table, two foot-peddled Singer sewing machines, Kesu and Porinju on stools behind the machines. Kesu adept in stitching lady's garments, Porinju in gentlemen's.

In the main section of the store, Mathayi sat cross-legged on a cushioned rug with a cash box nearby. Behind him were three walls of multicolored fabrics rolls tightly arranged on wooden shelves. Each roll was several yard lengths of clothing, wrapped around three by one feet wooden planks. At the far end of the right-side wall, a small section of the shelf was with glass panels in front, the enclosure exclusively set apart for silk sarees and other silk material. When a customer came into the store, Mathayi stood up, pulled down two or three rolls of fabrics for the buyer to select. He held a small section of the cloth in both of his hands, forcefully stretched it to demonstrate sturdiness of the material. At the buyer's approval, he measured the cloth with a yard stick, made a scissor nick in the fabric, ripped it down to the other end making an ear-splitting shrill. He folded the severed clothing, threw the bundle to Lonay's table. Lonayi took the measurements of the customer, jotted down the numbers in his notebook; cut the clothing to pattern and handed it over to Kesu or Porinju for stitching.

Every garment worn by Manoor villagers were made of fabrics from Mathayi's shop and have been passed through Lonayi's cutting table and the Singer machines of Kesu and Porinju. Mathayi's cloth shop was well known in Manoor, ruefully however, by an unsavory name: Goat Face's shop. The unpalatable moniker befell on Mathayi several years ago, totally unsolicited.

It was only a few months since the shop opened its doors for the first time. Though mixed with anxiety, Mathayi was very enthusiastic about his new business venture, he did everything possible to make it survive and flourish. He was at the store before any one of his employees, dusting the display shelves, making the shop presentable. Every morning, he covered the one-mile distance on a ditch road between his house and the main road in a few minutes. Midway on his route, there was a tall tree on the roadside. In summer, it was laden with dark violet berries. Local children loved the sweet pungent taste of the fruit, they waited under the tree for the berries to fall to the ground. Every time a bird landed on one of the tree branches, a hail of berries rained down, the kids raced to gather them. One morning, Mathayi was hurrying to his shop. Strangely, there was no chatter and chirrup of children under the berry tree, there was no one there except a twelve-year-old boy, leaning against the trunk of the tree with a forlorn look. There were no berries falling to the ground, no birds up on the tree. Mathayi had not seen this boy before. As he came closer to him, the boy's eyes widened, he stared at Mathayi's face – large melancholy eyes, ears sticking out, a long, but flattened nose, his wide mouth appearing to extend to the ears, his hardly perceptible lower jaw almost disappearing into the shadow of the upper jaw:

"Goat, Goat face"

The boy said, loudly, trying at the same time to restrain himself. Looking at Mathayi's face, it was an inspired exclamation, a spontaneous expression of what conjured up in him. Mathayi never thought the boy's call had any reference to him. Even in his innermost subconscious, he did not have an association between himself and a goat. Ignoring the boy, he walked on. Next morning, Mathayi was on his way to the shop. As he nearly approached the fruit tree, suddenly he heard a shrill call, coming in multiple voices, but in concert:

"Goat Face, Goat Face"

This time it was from behind a bush. Mathayi looked at where the voices emanated from, he could not see any one, he heard, however, boisterous giggles from the bush. He was puzzled a little but moved on. He had a shop to keep open for business.

The catcalls and mocking titter continued for several days. He, being the subject of taunting and name calling, Mathayi was very perturbed. He was consumed by the derision. The name "Goat Face" buzzed and rumbled in his head day and night. When he was about to slide into sleep and when he was half awake in the mornings, grotesque image of a goat head floated around in the visual environs of his mind.

It was the season of church festival and feasts in Manoor, a busy time at Mathayi's cloth shop. One morning he was hastening to his shop. As he was approaching the berry tree, he was nervously anxious and ominous, anticipating the catcall from the bush. He loathed to tread that stretch of the ditch road, wished he had not to. As he came closer and closer to the fruit tree, he felt giddy, heard thousand voices shouting:

"Goat Face, Goat Face, Goat Face......"

The voices became louder and louder, though there were no catcalls coming from the bushes. Goat heads were spinning in his head. Mathayi fell to the sandy road on his knees, planting his hands in front, he started walking on the fours, animal like. Every few feet, he was bleating. By each step, the clutter and clamor in him ebbed, everything calmed down, no voices, no goat heads spinning. The boys came out of the bushes loudly laughing at him, a small crowd was watching the spectacle from where the ditch road joined the main street. As Mathayi reached the junction, he stood erect and walked towards his store as usual. That day, the name, "Goat Face" was forever imprinted in the cultural consciousness and commercial lore of Manoor.

At his fabric store, Mathayi saw Yacob sitting on the steps of the store, a gramophone near him. He was waiting for the store to open. Yacob was Mathayi's younger brother. He came to the store occasionally, placed his gramophone at one end of Lonayi's cutting desk, played vinyl recordings of Hindi film songs. Invariably, a small crowd used to gather around the turntable, mostly to hear the music, but also to look at the device. They had seen only the older kind with a huge horn, shaped like a bellflower, that was the first time they were seeing a gramophone without a horn and more like a box. Yacob sat very close to the turntable making sure that no one touched the device. Sitting among the throng but still aloof from them, he was enjoying the glow as the proud owner of the pricey contraption.

Yacob had brought along the gramophone when he returned from a faraway city in the North-Western part of the country. Running away from Manoor, he had spent a few years there. He had left the village in shame and humiliation when a woman slapped him across the cheek. He had not reached his twentieth birthday then, nothing much to do, leading a carefree life. He spent most of his time at Bhanu's coffee shop sitting on a bench closest to the roadside, perusing everyone coming along the street. Occasionally he would leave his perch to cruise the road up and down. Whenever Yacob saw Devayani, the village midwife, rushing along the road with an assistant tailing her carrying the medicine bag, he and everyone else knew, a woman was in labor somewhere in the village. Devayani was a familiar face in Manoor. She had attended every childbirth in the village over the last several years. When she appeared first in the village with a shapely figure, chiseled features, shiny dark complexion and a singsong southern accent, villagers used to call her "dark goddess" but the advancing age had taken its toll on her gait and appearance. Devayani's reign of dominance in the midwifery of the village, however, was soon to end with the arrival of a challenger in the persona of young Vasanthi, a new midwife. Her youth and the corollary inexperience was compensated for by her looks. Tall and wheat fair, a small measure of plumpness complimenting her alluring figure. Her thick ebony hair braided and coiled into a bun covering the entire back of her head, always wearing clothing considered modern for the time. The villagers' loyalty and sympathy were still with Devayani, nonetheless, they were enamored by the fresh air and youthful vigor of Vasanthi.

When Yacob saw Vasanthi first time on the road, he was dumbfounded by her lure and charm. His eyes followed her until she receded into the far horizon of the road. Sitting on his usual bench at the coffee house day after day, he waited for her to come along the road. But her advent on the street in front of the coffee shop was unpredictable, her service calls to women in labor was at random. Many a day, he returned home without seeing her, feeling not having achieved anything, a day having wasted. On the propitious days when Vasanthi did grace the street, Yacob allowed himself to immerse in her alluring mystique. On one of those days, Yacob had a frenzied impulse: leaving the bench in a haste, he started following Vasanthi. She was on an urgent call walking fast. As he came a few feet behind her, he said,

"Whenever I see you, I wish I am pregnant and in labor"

His admiration for her desirable beauty, came in a ludicrously absurd way. Vasanthi was not amused, she was too enraged to chuckle or smile at the unintended humor in his entreaty. She turned back in a fury, slapped him across his face, threw a disparaging look at him and moved on uninterrupted. Yacob never knew Vasanthi's healing hand could hit him that hard. Nonetheless, much more than the pain and sting of the slap, he was squirming with shame and humiliation. He felt his whole being dissolved and dissipated into the ground under his feet. His friends were watching the scene from the coffee shop, he was mortified to meet their eyes. He started to walk home, ignoring them.

That evening Pylee came home enraged; he had already had heard about the incidence in front of Bhanu's coffee house in the morning. Yacob got a protracted verbal thrashing from his father. He ate his dinner alone in silence. When everyone woke up next morning, he was nowhere to be seen. For many days, the family searched for him far and wide, but to no avail. After a few months, however, everyone was relieved when a letter arrived at Pylee's home, it came from the city of Lahore in the northwestern region of the country. Yacob had written glowingly about his circumstances there, though he was working as a waiter at a restaurant. The family received letters from Yacob regularly for a while, then they halted, abruptly. It made them worried and concerned. Their anxiety heightened as they heard of the rumbling of rioting and violence taking place in Lahore and the neighboring city of Amritsar. The source of the news was Devassy's radio, the only one in the village.

India was being partitioned based on religion and the world witnessing the simultaneous birth of two independent nations after a prolonged period of British rule. The pangs of partition were widely experienced by the people of both countries. For centuries, adherents of Hindu and Muslim faiths had been living in peace and harmony, overnight they became bitter, sworn enemies. There were widespread violence, murder, rape and house burning. The majority community wanted to drive away or annihilate the religious minority. Hindus in Pakistan were seeking peace and security in India while Muslims in India were dreaming safety and tranquility among their brethren in Pakistan. From Pakistan, there was an exodus of Hindus in millions to India and Muslims from India to Pakistan. Their trek between the two countries was arduous and wretched; murder, rape and other atrocities against each religious sect continued on the way to their aspired homes. During the mass migration, thousands perished from disease and starvation and many at the hands of their erstwhile neighbors and friends.

Many Hindus in Lahore fled the city, but some were unwilling to leave their hearth and home, their beloved city; however, the Muslim majority did not want them any more in the city. They were more than explicit in expressing their hostility. Every day, they went on a murderous rampage of rape and house burning.

When a pack of religious zealots burst into the restaurant of Yacob's employment, he was at the storage area in the lower level of the eatery. Hearing the shouting and commotion on the upper floor, he came up the creaking stairs. He peeped through the crack of the door to see the seething face of the intruders, reddened with rage, and a frightened, petrified Mahesh, the restaurant owner and his boss. For some inexplicable reason, Yacob saw the trespassers ordering Mahesh down to the storage. He climbed down in a hurry, hid himself among gunny bags of rice, potatoes and onions, threw a dirty sheet laying around on himself and tried not to breathe. He heard the band of ruffians demanding to know where Mahesh's family lived, he was silent. Enraged, they slapped him repeatedly, kicked him in the stomach. Mahesh was mum, the assailants were relentless in their assault, Mahesh was steadfast in his weeping silence. Infuriated, one of the attackers pulled out a large dagger, stabbed Mahesh again and again. Yacob saw Mahesh dropping to the floor, blood gushing out of him forming pools on the floor, lying motionless, his eyes wide open. The murderers clamored upstairs, Yacob thought they had left the restaurant. He emerged from his hiding and came up to the first floor. The restaurant was engulfed in smoke, tongues of fire rising everywhere. He dashed out through the open door defying the smoke and fire. Meanwhile, one end of his clothing had caught fire, he fell to the ground and rolled to put out the flame. Even before he got back on his feet, he was running as fast as he could. He wanted to move away from the restaurant as quickly as possible. The whole building was on fire, the flames licking the sky. As he turned back and hastily glancing from a distance, saw the buildings neighboring the restaurant also aflame.

Yacob continued to sprint along the street until he came to an intersection. He saw a group of people coming along a crossroad, men, women and children. Some men carried crude weapons like sticks and spears, one of them had a musket. Recognizing them as Hindus, Yacob joined the group without causing a stir. None in the set paid any attention to the new entrant to the group; with mixed emotions of anxiety, fright and terror writ large on their faces, they were oblivious of their surroundings, they just longed to be safe and away from Lahore. After walking some distance, Yacob witnessed a scene that he never expected: an endless column of people, bullock carts and makeshift carriages, hurriedly moving along a route in a south-east direction, towards the Indian border. The group and Yacob, the unacknowledged member of the flock, joined and mingled with the convoy fluently like the confluence of a tributary to a river. The band soon dissolved and dissipated into the moving crowd. Yacob was left walking alone among the throng. Moving into the crowd, Yacob had no possessions, only the cloths he was wearing: a pair of pants and a shirt partly eaten by the flames. He was hungry and thirsty, desperately needed some water to drink. Then, he heard a bullock cart behind him, he stopped briefly for the cart to come alongside. It was an elderly woman and her three daughters in the cart along with household goods. With folded hands, Yacob asked them for water. At first, the women looked at him suspiciously, then the mother poured some water from a tumbler into the cupped palms of Yacob. A young woman, presumably the oldest among the daughters was at the reins. Yacob saw her having hard time controlling the oxen, the cart was moving very slowly. Yacob offered to drive the cart, perhaps in gratitude for the water or having a ride himself instead of walking under the scorching sun. The woman gladly accepted the offer and moved to the rear of the cart. With Yacob in the driver's seat the wheels of the bullock cart turned a little faster, his verbal commands, shouted and cussed, seemed to spur the bulls to quicken their steps.

As they were nearing the Indian boarder, Yacob slowed down the bullock cart and started talking to the oldest daughter. He gave her a few pointers to control and perk up the animals. When the cart crossed the border and was on the Indian soil, Yacob jumped down from the driver's perch and was getting ready to say farewell to the mother and daughters, his erstwhile cart mates. He thanked them for the ride and uttered some niceties. Then he saw the mother reaching the back of the cart and pulling out an oblong box with the help of one of the daughters. She lifted the box and handed it over to Yacob standing near the cart.

"We don't need it anymore, getting it out of the cart would give the girls some more room; we still have a long way to go" She explained.

Yacob was a bit puzzled, he accepted it anyway. On the lid of the box there was the lettering "HMV" in faded gold and the insignia of a white dog curiously listening, perhaps, to music from the horn of a turntable.

"A gramophone" Yacob said to himself. Holding the machine under his right arm, he started walking towards the Amritsar railway station, for his journey home. When he looked back, he saw the bullock cart moving away to a refugee camp, miles away.

# *Ten*

Pylee's household was stirred up a bit after the arrival of Kochumary as a new member. Her privileges and novelty as a new bride did not last too long. Everyone in the family gradually grew less comfortable in her presence. Until then no conflicts or dissent marred their regimented lives, under the command of Thandamma, stern and stringent. It was the calm and tranquility of a tyrannical reign, however. Inexplicably, they had gotten accustomed to the silence and stillness of their household. Kochumary, on the contrary, was a free spirit, growing up as the only girl of her parents, she always got her way. Her parents viewed her independent streak in a pampering sort of way. She felt stifled in the air of her husband's joint family.

One day, Kochumary committed the first blunder of her fledgling married life: she cooked and packed lunch for her husband, an innocent routine common in many families, but her act did not have Thandamma's assent and seal of approval. On that morning Kochumary saw the top of the rice chest vacant, Thandamma was in the shower, her usual oil bath extending to an hour or more. Kochumary opened the rice box, took out rice and other provisions for making lunch. She brought vegetables from the yard and got busy in the kitchen. By the time Thandamma was back on the rice coffer, Chakoru was leaving the house for work, a package under his arm. He left a spicy aroma of cooked food in his wake, it lingered all around the house. Thandamma sniffed and instantly got the clue, many unsettling thoughts gushed into her mind. In a moment, all of them collated and came out as a shouted question to Kochumary,

"Who cooked in the kitchen?"

Kochumary looked at Thandamma silently, guilt and supplication on her face; she was diminished into an erring school kid in the headmaster's office. What followed was an eruption, a torrent of words, abusive accusations:

"You are disrupting the family, trying to take over the household; remember, you came into the family only yesterday, you would not be allowed to interfere with the discipline and decorum of the family".

Kochumary was barred from entering the kitchen, she would not be allowed anywhere near the rice box.

Thandamma declared a war on Kochumary. She faulted her on everything she did, long-winded broadsides and reprimands followed. Kochumary adopted a passive response to the attacks for a while, then, true to her nature, she began to resist the older woman's offensive. It only infuriated Thandamma even more. As they were caught up in the struggle every waking hour, both women complained to their husbands, sought a remedy for their grievances. Kochumary was very determined and direct: she wanted to move out of the house, set up a house of their own, nothing less. For Chakoru, however, it was an unthinkable proposition, he could not imagine a life outside the protected environs of Pylee's household. Kochumary, however, was tenacious and steadfast in her dictate. Bedeviled, Chakoru decided to present his wife's proposal to Pylee for advice. Meanwhile, Thandamma was relentless in Pylee's ears with her grouse and frustration about Kochumary. As an easy way out of the dilemma, Pylee sided with Kochumary's wish. He found a house and helped set it up for his younger brother and wife. It was in this house where their first and only child, Rosy, was born and grew up.

Chakoru worked hard. His whole life was centered around his job at his brother's shop; he did not have any other interests or vices except having a drink once in a while. His wife and child always had enough to eat, he provided for all their needs. Nevertheless, Kochumary felt he lacked something every wife expected of their husbands: personal attention and occasional tender moments with the family. Over the years since their marriage, she had accepted and gotten used to his behavior, tweaked her life around him so that none was too uncomfortable. Later on, however, she felt her husband had become increasingly aloof and detached. In her subtle ways, she tried to bring him back to the day today life of her family. It only made him angry, he shouted at her, asked her to leave him alone.

It was the teenager, Rosy, who saw it first time: her father talking to himself, wildly gesticulating. Many a morning, he would get up early and sat on the steps of their house, silently staring far away, beyond the coconut palms and paddy fields, then abruptly breaking into soft soliloquies and hand motions. Chakoru started eating alone most of the days; whenever he did dine with his family, Kochumary noticed him blinking incessantly, not uttering a word, being restless.

Chakoru left home every morning as he used to, but Kochumary came to know from Pylee, he did not show up for work at the shop for several days. One evening, he did not return home as usual. Kochumary waited for hours. Worried and perplexed, she set out searching for him. She, finally, found him at Pylee's house, sprawled on the verandah of the house, vacantly staring at the ceiling. He refused to go home with his wife, but with Pylee's prodding and gentle chiding, he followed his wife home. As soon as they reached home, however, he turned violent, chased Kochumary, threatening her with a large stick. She shut herself in a room to escape his wrath, Rosy, taking refuge in one corner of the room, started to weep, frightened, bewildered.

That was not to be the only time Chakoru strayed and ended up lodging at Pylee's home. Many evenings, he wandered and found himself sitting on the steps of his brother's house, indolently or stretched out on the verandah. It was almost like a homing instinct interrupted temporarily, now reactivated again. Thandamma did not like the intrusion. At Pylee's persistent prompting and pleas, he reluctantly retreated home, nonetheless, he was hardly cognizant of a wife and daughter waiting for him at home. As time progressed, his home too receded and disappeared from his perceived consciousness. He stopped coming home.

For Kochumary, his being away was less troublesome and agonizing than his being home. Still she worried about him: where does he spent his nights, how does he feed himself. She came to know from Pylee that Chakoru spent most nights in an abandoned log shed, behind Bhanu's coffee stall. Kochumary started sending food packages for him with Rosy. He grabbed the pack, clumsily gobbled up the food, not looking at his daughter's face.

Chakoru hardly communicated with anyone except to himself and the imaginary characters he was constantly conversing with. People moved away from him, considering him deranged. Children watched him from a distance with frightened curiosity. Then one late evening, Ravunny appeared on the scene: tall and wiry, slightly overgrown black hair, an arching mustache grazing all the way down to his lower lip. He came in to Bhanu's coffee shop, ordered a cup of tea. Even before his tea was served, he was spiritedly talking to himself, often pounding the coffee table. As a waiter placed the tea on the desk, the tumbler of tea wobbled, almost spilling the tea with his strikes on the table. Other customers at the shop gawked at him curiously, bemused and baffled. As it was closing time for the shop, Ravunny lounged on one of the benches as if it was his own bed. One of the servers at the shop quickly chided him out of the shop, directed him towards the log shed in the back. As he found his way to the shed, Ravunni saw Chakoru in one corner murmuring to himself, groaning loudly every now and again, spewing vulgarities. Ignoring Chakoru and away from him, Ravunni curled up among dried leaves and other rubbish.

When Chakoru woke up in the morning, he saw Ravunny standing in the middle of a small clearing in front of the shed, a polished wooden stick with a metal hook in his hand, shouting orders at the top of his voice:

"Right, Kesav"

"Left, Kesav"

"Move on, Kesav"

Those were the mahout's walking commands for an elephant. He was giving the commands to a tamed elephant and talking to the elephant's owner in between. The animal and its owner, however, were unreal, living only in his psychotic imagination. Now and then, Ravunny swirled the wooden wand used to control the elephant by the hook. As it came to be known later, Ravunni was the mahout of a male elephant named Kesav owned by a rich family in a faraway village. During a hot and humid summer, Kesav went into **"*Musth*"**, the testosterone driven madness and aggression in male elephants. In the rage and ferocity of its insanity, Kesav trampled and killed the assistant mahout. It was the gruesome brutality and carnage of his assistant's killing that threw off Ravunny's mental balance, drove him into lunacy.

Chakoru came out of the log shed and started moving around Ravunny; however, their eyes did not meet, nor they acknowledge each other. They were talking nonstop to themselves or others who were not there, but very much in their delirious brains. Nevertheless, they seemed to be comfortable in each other's presence, developing an unexpressed comradery at a surreptitious level. Ravunny shared Chakoru's food parcels from home, seldom offered, but Ravunny helped himself to the food any way, as it was there. Chakoru hardly cared. Day or night, Chakoru scarcely ever moved out of the shed. Ravunny occasionally went to Bhanu's coffee shop, had a cup of tea and returned with a retinue of children following him, boisterously laughing at him, calling him names.

Chakoru and Ravunny shared the log shed for a number of days, living in their individual neurotic worlds. Then one day, they both disappeared, never to be seen again. No one knew where they went.

With Chakoru stopped working and finally vanishing from their lives, Kochumary and Rosy were left without support and sustenance. It was the patriarch of the family, Pylee, provided them with food and other necessities. He was very concerned about his younger brother's family and constantly searched for a way to assure a steady income for the family. Then, one day, he came to know Paru Amma closing down her food stall at the toddy shop. It was an opportune moment for Kochumary to jump into her own modest business, he thought; after all, she was an excellent cook. He discussed the idea with his young sister-in-law. Initially, she was reluctant to embrace the proposal, she had no experience in business, leave aside dealing with clients at a drinking place. However, she could not overlook her dire circumstances, the urgent need to find a way to feed her daughter and herself without depending on any one. With Pylee's persistent motivation and his offer to come up with the seed money for the venture, Kochumary agreed to open the food counter at the toddy shop, all her own.

Kochumary's house was at the end of a long pathway, cramped and narrow, two people hardly could walk along abreast. The lane was strewn and speckled with smooth pebbles. During monsoon rains, tiny streams swept away the sand leaving the nuggets on the path. Wild shrubbery lined the sides of the alley. Midway along the pathway to Kochumary's house was a smaller house tucked away under a huge mango tree. The house and the surroundings were clearly visible from Kochumary's house as her house was on a slightly elevated ground. Kochumary viewed the house under the mango tree with some unease and apprehension. She was much troubled by what went on around the house at night; people going in and out of the house at odd hours, occasional loud squabbles, skirmishes.

The house under the mango tree belonged to Sankuru, the man in charge of fireworks at the temple. His pyro techniques were limited to only one kind, a crude gunpowder explosion. Routinely, he struck and compressed gunpowder into the central hole of a cylindrical steel ingot with a wick hole on the side, he topped the gunpowder with crushed stone, hammered and compacted it further. The assembly was then placed in an isolated location of the temple compound, a thin thread of gunpowder was placed on the ground leading into the wick hole. On the ready, Sankuru carefully ignited the powder trace on the ground and run away as fast as he could, the device exploded with a deafening sound, it shook the village, reverberated all around. Locally the explosion was known as "Vedi"; the villagers called the temple pyro technician, "Vedi Sankuru". The worshipers at the temple offered Vedi in honor of their favorite deity; they paid for the Vedi at the temple office. The intensity and urgency of the divine favors they were seeking determined the number of explosions offered. More often, they are for the recovery of someone sick, happy marriage of a daughter or the celestial gift of an offspring. Sankuru made sure the explosions went off at the appropriate moment of the religious ceremony being conducted in the temple, mostly at the very end of the service. Many at the temple, shuddered at the blast; children and the weak, closed the ears with their palms.

Though illegal, Sankuru made his own gunpowder in the temple premises. He burned a selected variety of wood to make charcoal, pounded and ground it into a fine powder. On the days when he prepared the charcoal powder, he assumed an unearthly look; head to toe, he was coated in black soot, his facial features were not discernable, his countenance was a frightening dark blur. He mixed in the necessary chemical ingredients to the charcoal powder and milled the mixture on a granite slab grinder as a last step to produce the explosive concoction. During this maneuver, he did not allow anyone near or around him; it was a grave and solitary operation. On one of those solemn days, when Sankuru made the gunpowder, something unimaginably terrible happened. It was a sunny midafternoon, he had done with the final steps of putting together the gunpowder, he was storing the explosive in keg like containers. Suddenly, there was an earth-shaking explosion, like a bomb blast. Everything around him exploded, an infernal ball of fire engulfed the shack he was working in. Sankuru was flung off several yards. When the villagers rushed to the scene, they saw him hardly alive, his body mangled, badly burned. They put him on a makeshift trolley brought in from somewhere, carted him to the Vaidya. One look at his patient, the country medic declared his inability to be of any help, Sankuru's condition was far beyond his capabilities. Somehow, he had to be taken to the hospital miles away, he said. The only transportation they could find in the village was a bullock cart. After a long, arduous journey along the rough country road, he was admitted to the small hospital.

Sankuru was at the hospital for more than five months. When he was brought back home, his wife, Ayya, was shocked and saddened to see the condition of her husband. His body was speckled with unsightly burn marks, pinkish white patches on his dark brown skin. His left hand and the legs were rigid, unbending. He could hardly stand on his own. Ayya took care of him lovingly, told him tearfully how tough it was without him and an income.

Unable to walk and move around, Sankuru was confined to a side room of the house. He saw his household largely unchanged during the time he was away; however, he was at a loss to figure out the frequent visitors to his house after night fall. He could hear them in the adjoining larger room, veiled conversations, occasionally, hushed laughter. As the days went by, Sankuru made out the nature of the nocturnal happenings taking place in his own house: Ayya was entertaining her clients and she had no dearth of customers. It was a cruelly painful revelation for him, driving him into depression, periods of silence, food aversion. Ayya had an effective remedy for the problem: she served him expensive liquor with dinner. The ordinary toddy, she thought, was not good enough to expiate the pain he was enduring, to keep him inebriated and finally lull him into deep slumber. In the drunken stupor, Sankuru learned to close his eyes and ears to what was taking place in the next room.

Kochumary was very perturbed by what went on at Sankuru's house at night. She, nevertheless, could not do much about it. She consciously tried to block it off from her mind, though the view was right in front of her house. Kochumary, however, could not escape some undesirable and unexpected consequences of her sharing the neighborhood with Sankuru. One late evening, Kochumary and Rosy were getting ready for bed. Unexpectedly, there was a knock at the door. As she opened the door, she saw two men standing in front of her, one very much past his youth, the other hardly old enough to shave, islands of curled up whiskers on his face. They asked her for some water to drink. Kochumary was not very charitable or munificent. "What are you doing at this part of the village, at this late hour?" she asked, sternly.

"We are looking for some fun"

"You are looking for that kind of fun here! this is where decent people live"

"Like Ayya?"

The older man said scornfully, sneering at her; he then continued,

"We just had been to her house, the bitch is too busy; could we come in, we pay you good"

The man said, salaciously looking at the mother and daughter. Kochumary could not believe he dared to proposition her. She felt violated, she was seething, but did not show it outwardly.

"You wanted water, didn't you, I would go get some, you stand right there" Kochumary went to the kitchen leaving Rosy there, but the young woman could not stand the men leering at her, she too withdrew into the kitchen. Kochumary came back within minutes, holding a large machete in her hand. She menacingly swung it at the men.

"You scoundrels, run away at this minute, otherwise your heads will roll in the mud",

She roared brandishing her weapon at them again. Alarmed, taken aback, the men bolted into the darkness, hurling shouted curses at her.

Kochumary was unsettled and flustered by the events of the previous night. Though she routinely left for her food counter late in the morning, she returned home only well past into the night, after the toddy shop shuttered its doors. She was apprehensive of leaving Rosy alone at home. In her absence, anything could happen as it occurred the night before. She was concerned and anxious about her daughter's safety.

At the food counter, Kochumary was not her usual self, gone were the, naughty, impish smiles, teasing small talk with the customers, the perky playfulness. She was pensive, the faces of the ruffians turned up at her house at night were still milling in her mind, making her fret and enraged at the same time. She was affronted that they bracketed her house with that of Ayya. In their ignorant blindness, they could not have recognized the respected from the rest, she tried to console herself. That thought, however, was quickly pushed aside by her seething rage. One of the regular customers at the toddy shop walked by. Seeing Kochumary's long morose face, he quipped tauntingly:

"Why the glum face? Is Chakoru back?

A quick retort of choice invectives from Kochumary hastened him, hurtled him through the shop door.

Kochumary was afraid that every moment she was away from home, Rosy was unprotected, unsafe. Her daughter was the very center of her life. She braved every hardship of the day mostly for her: the long walk to the toddy shop, carrying the day's provisions on her head, dealing with the drunken customers, bandying words with them, the trekking back home at night. Not having received love or affection from Chakoru, Kochumary had grown accustomed to seek and receive much strength and comfort from her young daughter. Over the years, they had developed a degree of mutual dependence for emotional support. Kochumary could not imagine anything untoward happening to her daughter, she wanted to protect her by any conceivable means. She longed to see Muthoma, urgently. Muthoma was not a regular at the toddy shop, nevertheless, he came in at least once a week, mostly late in the evening. The day of his visit, though, was unpredictable. Kochumary eagerly waited for him to come in, settle at her counter, drink toddy, order his favorite dishes to go with it. She had to wait a couple of days for Muthoma to show up. She had a number of things to discuss with him and above all, she had a favor to ask of him. While walking towards the toddy counter, Muthoma smiled at Kochumary, acknowledging her, returned with two earthen pots of toddy, planted himself on the offered short stool. Kochumary could not wait for pleasantries. She straight away started to narrate the incident that took place at her home two days back, preceded by an abrupt, excited introduction:

"You won't believe what happened to us on Friday" She went on to elaborate the frightening event: how the hooligans came to her house, propositioned her and her daughter, how she warded them off by swinging a machete at them. She continued to vent her deep concern and fear about Rosy's safety in her absence; then without a prologue, but slightly gasping with emotion, she asked Muthoma,

"Could you, please, be at our home in the evenings?"

She paused for a few emotional seconds, then proceeded,

"Only for two or three hours, until I come from work; I don't want Rosy to be alone."

"She would cook dinner for you"

Kochumary did not have to indulge much in entreaties or persuasion with Muthoma. He readily agreed with an assuring smile. She was gratified Muthoma willingly acquiesced with her request. However, keeping to herself, sharing with no one, she also had an ulterior motive in inviting Muthoma home: spending time together, getting to know each other, Rosy and Muthoma would fall for each other, she hoped. Though a bit old for Rosy, Kochumary considered Muthoma a suitable mate for her daughter, she would gratefully welcome him as the man of the house.

It was sundown when Muthoma arrived at Kochumary's house. Rosy opened the door, offered tepid greetings to Muthoma and withdrew indoors. Muthoma settled down on the verandah, sitting on a small bench. He looked into the thickening darkness down the slope. He could see the silhouette of the house under the mango tree against the blackening sky; gradually the silhouette melded into darkness, the house becoming hardly discernible. Occasionally, he saw a solitary lighted torch moving towards Ayya's house, being put out near the house; then lit again after a while to move away along the pathway.

Muthoma could hear Rosy in the kitchen. After a while, she appeared at the door announcing dinner. She had set the table in a small room adjoining the kitchen. The table was a small board rising only two or three inches from the floor, resting on four wooden blocks. On the table was a plate of steaming rice, fish curry and sautéed vegetable in small bowls and a tiny thimble of red hot pickle. Squatting on a grass mat behind the table, Muthoma had his dinner. He complimented Rosy for her cooking; from the kitchen, she acknowledged him with a smile. Muthoma went back to the bench on the verandah. Before long he saw Kochumary walking towards the house, an empty basket on her head.

Kochumary was happy her plan was working out well. Every day, she went to her food counter with the assurance that Muthoma was at home in the evenings and Rosy safe. Nevertheless, she was not sure if Rosy and Muthoma were getting any closer romantically, if her little secret scheme would ever succeed. She did not know their relationship was just less than cold. When he came home at dusk, Rosy welcomed Muthoma with a few pleasantries, they exchanged a couple of sentences, mostly about food during dinner; that was the extent of their everyday communication. Rosy spent nearly all her time in the kitchen or one of the other rooms. Muthoma sat on the bench on the porch looking into the darkness outside. He himself did not know how he occupied himself sitting there silently. Perhaps, he was purging his mind vacant, meditating without trying.

One evening, when Muthoma came home as usual, the front door of the house was locked, Rosy was not at home; she might have stepped out, he thought. He took his seat on the bench and waited. Not before long, he noticed two figures stirring at the small wooden gate of the house, a few feet away; they were scarcely visible in the twilight. Soon, he could make out one of them departing and the other walking towards the house. As the figure came closer, Muthoma instantly realized it was Rosy, but wondered who it was that walked away. He greeted her and casually asked,

"You had someone with you?"

"Please don't tell Amma" Moving closer to Muthoma, Rosy begged, there were fear and panic in her voice.

"Why, Rosy?"

"She had told me not to have any male friends; she would kill me if she comes to know"

"So, that was your friend, the one left you at the gate?"

"Yes, it was Anto, we know each other for a long time"

"You won't tell Amma, would you? You have to promise me"

"Alright, I won't tell, don't worry"

Muthoma smiled, the barrier of silence between them lifted. Rosy went to the kitchen, got busy making dinner.

Unlike on previous days, Rosy was garrulous and chatty as she served dinner, she had relented her reticent demeanor. Eloquent and articulate, she could not stop talking about her newly revealed friend. During the days followed, Muthoma's dinner times gotten livelier. His time on the bench was not any more hours of loneliness and silence, no more sliding into inadvertent meditations. Rosy was there picking up and continuing her narrative from the dinner table. Gradually, Rosy unfolded the story of her relationship with her friend: how their furtive liaison grew and flourished over the years, without affording even an inkling to Kochumary. Her animated account was exuberant.

It was the beginning of school year; Chakoru was taking his only child to enroll at the elementary school. Kochumary had dressed Rosy in the best frock she had. As they stepped out of the house it was drizzling. Chakoru cut a broad banana leaf from the yard, held it over the little girl's head as they walked to the school. It was the first day of the school, they were rather late to arrive at the school. By then, the first-grade class already had assembled, the tiny tots in their seats on the short benches, their slate boards and books neatly stored under the benches. Chakoru left Rosy at the class entrance and went home. The teacher was busy reining in an unruly group of children, she could not pay any attention to Rosy at the door. Bewildered, lost and left to her own devices, Rosy entered the class gingerly, sought a seat on one of the benches, but there were no vacant seats, children had crowded on every bench pressing against each other. Then a boy sitting at the end of a bench silently beckoned her, he gently pushed the child next to him making a little room on the bench for Rosy. She squeezed herself into the space. The boy was Anto: slim, dense dark hair, a prominent nose, round eyes wide open in perennial amazement.

The first-grade teacher was Eliamma, a slight middle-aged woman, narrow ovoid face, dark complexion, her hair tied into a tight tiny bun, squeaky high-pitched voice. Her attire was the traditional *mundu* and slackened white blouse, a short length of muslin draped her upper torso, sari like. The teacher struck her table repeatedly with a thin cane in her hand, drawing children's attention, ordered them to pick up their slate boards. With some commotion and clatter, the toddlers alighted the benches, picked up their writing boards - rectangles of slate in wooden frames. On the chalkboard, Eliamma wrote the first letter of the vernacular alphabet, asked the class to write it on their own slates. Rosy with her slate in hand, looked around, puzzled. She did not have the slender sliver of slate used to write on the writing board. Just as careless he was to leave Rosy at the class door to fend for herself, Chakoru had not bought everything his daughter needed for her first day at school. Little Anto quickly realized his bench mate's predicament. He had a brand-new slate pencil. With some efforts, he broke it into two, gave one piece to Rosy. Rosy easily copied the letter on her slate from the chalkboard; Anto was struggling to do the same, Rosy turned to him to help. She ended up nearly drawing the letter on his slate; happy, they smiled at each other.

Rosy and Anto sat next to each other in every class until fourth grade when girls and boys were segregated in their seating, their friendship, however, continued. They played together during recess, shared their snacks, mostly a few nuts or tender mangos Anto plucked on his way to the school. Their amity and closeness extended to their teenage years and beyond. Even when Anto went to the college in a faraway city, the relationship was uninterrupted, it was preserved through letters. Once, an envelope Rosy received from Anto contained no letter, instead, a poem. He needed to know what she thought about it. Rosy had read one or two short stories he had written, but never knew he had a penchant for poetry. Even before she could grasp and assimilate the verse to form an opinion, another poem came in the mail, then a few others in quick succession.

Rosy felt and sensed herself in every stanza Anto wrote; but Anto insisted he had no particular person in mind when he wrote the lines; he was not even writing about a living soul, most of the times. Rosy, however, lost in her own thoughts, was thrilled how she was infused in every poetic rhythm emanating from his creative mind, even when he was not conscious of it; how she was intertwined with every thread of his lyrical sensibilities. Her intimate musings delighted her, intensified her feelings for Anto.

Many of the topics Rosy chattered about went over Muthoma's head, especially her effusion about Anto's poetry. The last time Muthoma encountered poetry was in Desu master's class years ago. He was to recite poems by heart, every time, however, he lost the poem midway through the recital, he could remember only the first few stanzas of the poem. Nonetheless, Muthoma was impressed by the portrait of Anto emerging from Rosy's rendition, there was an endearing quality to the picture.

"You have a good friend; I sort of like him already, I would like to meet him, could I?"

"Certainly, let me talk to him"

After a couple of days, Muthoma was on the verandah, as has been his routine for the last several days. It was already dark and dusky outside, a faint moonlight softened the darkness, a flake of moon in the sky. Rosy was not at home. Then, unexpectedly, he saw her walk in through the gate, a man alongside.

"This is Anto"

Rosy introduced her friend. Muthoma smiled at his visitor heartily; his pleasantries were rather circumscribed. Anto, in a dark grey pants and shirtsleeves, a young man in his early twenties; tall, slightly curly hair, a serene face with a proclivity to break into a smile intermittently, then quickly returning to a tempered seriousness. He politely answered Muthoma's enquiries, which were not many. Nonetheless, Muthoma was immediately awed and surprised to realize Anto was Devassy's son. He knew the prominent family but did not know much about the doyen's children. As they saw Muthoma falling into silence with a benevolent expression on his face, Rosy and Anto began chatting with each other, in spite of Muthoma being around. After a while, Muthoma got up to leave. Rosy was instantly alarmed, Muthoma read the deep concern on her face.

"Don't worry, your mother would be here soon"

"She would get angry, I am scared" Rosy was almost in tears.

"It is important that she meet Anto"

"She won't like to see us together, I have already told you"

"Don't be frightened, I would explain everything to her, by the time she sees you, she would be calm and friendly, trust me"

Leaving Rosy and Anto on the verandah, Muthoma walked through the wooden gate and on to the pathway, unlit, shadowy.

At the junction where the footpath met the main road, Muthoma saw Kochumary walking towards him, an empty wicker basket in her hand. As she came closer, face to face with Muthoma, she was visibly surprised to see him there.

"Are you leaving already? Is Rosy alright?" Kochumary asked.

"She is alright"

"Is she alone?"

"No, her friend is with her"

"A friend?" Kochumary was alarmed even more.

"He is a good man; a suitable boy, from a good family, well educated; Rosy would be safe and happy with him, you will see"

Muthoma set out to walk away with an impish smile, as if trying to stash and hide something pleasant.

Kochumary started to walk towards her home, puzzled and confused, wondering what was in store for her at home, uneasy and apprehensive to meet Rosy's friend.

# Eleven

The nondescript ferry jetty on the northern banks of Emmau River. It was not daybreak yet, there were hints of glow in the eastern sky, however. The golden rays of the sun, still in the depths of horizon, set the edges of greyish morning clouds aglow. One could hear the gently lapping waves of the river, intermingled with the chirr and croaks of insects and frogs. A stench pervaded the air: coconut husks rotting in the shallow waters of the river.

A small wooden boat, coated in tar, was gently bobbing in the water. The vessel had only two seats, wooden planks set across the breadth of the boat, one seat for the rower, the other for a passenger. Standing over the boat in ankle deep water was Kunjayi, carefully tending the vessel. The boat was his own, he did not work on the ferryboat of Lona anymore. He operated a private ferry for passengers willing to pay a higher fare for personalized service. Every day, Kunjayi was at the jetty even before dawn, he was there early to net the travelers needing to ferry across, before Lona's public ferry start plying the river, that would have been well after the sunrise. Kunjayi was standing erect, his frame not bent as it used to be, he looked taller because of his upright posture. He was no more dependent on bicarbonate powder for his heartburn. A small business of his own, a generally improved health and better appearance, Kunjayi was a changed man. All these because of the loving care of his only daughter, Chamy. The welcome changes, however, did not happen all at once. Before his life turned around for the better, Kunjayi had to go through an onerous period of anxiety and worry, all about his daughter, Chamy.

It was two years ago, on a hot and humid summer night. Lona and Kunjayi had berthed the ferryboat. They had done their last trip from the other side of the river; the ferry was closed for the night. Kunjayi placed the oars on Lona's porch before going home. Just as he was stepping down from the porch, unexpectedly, Lona called him back, invited him to come in. This, never had happened before – the hospitality, the intimacy. Though they knew each other for long, their relationship at best, was that of an employer and employee and at worst, cold and callous. Kunjayi was much puzzled and surprised. He entered the house, anyway, gingerly. He saw no one else except Lona sitting at a small table, his face grim and dour. There were four pots of toddy on the table. Gently nodding his head, Lona welcomed Kunjayi; with a wave of his hand, he signed Kunjayi to help himself to the drink, but no word escaped his mouth. As Kunjayi started to drink the toddy, Lona's wife, Chinnu came from the kitchen with a dish of steaming crab curry.

"Do you like crabs, Kunjayi?"

Lona asked, not leaving his seriousness, still no amiability in his voice. Kunjayi smiled heartily in agreement, he could feel and taste the curry in his mouth. Lona emptied his first pot of toddy, then went inside to return with a tall bottle of clear cashew liquor. He poured a glass for Kunjayi and one for himself. Kunjayi was overwhelmed; it was not that often he gets to taste a drink like cashew liquor. He downed his drink, started to munch on the crab chunks. Lona was on his second cashew drink, he served another glass for Kunjayi. Kunjayi appeared to have overcome with inebriated emotion, he struggled down from his seat, stumbled on to Lona, hugged him noisily,

"You are my brother I never had."

he declared, sobbing.

Lona hugged him back, laughing boisterously. Writhing back to his bench, Kunjayi tripped and fell to the floor, somehow heaved himself back to his seat.

Suddenly, Lona broke into a song, belting it out incoherently at the top of his voice. Hearing the cacophony, Chinnu came rushing to the front room. She was alarmed and embarrassed by the scene in front of her. She hastily went inside to return with an unlit palm-leaf-torch, gave it to Kunjayi, urged him to go home. Kunjayi gathered himself clumsily and exited Lona's home. His steps were grossly unsteady, he could hardly balance himself. He dragged along the darkened road and somehow, he arrived home. Strangely, the front door of his house was not locked from inside, as usual. As he groped on the door, the double door parted to open wide. He saw his bed already been made: a grass mat rubbing the wall in one corner of the room, a pillow and a sheet with parsley design. He plumped on to the bed, started to snore in an instant.

When Kunjayi woke up in the morning, he felt something amiss in the house; there was no clang and stir in the kitchen, an eerie silence in the house. Every morning when he wakes up, Chamy used to come with a glass of black coffee for him, today not even a whiff of coffee in the house; he felt it very strange she was not there as usual. He called out for her aloud; no response. She might have gone for work early, this is not the first time she had done so, Kunjayi tried to console himself. She had an office-cleaning job at the local bank. Though the villagers liked to call it a bank, in reality, it was a pawnshop.

When men were down on cash, they wrested the meager jewelry of their wives, rushed to the bank for ready cash at an exorbitant interest rate. Besides cleaning the office, Chamy also used to do odd jobs at the bank: making coffee and tea for the two clerks and the manager. She was always there at the bank, even though the cleaning takes her only an hour or two in the morning and roughly as much time in the evening. At the bank, everyone liked her being around.

Kunjayi left for work at the ferry worrying about his daughter. While leaving the house every morning, he used to see Chamy at the doorsteps watching him, but not on that day, it made him perturbed and fretful. At the ferry, he was pensive, he was anxious to end the workday and get back home. On his way home, he did not stop at the toddy shop as usual; he was in a hurry to reach home, make sure Chamy was back and safe. At the house, however, Kunjayi saw the front door remaining locked as he had left it in the morning. Ominous thoughts started to seep into his mind. Unnerved, he sat on the steps for a few minutes, then, he started to walk towards the bank.

There was no one at the bank, all had gone home, leaving the small brick building in darkness. Dejected, panicked and not knowing what to do, Kunjayi started to walk home. Then on the bare, darkened road, he saw the shadow of a person moving towards him. When the figure came closer, Kunjayi recognized the man; it was Chacku, one of the clerks at the bank.

"Any news from Chamy" Chacku queried.

"I don't know where she has gone; I just had been to your bank looking for her"

"Don't you know she ran away with George, our manager?"

Kunjayi was taken aback, he could not believe what he just heard, he was about to faint, he moved to one side of the road, wearily sat on a parapet.

"There is nothing to worry, Kunjayi. It is a good match, it would be very good for Chamy"

Chacku said, then, went on to extol the merits of George and what an excellent catch he is for Chamy. George was from a well to do family in a faraway city, well educated, having a good position at the bank. His parents could have arranged his marriage from a wealthy family with a sizeable dowry; it was Chamy's and your good fortune, he fell for her.

"Don't you fret and worry unnecessarily; they would be back soon"

Chacko patted Kunjayi on his back, consoling him, before moving on. Kunjayi was hardly consoled or comforted. He could not comprehend how Chamy could leave him alone and disappear. She has never been away from him, from her early childhood after her mother passed away. She could have given him some indications before she eloped.

Kunjayi sat on the parapet some more time, brooding, then went home heavyhearted. He did not think about dinner, he curled up on his bed trying to sleep; but, his deprivation and melancholy, feeding on each other, only intensified.

The village was abuzz about Chamy's elopement with George. Some marveled at her good fortune, others were aghast at her unbecoming conduct.

For three days, Kunjayi did not hear anything from Chamy. On the fourth day of her missing, he was returning from the ferry. From a distance, he saw light and movements in the window of his house. Puzzled and apprehensive, he came and opened the front door. What he saw indoors, surprised and filled him with disparate emotions: Chamy rushing out form the kitchen to greet him, George leaning on the wall squatting on a grass mat. Kunjayi darted an angry look at his daughter, keeping a stern silence. Chamy came forward to lock him in an embrace, sobbing,

"I am sorry, Appa, I left you alone, forgive me."

By this time, George got up, came near the father and daughter.

"Appa, we are married, this is my husband"

Kunjayi was still unrelenting but kept patting Chamy on the back. He saw a thick gold chain around her neck with a *Thali*, the golden talisman in the shape of a teardrop with a sculpted cross. Ritually adorned on them by the groom at nuptial, it was worn by all married Christian women.

"What did you eat during the last three days, Appa?

Kunjayi did not reply; he himself did not know the answer. "We can't leave you alone here, we came to take you to our home in town"

George nodded his assent. Kunjayi was not enthusiastic about his daughter's proposal, he was worried about his job at the ferry, uneasy about life in a town. He was more attuned to and treasured his life in the village: early morning walk to the ferry, chatting with the regulars on the ferryboat, silent inter-actions with Lona, returning home late in the evening with a break at the toddy shop. Nevertheless, Chamy was persistent. With her love and prodding from George, Kunjayi relented, agreed to try the plan of his daughter and her new husband.

Kunjayi spent about three months at Chamy's new house in town, a comfortable house near the market place. George's was a joint family, his old parents living with him and Chamy. Besides the loving care of his daughter, Kunjayi was happy the way he was treated by George and his parents. Chamy, nevertheless, was very concerned about the run-down health of her father. His heavy drinking and irregular eating habits had taken a toll on his physical wellbeing. He was constantly plagued by acid reflux, lack of energy made his gait stooped and frail. Soon after his arrival at her house, one of the first things Chamy did was to arrange him to see George's family physician, Dr. Varghese. Though the doctor made house calls, Kunjayi accompanied by George was seen at his home, which doubled as his office. Dr. Varghese talked to his patients exclusively in English, even though none of them knew a word of the language. His long-time nurse, Sossama, translated him to the patients. He had no difficulty grasping what the patients told him in Malayalam, as he too grew up speaking the same vernacular. Taught and trained by English teachers at the medical school, he insisted his services should be dispensed only in the language of the elite, the medium of science.

Dr. Varghese sent Kunjayi home with prescription for a number of medicines, strict directives for his diet, his day today activities: no alcohol, only non-fermented toddy to quench his craving for the booze, regular morning exercises. Chamy made sure her father closely adheres to the doctor's instructions.

For Kunjayi, it was a struggle; he thirsted for toddy, abhorred **neera**, the unfermented toddy, loathed the morning exercises, longed for a hearty meal, not the restricted and measured ones. By the end of a few weeks, however, the involuntary and imposed treatments and daily routines had some gratifying results. Kunjayi felt it more than anyone else did. He could throw away the small plastic pouch of sodium bicarbonate he always carried with him to combat his stomach pain. His bearing improved; standing erect, he appeared taller.

It was nearing three months since Kunjayi came to spend time with Chamy and George. Feeling fit and energetic, he wanted to return to Manoor, go back to work at the ferry. Chamy was reluctant to let him leave. She relented, however, as her father persisted and insisted on going back to his village.

Kunjayi returned to Manoor with zest and enthusiasm to resume his work on the boat. When he arrived at the ferry,

Lona was at the helm of the wooden craft laden with riders, ready to leave the jetty. Lona peered at him silently, measuring him, scrutinizing him, a surprised look on his face. At the rear of the boat, where Kunjayi used to sit and row, Kunjayi saw a sturdy young man sitting, oar in his hand.

"I am back, can I get on the boat to start working?" Kunjayi asked Lona eagerly.

"No. You see Shanku sitting there; he has taken your place"

"Are you firing me!"

"No. You have already been fired when you did not show up for work for the last three months"

Crest fallen, saddened and piqued, Kunjayi returned home. When George heard about what happened to his father-in-law at the jetty, he was unsettled too. To console and placate Kunjayi, it was he who came up with the idea of a water taxi. Kunjayi quickly embraced the plan. There was an element of vengeance in the minds of both men.

The next day, George took Kunjayi to a small boat yard down the river. The yard was owned by a carpenter. His specialty was carving out boats out of logs. His turn out of boats was very slow, however, taking one or two months to build one vessel. Kunjayi and George were happy to see a small boat in the yard, built, painted and ready for sale. George bought it straight away for Kunjayi. Together, they paddled it to the ferry jetty.

Kunjayi was still waiting for his first passenger to show up. He had finished tidying up the boat, he stepped into the boat, sat on his seat looking expectedly towards the country road slanting to the riverbank. It was dawn, eastern sky was brightening up, tiny waves on the slow flowing river glistening in the rays of the rising sun. A cool westerly breeze wafted away some of the stink of the decaying coconut husk.

"Hallooooooooooooooooooooooo"

Suddenly, Kunjayi heard someone hollering from the other bank of the river. He could not see anyone on the other side, there was a thin veil of fog, it was still dark. He felt something strange about the call itself. He was quite familiar with the local people's call for a boat,

"Poooooooooooooooooooooooohai" they go.

He had heard George saying Hello to Dr. Varghese, not anyone using it as boat call. Puzzled a bit, Kunjayi started to paddle towards the caller, his first customer of the day. As he came closer, he could see a tall figure waiting at the bank.

"Hello" the figure said again, this time pithy and as a greeting; then he introduced himself,

"I am Simon, perhaps you remember me"

Kunjayi did not understand the salutation nor the introduction. He just smiled, the other person did not see it in the dark. The traveler gingerly stepped into the boat, took his seat facing Kunjayi. In the faint light of the dawn, Kunjayi could see a tall, fair-skinned man trying to accommodate himself in the tiny boat and not so ample seat. He was wearing a dark pant, white wrinkled shirtsleeves, carrying a large cloth bag. His face oval, the long hair mostly grey, a thick untrimmed, salt and pepper beard. From his hairy visage, Kunjayi could feel a pair of shimmering eyes casually looking at him. He was silent during the entire ride across the river; he seemed to be enjoying the peace and tranquility of the morning while watching Kunjayi's oar rhythmically hitting the water, propelling the boat forward.

As the boat reached and berthed at the riverbank, the traveler gave the requested fare to Kunjayi. While he was giving the fare to him, he asked Kunjayi where Varu's house was. Kunjayi was surprised and raved to hear the visitor speaking Malayalam, haltingly with heavy English accent. Kunjayi in a gush, gave him the directions to Varu's house. Hearing Kunjayi's description, the traveler immediately realized the route was already familiar to him, Varu was still living in the same house of his parents, he had not moved elsewhere as he feared.

By the time Simon started walking along the road, the predawn darkness had partially been lifted. He felt an immediate familiarity with the landscape in front of him. The road was still unpaved, in places the gravel sparsely embedded in the sand. On the embankments on either side of the road, there were fences of braided thorny bamboo branches, thickets of wild shrubbery behind them; in places, the hedge laden fences were bulging and leaning out onto the road. Scent of wild flowers in the morning air.

As he continued to stroll, he felt nothing much has changed along the country road since he left several years ago; many of the landmarks he was acquainted with remained the same as they were before, they seemed to be beyond the vagaries of time. The roadside houses stood asleep, still and silent, no glimmer of light in the windows. The people of Manoor and surrounding villages were not early risers, they led their lives unhurried, leisurely. Simon had been to some of these houses and acquainted with the families, but he found it difficult to single out those houses. As he moved along, he came across a house with tiled roof, a wrought iron gate painted in black and red, images of two hooded serpents intricately designed into the ironwork. He did not have much difficulty identifying that house: the house of Vishnu, the snakebite healer. He treated snakebites by traditional methods he inherited through generations. Simon remembered the day he brought a snakebite victim to Vishnu. It was a dark night in the monsoon season, the earth was slush and drenched in incessant rains. He was busy working in his tiny room adjacent to the Manoor church. Hearing people outside calling out for help, he came out. A parishioner had been bitten by a snake, he is sinking fast. Simon rushed to the parishioner's house. Along with others he carried the bitten on a makeshift stretcher to Vishnu's house. The snakebite healer asked the patient a set of formal questions: which direction he was walking when the snake bit him, which way the snake slithered away after biting him, did he walk to south or north after snakebite. He carefully listened to the answers and quickly came up with identity of the slithering culprit: a **Vellikettan**, a krait. He followed the announcement with a Sanskrit verse outlining the nature of the species:

"Small, beautiful to look at

A deep chalice of poison, a killer"

The healer signed Simon to follow him; he went out to his garden of medicinal plants, Simon at his heels with a torch illuminating the plants. The snake physician carefully selected a few plants, gathered their leaves and returned to his house. He extracted juice from some leaves, made a paste out of others. He made the patient to drink the juice, the patient grimaced drinking the acrid extract, he applied the paste on the bite site on the patient's lower left leg. He, then went into a deep meditative spell. Eyes closed shut, he was motionless, except his lips murmuring inaudible mantras. He woke up after a few moments to recite the restrictions and taboos the patient was to follow: nothing to eat or drink for twenty-four hours, avoid meat and fish for a week, make an offering at the church at the earliest. Simon was amazed to see the snake bitten parishioner at the church the following Sunday.

As he kept on walking towards Varu's house, not far from Vishnu's house gate, Simon saw Emmau post office, a cramped space next to a tea shop, the door secured with an outsized padlock, the red mailbox hung from a wooden post. Manoor village did not have a post office of its own, the villagers had to come to Emmau for their postal needs. The postmaster was an atypically tall man awkwardly trying to accommodate himself in the tiny office space at his disposal, his discomfort often reflecting in his demeanor. His bristling mane was parted in the middle, thick-rimmed glasses on the nose, a dot of sandalwood paste on the brow. The postmaster always looked stony and harsh, never failing to wear the gravitas of his position as a government employee. The postmaster was famed in Emmau and the surrounding villages, not because of his rank in the postal department, but rather a peculiar behavior he was known for: whenever he dispensed stamps to a customer, he had an irrepressible habit of reading every inscription on the stamp, repeatedly and not very silently – an effort to convince himself the article was of legal issue and exact value. There were instances when he had snatched back the stamps from a client for one more final scrutiny before they were given back to the customer.

Beyond the post office, after a slight bend on the road was Emmau village center, marked by four shops in a row; a tiny grocery store, a vegetable stall, a coffee house and a slightly bigger shop, widely known in the villages, simply as "The Store". The store carried more modern merchandize, items not available at the local grocery or Apputy's grocery in Manoor. The well to do of the villages, when they needed toothbrush and paste or greeting cards, they always came to the store.

At a short distance from the village center, Simon walked past the Emmau parish church; a serene structure nestled among coconut palm trees; white washed Gothic façade displaying distinct influence of Portuguese church architecture. Years ago, Simon used to be friends with the parish priest at that time. He distinctly remembered the pastor, a lean bespectacled man, a mischievous glint always in his eyes. The father knew a smattering of English and loved the language. He wanted to learn it further, longed to be proficient in it and he sought Simon's help; Simon was only glad to oblige.

He spent hours with the vicar, teaching him words, phrases, diction and other intricacies of the lingo. Half way through the lessons, the priest was enthralled by the progress he had made, could not wait to share the newly acquired tongue with his flock. On a Sunday morning, he ascended the pulpit, delivered the sermon in English with a verve and ebullience not normally present in his homilies. He was gesticulating in the air, his undulating eloquence marked by sentences culminating in measured crescendos. The worshipers looked at each other, taken by surprise, unable to decipher anything he said. As he closed the sermon, there was a satisfied smile on his face; that was a moment he had been dreaming about for a long time, never imagined that he would ever realize it. On that day, if Simon was present in the church, he would have had a few things to say about his student's grammar and diction. The parishioners were left wondering whatever happened to their vicar until he delivered his entire sermon, once again, in Malayalam.

Manoor was only a short distance from the church. As he entered the village, Simon felt at home, he was on more familiar grounds. Varu's house was closer to the periphery of the hamlet. Simon did not have much difficulty finding the entrance to the yard leading to the house. It used to be a trench dug into the embankment slanting on to the road, now it is shored up with masonry, small steps leading up to the yard. When he came up to the yard in front of the house, he noticed that hardly anything had changed since he left the country a number of years ago: the jackfruit tree on one side of the house had flourished a little more, the seasonal abundance of the large fruits crowding on the trunk and large branches; the mango tree rubbing against the house looked taller, grown a bit wider in expanse, laden with tender mangos. The tall coconut tree with a "S" shaped bend several feet up in its slender bole, stood towering above Varu's house. The tree with a disproportionately small head of leafy plume and coconuts was a landmark on the village road. Varu's house was often referred to as 'the house under the twisted tree'.

Varu's house was calm and quiet, nothing stirred or heard around the house. As Simon came closer to the house, he noticed someone on the verandah, sound asleep on a bench, covered head to toe in a checkered sheet, snoring loudly, chest rhythmically heaving up and down. Simon coughed a couple of times to make his presence known, no response. With his palm, he struck the cement floor a few times making a clapping sound, the reaction was only a momentary jarring distortion in the snoring. Simon moved closer to the sleeping figure on the bench and said loudly,

"Hello"

"You have visitor from far away.,"

he said in Malayalam.

In a huff, Muthoma pulled away the sheet from his face, sat up in haste. Alarmed and perplexed, he looked askance at the stranger smiling at him.

"Don't you remember me, I am Sheemon upadesi!"

Though haltingly and accented, Simon had fully switched on to the local language by this time. In Malayalam, almost all Biblical names have language-adapted synonyms: Simon is Sheemon, Paul is Paulose, Mathew is Mathai, David is Devassy etc. The word Upadesi meant a mentor or counsellor. The name was distantly familiar, but Muthoma had hard time placing the visitor. Varu was waking up in the house, lazily, reluctantly. Hearing a stranger outside, he came out of the main door of the house.

"I am Sheemon upadesi; do you remember me?"

Simon asked looking at Varu expectedly. Varu recognized the name immediately; however, stared at Simon for a moment, trying to delineate his face behind the overgrown beard and hair, align it with the visage he had in his memory.

Varu and Muthoma were young boys when Simon was an everyday presence in Manoor. Later on, however, they had heard a lot about him from their parents, especially from their mother. For many years, Simon was interwoven with the village fabric of Manoor. The villagers never thought of him as someone from somewhere else; they never ever considered him as a stranger, a foreigner. They were not conscious of how and when he entered their lives, grew on them. They felt he was always there with them. Such was the seamless relationship he had with the people of Manoor. Simon, however, still remembered how he began his life in the village: it was in the middle of night, the atmosphere awaiting the advent of monsoon was humid, oppressively hot. Simon knocked at the door of the rectory of the Manoor parish. For a while, there was no response, then he heard some movements inside. The eighty-year-old vicar, Fr. Joseph opened the door. Tragically, however, the priest fell to the tiled floor tripping on a doormat. His right knee buckled and badly sprained; he was in acute pain, could not get up and stand on his own. For a moment, Simon was perplexed, then he lifted the vicar, put him on his shoulders, walked on to the road looking for help. In a strange land he landed only days back, he did not know where to find medical help. He went to the first house on the road side with a lighted window; that was Pappachan's house. He was surprised to see their vicar groaning in pain, on the shoulders of a foreigner, never seen in the village before. Simon told Pappachan what had taken place in English, but seeing incomprehension writ large on Pappachan face, Simon tried to describe the events signing crudely by his face and hands. He never imagined, signs and gestures were going to be his mode of communication with the villagers for many months to come. Pappachan hollered to his neighbors, awakening them from their sleep. Soon a small crowd gathered on Pappachan's courtyard, alarmed at the condition of the priest. There was not much discussion about what to do next: they propped up the vicar on a chair, carried him to the vaidya's house. The vaidya's house, everyone asleep, was in total darkness except an oil lamp flickering at the base of a masonry pedestal, a **tulsi** plant on it. Hearing the commotion outside, the physician came out, but, declined to see or treat the patient: the auspicious time dictated by the configuration of celestial bodies has long been passed, it is forbidden to provide care for the afflicted when the planetary positions are not favorable; the patient should wait until sunrise for the next propitious moment to present itself. The pastor and Simon were directed to retire and wait in an adjoining out house. The parish priest was still moaning in pain and discomfort. Simon ferreted and searched the large canvas bag he was carrying along. He fished out a small plastic box; his sister, Elena, had packed some first aid supplies and medicines before he boarded the ocean liner from England. From the box, Simon picked up a small bottle of analgesic tablets, gave a couple of the tablets for the priest to swallow. After a while Fr. Joseph got some relief, his pain ebbed. Simon felt it time appropriate for letting the father know why he came to Manoor. Though his command of English language was limited, he understood what Simon was telling him. The vicar was overjoyed that the religious authorities in Madras had taken note of his advancing age, sent Simon to assist him in his pastoral work. Helped by the painkiller, the father soon fell asleep. Simon curled up on the floor, his head resting on his cloth bag.

At the crack of dawn, the vaidya came to the out hose, examined his patient, prescribed the treatment: morning and evening massages with medicinal oils, a few oral medications;

prognosis good, but, it might take several days of stay at the vaidya's house before Fr. Joseph could stand up and walk. Realizing that he would not be able to return to the parish church any time soon, the vicar gave Simon the key to the rectory, instructed him to remain there until his return.

Hearing what had happened to their vicar, many parishioners came to the rectory the next morning, enquiring about him. Only Simon was there to face them, explain the incident of the previous night. He was left with only sign language to communicate with them. After the labored practice of the art during the night before, he was a bit more at ease using it; nonetheless, he was severely handicapped, he realized. Simon's morning visitors were very appreciative of his struggle to converse with them, they enthusiastically filled in to make sense of what he was trying to say. That was how Simone came to know many of the Manoor inhabitants. They became increasingly comfortable with their foreign visitor, his easy ways, his eagerness to be of help. However, he was severely frustrated by the language barrier, unable to delve deeper into the villagers' lives. He could serve them better if he could communicate with them better. He must master the local language somehow, it was essential. He would discuss it when Fr. Joseph returns.

Devassy was resting on an easy chair on the front porch of his house, reading a book, dozing off intermittently. The chair with extended leg rests on both sides creaked when he stirred in it. He raised his head from the book hearing the iron gate at the end of the walkway from the road clank open. He recognized Simon walking towards him. Devassy stood up to welcome the visitor, extended his hand for a warm handshake. Simon had a letter from Fr. Joseph addressed to Devassy: Simon was a godsend for the parish; he should learn Malayalam as quickly as possible; there was none other than Devassy qualified to teach him the language; get on with the job right away. Devassy was overjoyed the priest had entrusted him with the task. He had already met Simon, developed a liking for the Englishman, but more than anything else he admired his clarity of language and his diction. Devassy had been an Anglophile ever since his college days. Having been taught a number of classes at the Jesuit college by priests from England, he was familiar with their punctilious pronunciation and intonations. Over the years, he assiduously tried to inculcate them into his own diction, achieving, however, only a limited success. Conversing with Simon was exhilarating for Devassy; he took it also as an opportunity to improve and brush up his own articulation.

Simon was a quick study. He came to Devassy's house every day except Sundays. On most days, Devassy's classes extended to two hours or more. He felt it challenging to introduce Simon to a language far removed from his own Anglo-Germanic linguistic roots and the intricacies of Dravidian phonetics of Malayalam. The teacher and his student often found it unyielding, but they both were persistent, singularly motivated for their own individual reasons. Devassy adopted the method of language immersion in his single student classes, he spoke only Malayalam during the entire sessions, rarely, however, he switched to English to explain something to Simon, only when there was no other way. He drew pictures extensively on a slate board, acted and mimicked to put an idea across to his student. Many a time, he was surprised at himself, he never knew he could act when there was a need.

After the language lessons, Devassy and Simon used to sit and chat for a while, invariably over cups of coffee served by Devassy's wife or one of his servants. One day, Devassy had an anthology of Shakespearean plays on his desk. After finishing his cup of coffee, he opened the book, he had already bookmarked a page. He wanted Simon to recite a passage he had selected, Simon was only glad to oblige. His voice reverberated in the room, his diction and cadence precise. Devassy almost felt levitated, he could not but join Simon in the rendition. Soon they were engaged in a full-throated recital of the Bard's stanzas, in unison, doing all they could to be in tune with each other. They rumbled the monologue from "King Lear", the king's self-loathing entreaties to bring down the nature's destruction on himself,

"Blow, winds, and crack your cheeks! rage! blow!

You cataracts and hurricanoes, spout.

Till you have drench'd our steeples, drown'd the cocks!

You sulph'rous and thought-executing fires,

Vaunt-couriers to oak-cleaving thunderbolts,

Singe my white head! And thou, all-shaking thunder,

Strike flat the thick rotundity o' th' world,

Crack Nature's moulds, all germains spill at once,

That makes ingrateful man!"

Before they realized it, reciting Shakespearean verses became a routine, every day following the language lessons. For the passages, they had a proclivity for tragedies. Devassy and Simon selected the stanzas at random. One day, it was the long and extended second monologue of Macbeth; some other day, it was the second monologue of Romeo and Juliet, Romeo's love-torn rendition of Juliet's beauty, invoking the imagery of celestial bodies; yet another day it was the fifth monologue of Othello, the Moore's conflicted lamentation prior to his killing of Desdemona. Notwithstanding the contents of the verses, when recited together, they enjoyed every one of them, Devassy especially. The verses took him back to his college days. Shakespeare, then, was a tough challenge in the classroom, but a delightful company, nonetheless.

Though Devassy did not think in those terms, Simon reciting Shakespeare with him was a sort of remuneration for his language lessons. After three-four months of strenuous efforts and under Devassy's creative teaching methods, Simon was able to speak Malayalam, not very fluently, but capable of holding a meaningful conversation in the language. He vigorously practiced it with the parishioners and whomever he came across. They were fascinated by a foreign visitor, coming from across the seas, speaking their own language. They were amused a little too, his faltering, heavily accented way of speaking. Fr. Joseph, however, found it much easier to converse with Simon in Malayalam than struggling in his own fragmentary English.

There was a tile roofed single story building between the church and the cemetery, a silent desolate place. No one went there except when there was a funeral. Most of the rooms in the building were utilized for storing unused furniture and other items. At the far end of the building, there was a small room facing the back of the church, two stained glass windows of the church clearly visible from there; pigeons fluttering around, cooing day and night. The parish had given the room to Simon as his modest living quarters. Ever since he moved in there, that corner of the church campus livened up a little, some movements, visitors coming to his room. Most of them were parishioners seeking his help and counsel. Some of them came there to invite him to a forthcoming wedding, others were there to inform him of someone seriously sick or a death in the family. In any circumstances, Simon had something to offer to help the situation. In marriage ceremonies, many families wanted him to be in the groom's party of close relatives going to the bride's parish church for the formal blessing of the union. Simon very much enjoyed the pomp and merriment of the occasion. He invariably accompanied most funeral processions in Manoor. Following the burial, he walked with the mourners to the home

of the deceased; at home, he sat among the grieving family, silently listening to them as they reminisced about the departed;
in some of the bereaved homes, there was only a suffocating
silence enveloping everyone, he joined the stillness absorbing
some of the brimming pain and anguish in the room. By par-
taking in the joy and pain of the villagers, Simon felt intimate
and one with the pulse and life of Manoor.

In spite of his bedraggled appearance, the long beard and
hair, disheveled cloths, Varu did not take too long to recognize
Sheemon upadesi, his parent's friend, a frequent visitor to their
house. He invited him in. Sitting on a wooden bench, Simon
was scanning and scouring around the house, brushing up his
own memories about the house, looking for familiar objects and
their placements as he remembered from the past. Meanwhile,
Muthoma came to the room, still looking sleepy, a *mundu*
loosely wrapped around his waist, a banian not fully covering
his upper torso. Recognizing him, Simon invited him to come
sit next to him on the bench. Varu left the room to fetch a cup
of coffee for the guest. As Muthoma came to sit on the bench,
Simon looked at him intently, lowered his voice and said,

"I came all the way from England to see you; I urgently
need some help from you" Muthoma was puzzled. As he
looked at Simon dubiously, Simon went on to elaborate,

"I have some personal possessions locked away in the room
I used to live in, adjacent to the church. I wrote to the church
authorities many times requesting them to open the room for
me, allow me to take away everything that belong to me. They
have steadfastly refused every time. Those items are intimate
part of me, I have to repossess them at any cost."

Though intrigued, Muthoma was not engaged in what
Simon was saying. "Some of the objects in that room are related to you as well. You would realize it when you get to know
the stories behind them" Muthoma was further bemused.

"Wouldn't you help me, Muthoma"

Simon asked Muthoma with some intimacy. Muthoma was impassive, a vacant smile on his face; after a while he walked away from the room leaving Simon fazed, at a loss.

Hoping Muthoma would come back to offer him assistance, Simon patiently sat on the wooden bench, but he soon saw Varu and Muthoma leaving for work at the butchery. He was a bit stung by the insolence of the brothers.

It was well into the morning, Simon saw Cherichi, Varu's wife, walking towards a corral at the far end of the back yard. She held a bronze jug resting in the curve above her waist, she was on her way to milk the cow. Simon stepped out of the house, caught up with Cherichi, she was startled a little, hearing footsteps behind her. Simon was there, offering to milk the cow for her. Cherichi accepted the assistance reluctantly, gave the jug to Simon and returned to the kitchen. In the cow shed, there were a cow and two goats, the white cow had large blotches of black all over her trunk. The goats stood motionless staring at Simon, they were baffled, perhaps, by the stranger in the house. Simon crouched beside the cow, positioned the jug beneath the animal, getting ready to milk. The moment he touched the udder, the cow kicked him violently, she was resisting the unfamiliar touch. Simon fell headlong to the floor, wet and dirty with urine and dung. When he struggled up, his clothes were dripping bovine excreta, he shook them off from his garb, got back to the business of milking. This time, the animal was calm and quiet, no throwing of her powerful hind legs into the air, allowed Simon to rhythmically squeeze out the milk from the teats. She was eager to relieve of the milk puddled in her.

Simon came back to the small courtyard in front of the Cherichi's kitchen. He was reluctant to step into the house, he was dirty and soiled all over. He handed over the pot of milk to Cherichi, she was overwhelmed by the whiff of stench emanating from him, she retracted herself, intuitively. Cherichi was amused looking at her guest, but did not show it outwardly, she laughed within herself. She went inside to fetch soap and a towel for him. By the time she returned, however, Simon had already left the courtyard. Cherichi saw him walking towards the pond at the periphery of the compound. He was very familiar with the freshwater pond; he had bathed in it many times, several years ago. Those memories still fresh in his mind.

At the pond, Simon undressed, jumped into the shallow water, bathed and came ashore. He painstakingly washed his clothes by soaking them first and striking them on a block of stone he found nearby at the bank. Intermittently, he dipped them in the pond water, washing off the dirt. Simon spread the washed clothes on wild bushes on the side of the pond to let them dry in the sun. It was nearing noon; the blazing sun was at the pinnacle of the sky, reflecting in the pond like a radiant silver plate corrugated by the gentle waves on the water. Though it was scorching hot, Simon knew it would take a while before his clothing was dry, ready to wear. Only a few feet away from the embankment of the pond, there was a large rock jutting out from the water, its darkened sides streaked by white bird droppings. Simon plodded through the shallow water, heaved himself to the top of the boulder, sat there in his underpants, cooling himself in the gentle breeze. In the water below, he watched fishes swimming around, most of them small ones, pursuing and wrangling for specks of food floating in the water. Then he saw a large, twelve-inch fish moving into the midst from nowhere. She glided in smoothly and unhurriedly, her fins wagging just enough to float and propel her, a regal entrance. The smaller fishes milling around in the water parted to give her way, she, however, ignored them, for her they were nonexistent. Self-absorbed, she swam in a circular fashion, bearing her royal gravitas. Simon, however, saw dinner in the royalty. He alighted from his perch, came ashore to search and find a slender but strong twig. As he got back on the partly submerged rock and waited for the large fish to come closer to his roost. As soon as the fish came to a striking distance, he darted his stick at it, harpoon like. The tip of the rod struck the fish on the dome of her head, between the gills. The fish shuddered, convulsed for a moment before collapsing to one side, dead. Simon had learned rod darting from the natives when he spent some time in Congo years ago. He was gleefully surprised that the technique still worked in his hand. As Simon understood, the crux of the method was to hit the most vulnerable point of the piscine anatomy. He jumped into the water, retrieved the fish and came ashore. He collected a leaflet from a fallen coconut palm frond on the ground, strung the fish on it, running the leaflet through its gill and mouth and tying a knot above to prevent the fish slipping down. Simon saw his clothes flapping in the wind, they are dry, ready to wear. He put them on, walked towards the kitchen. Seeing the fish, Cherichi was puzzled and happy at the same time. She got busy cleaning the fish for making her favorite dish: fish curry with raw mango slices.

When it was dinnertime, Simon saw Muthoma sitting on a wooden bench just outside the kitchen; Simon did not know he was waiting for his dinner. Simon asked him to come in, join everyone else, Muthoma was reluctant. Varu was too embarrassed to go into the events of the past and explain to Simon that for the last several years, Muthoma always ate alone on the small kitchen porch. As the situation demanded, Varu too insisted on Muthoma to come in for dinner. Muthoma walked in hesitantly, took his seat at the far end of a very short table rising only a few inches from the floor, Varu sat next to him on a grass mat. Both brothers were baffled a little when they saw Simon bringing all the dishes Cherichi had cooked, arranging them on the table and finally settling himself on a seat, cross-legged on the grass mat.

After the supper, Simon sat on a bench for a while, he could hear Muthoma already snoring on the verandah outside. Simon did not know where to sleep and spend the night. Then he saw a narrow room on the left of the living area of the house, it was a storage, empty gunny bags thrown around haphazardly filled the space. He crawled into the room and stretched himself on the gunny bags, he was about to fall asleep. Varu, then, came with a roll of grass mat, a sheet and pillow for him. He made his bed on the floor. Soon, he was fast asleep.

Simon came to Varu's house only that morning. Without losing much time, he blended with the household, effortlessly. Now, he is a guest at the house, uninvited, unsolicited; but no one objected his presence. For Simon, that was welcome enough to feel comfortable.

# *Twelve*

It was mid-noon when Muthoma came to the deserted yard between the rear of the church and the cemetery. Under the blazing sun, the sandy ground was scorching. Barefooted, Muthoma felt his feet was about to blister, he tiptoed to the vacant building where Simon once lived. He located Simon's residence, a room at the far end of the building. The front door of the room was closed shut; the bolt on the door had come off its moorings and hung on the door by a single screw, a padlock clung to the loosened latch assembly. Muthoma tried to push open the door, but it was locked from inside, perhaps there was someone in there. He knocked at the door, no response. If someone had locked the door from inside and left, there ought to have another exit for the room, Muthoma mused. He walked around the building, looking for a possible entrance to the room. Just behind Simon's room, he saw a sundry of roofing material: braided coconut fronds, bamboo rods, leaned against the back wall of the room. Hidden behind was a window, left cracked open a little. Muthoma went to have a closer look at the window. He opened the shutters. To his surprise, there were no grills or bars for the window. If one could climb to the height of the window, it was not very difficult to get in and out of the room. Before someone noticed him scouting around, Muthoma left the premises.

For a couple of days Muthoma did not mention anything to Simon about his expedition. Then, one night, Simon was getting ready to retire, he had made his bed on the floor, put out the kerosene lamp, he was sitting on the bench, pensive. In the dim light, he saw Muthoma coming in from the verandah outside. He sat next to Simon and started talking in a hushed voice.

"We have to go visit a place tomorrow night, it is a place not very unfamiliar to you; no one else should know about our visit, let it be strictly between you and me"

Curious and bemused, Simon listened intently.

"We have to make a few arrangements before we go. Don't worry about it, I would do everything needed"

Not waiting for a response from Simon, Muthoma left the room, went to sleep.

When Muthoma and Simon arrived at the yard behind the church, it was pitch dark, even the starlight was occluded from reaching the yard; there was an ancient mango tree rubbing the outer wall of the cemetery, one of its massive branches extended to the yard, an obstructive canopy above. Muthoma had some familiarity with the location gained during his last visit. Having lived in the building for many years, Simon still had traces of homing intuition left in him to reach the doorsteps of his old home; they still had to grope through the dark. As they made it to the front door of the room, Muthoma asked Simon to remain there. He, then, slid into the darkness, felt his way to the back of the room, located the window hidden behind the roofing material. The window was a few feet above ground, at the level of his chest. Holding the window frame, he heaved himself up, thrusted his head and hands into the window and started groping for something in the room to hold on to. Clutching a solid wooden door frame he located in the room, he hauled the rest of himself through the window, taking care not to crash headlong onto the floor. He maneuvered himself to bring his feet to the solid ground of the room. It was total darkness in the room. From a small bag slung on his shoulder, he took out and lit a candle. The room appeared to be a storehouse for unused articles, replete with broken tables and chairs, wooden crosses used in the Good Friday ceremonial processions and towering over everything, a slightly torn ornate umbrella, large, colorful and fully unfurled. Muthoma made his way through the thickets of the retired objects, reached the front door. As he unlocked and opened it, Simon was looking at his old house and Muthoma in amazement.

Simon, entered the room, eager and expectant. Along with Muthoma, he ploughed through the hoard of scrapped and discarded articles, often trampling over some of them on their way. As they moved along, Simon was diligently scouring around for the very personal items he came all the way from England. In spite of rummaging around carefully, he could not find any for a while. Then, at the far end of the room, close to the wall, he saw a bare wooden cot. He quickened his pace, as if he found a long-lost friend among a crowd. Coming closer, he saw the network of coir crisscrossing between the framework of the cot, he felt an instant familiarity and intimacy with the old piece of furniture. He had spent many nights on it coaxing himself to slumber and comfort. Abutting the head of the cot was a cupboard, broken and doorless. Tucked between the cot and the cabinet, he saw a stack of canvasses. His heart almost gave way with excitement. He could see only the outer frame of the canvasses pressed together, covered in dust. However, he knew every one of them individually by the streaks of paint overran to the side of the frames, a unique signature.

"These are what I came here for, Muthoma. Thank God they are still here."

Simon told Muthoma, elation and excitement in his voice.

"Let us have a look at them, shall we; hope they are still intact" After a few moments Simon continued,

"And, perhaps, seeing them, you would get to undo a mystery: how you also are part of these paintings!"

Muthoma stared at Simon, confused and lost.

A lighted candle in his hand, Simon hurried to the front door, closed and latched it and shut the two windows of the room. In the middle of night, he was certain, no one would come to that part of the churchyard; still he was afraid the lighted windows could draw undue attention, someone might scent their presence in the room. As he was groping his way back to where Muthoma was, he noticed a few church candles on a stool, fat and tall, those candles might give more light and last longer, Simon thought. He picked up two of the candles and the stool. By that time, Muthoma was already seated on a three-legged stool he had found. Simon lit the tall candles, affixed them on the wooden cabinet, his immediate surroundings lighted up in soft candle light, air of the musty room imbuing with the aroma of burning wax.

Simon pulled his stool closer to the stack of canvases; he was uncertain about their condition after many years in heat and humidity of the room. He dusted them, fondled them, almost sensually. He drew out the first painting in the stack, placed it on the cot, leaning it against the wall. Muthoma looked at it perplexed, intrigued. It seemed to be a crowd scene that was depicted in the painting, may be a funeral, but there was no coffin; in the center, however, was a vacant space in ghastly white in a black and blue background. Surrounding the emptiness were a bevy of characters with a variety of facial expressions. One group was grimacing in a tortured agony, wide open eyes red and protruding, the facial muscles taut and strained; another group was in deep depression, down cast eyes, hair in disarray and brisling, arms and unclenched palms up in the air writhing in utter helplessness. Up above the bare space, close to the upper frame of the painting were a few scattered spectral figures, ill defined, cloud like, seemingly melding into the background. At the bottom of the picture, an aquamarine lake, calm and still; in the middle of the lagoon, a woman's head jutting out of the water, her hair floating on the surface, her mouth open in a loud scream, circles of violent waves boiling around her.

Simon looked at Muthoma for a response; Muthoma's reply was only his characteristic vacuous smile. Simon pulled out the next painting from the stack, placed it resting against the first one on the cot. Smaller in size, it was a nude. One glance at it, Muthoma's eyes widened, his jaws dropped in amazement, a range of feelings rushing on to his face.

"Amma"

A restrained cry of exclamation escaped him. It was as spontaneous and innocent as the first word of an infant. He had recognized the subject matter of the painting, but turned his eyes away from the portrayal in an instant. He felt uneasy and fraught the way she was pictured. He remembered her only from the waning days of her life, always modestly dressed, graceful. In the painting, she was radiant, endowed with abundant and ample physical beauty. The detailed study of her physicality unnerved him. He could not have identified his mother except for a pair of unmistakable birthmarks on her: a tiny black mole on her left lower cheek close to the corner of her mouth and another one, slightly bigger, on her long neck just above the collarbone. Simon was closely observing Muthoma for his reaction, seeing his mother's picture. Then, suddenly, Muthoma blurted out,

"She has no clothes" dismay and stifled vexation in his voice.

"Her nakedness is shrouded by her beauty, don't you see!" Simon intoned.

"How about this one"

Simon brought out the next canvas from the collection. The theme of the work was the same as the last one, but she was pictured fully clothed in the traditional white attire: a loose, almost translucent blouse and **mundu**. She appeared to have a dip in the family pond, her garments clinging to every curves and contour of her sculpted body.

"Look at her, how serene she looks, I loved her so much" As Simon finished his sentence, Muthoma's face grew tense and puzzled.

"She suffered a lot in her life; she betrays none of that in the painting, does she?"

"I don't know how much you know about all that she endured, it all happened before you were born"

"I still remember the day she came first time to this room crying, to complain about her husband, seeking advice and counsel"

"You know her husband, Marco, was a butcher, but he also was a cattle merchant."

Muthoma did not like Simon referring to his father as his mother's husband, he wanted to correct him, but did not, he allowed him to continue.

The butchers from the neighboring villages used to buy cows and bulls from Marco. He brought small herds of them from a town, faraway in the adjacent state of Madras. It was a business needing hard work, long and strenuous travels. Nonetheless, Marco made hefty profits from the transactions. Every month he journeyed to a far-off cattle market. On the day he was set to go, usually the second week of the month, Lillu, his wife, woke up very early, still hours before daybreak. She got busy in the kitchen, making breakfast for Marco and packing lunch for him. When it was still very dark, Marco left his house with a lit coconut leaf torch in his hand. He was walking towards the Emmau river jetty. A wooden boat and its oarsman waited for passengers. The boat would take them through the waterways to Thissur, the nearest town from Manoor.

When Marco stepped into the boat and took his seat, there was only a single rider besides him in the vessel, Kuryaku. He was a veritable commercial link between Manoor and the town of Thissur. From every households in need, he collected orders, orders for items unavailable in the village and can be found only in larger towns like Thissur: medicines to be picked up at the drug store, pastries from the bakery, cabbage, carrots and beetroots, all considered to be European vegetables, from the market. Kuryaku shopped for each item in the town, took the return boat, delivered them to individual households by sundown. Far from being loquacious, Kuryaku's presence was hardly felt in the boat, Marco did not try small talks with him and he too kept to himself. The boat moved along the river for a while, it was pitch dark, nothing visible along the banks of the river except the occasional oil lamp flickering in a hut. By the time it entered the backwaters, it was day break, the first rays of the sun glistening on the coconut tree lines far away. The water surface was blanketed by thickly growing **Kulavazha**, the water hyacinth. The boat parted the sheet of the aggressive water foliage to make its way. Sprinkled around were patches of water hyacinth in full bloom, its rich white and blue blossoms bobbing in the water. As the boat was passing beside one of these patches, Marco grabbed a few handfuls of the flowering hyacinths, hauled them into the boat. The oarsman did not object or made any comments, he knew it was one of Marco's routines during his monthly boat rides. Marco quickly separated the plants into single ones, distributed them into small flower pots he had brought along in a gunny bag, a single flowering plants in each pot. As the boat moored at the landing, Marco stepped out of the boat, hurried to the Thissur rail station, about a mile away. On the footpath, just across from the station exit, he arranged pots of hyacinth in a linear display; in an hour, his wares were all sold out. With his rolled-up gunny bag under his arm, Marco walked to the rail station and waited for the next train northward, he was to get off at Pollachi. Every week, there was a huge cattle market in that town, thousands of livestock being offered for sale. At the market, there were many agents offering their services to facilitate the purchase and sale of animals. Marco declined assistance from all of them, he managed everything by himself, the selection, bargaining and the final transaction. It was usually late evening by the time he had bought the number of animals he had budgeted and came for. He was very happy about his purchases on that day, ten in all, six bulls and four cows. Herding these animals all the way to Manoor, along the dusty roads, up the hills and down, was the most arduous and demanding part of Marco's monthly visit to the Pollachi cattle market. It took a week to ten days to make the trek.

Over the years, having made the trip several times, Marco was more than familiar with his route. He knew where he can have a quick meal and a drink, a roadside coffee shop where he can stretch himself for a few hours at night, feed his animals, tie them securely to nearby trees. On that evening, he had driven his small herd steadily for two or three hours, he had left Pollachi town and its suburbs far behind. It was well into the night, he was at an isolated stretch of the road. He knew his usual resting place was, at least, an hour away. He, however, was feeling parched and thirsty, but he walked on hooting wordless commands, herding the animals. After a short distance, the silhouette of a small house against the darkened sky came into his view. A few yards away from the roadside, the house looked isolated with a rectangular signboard, "Hotel" hanging in front, a bare bulb swinging in the breeze illuminated the sign. Marco's thirst retuned, his yearning for a drink instantly rekindled. Along with his animals, he started walking towards the house. At the footsteps of the house, he coughed softly to announce himself. A woman in bright colored saree appeared at the door; she invited Marco in, saying in Tamil,

"You might have come for dinner, go tie your animals, I would keep your food ready by the time you come back"

As Marco returned, his dinner, indeed, was ready: arranged in front of a grass mat was a mound of steamed rice, mutton curry, vegetables, a glass of water. A few feet away, the woman was sitting cross legged on the floor, waiting on him. She appeared into her late thirties, light brown complexion, an ovoid face, flashing large eyes, a shiny **mookuthi**, the nose ring, on her right nostril; she wore her black and straight hair in a loose chignon, a couple of tresses had been unloosed from the bun and played on her face. The **pallu** of her saree was tied around her waist, instead of letting it hang down on her back as was done normally. Marco was having the food with relish, he was uneasy, however; his every movement being watched by the woman. The silence hanging in the room added to the discomfort. Breaking the quietude, he said,

"I don't know your name"

"Anasuya, everybody calls me Anasu" she said with a shy smile.

"Anasu"

He repeated getting up from the grass mat as he had finished his dinner. He walked to the edge of the verandah to wash his hands, Anasu followed him with water in a brass vessel, she poured water on his hands as he cleansed them.

As Marco was getting ready to leave, Anasu said,

"You must be tired, you could spend the night in the hotel, I can give you a nice bed on the porch and breakfast in the morning. Together with the price of tonight's dinner, it would cost you only twenty-five rupees"

As Marco looked at her hesitantly, she said reassuring him,

"I could feed and take care of your cows and bulls as well for another five rupees".

The astute businessman he was, Marco took up on the offer quickly; a goodnights sleep was too good to forgo, someone else tending his animals was even more appealing.

As Marco woke up in the morning, he was being caressed by the pale, yellow rays of the rising sun, a cup of steaming coffee on a tripod next to his bed. Away in the yard, Anasu was giving food and water for the cattle. He savored the scene, he almost felt at home.

At home, Lillu was counting days. She knew exactly how many days it takes for Marco to tramp down from Pollachi to Manoor. As her husband returned one day late than usual, she did not hide her concern and displeasure. Marco, however, had many excuses ready for his tardiness. When Lillu persisted questioning him, he brushed her aside, angrily. Nevertheless, he was perturbed and disconcerted in his mind; he did not like to see his wife irate and vexed; he, however, did not know how to appease her. The guilt of spending a night at Anasu's hotel soothed him, somehow. The hours he spent at the hotel, the tranquil morning scene he witnessed at the inn, and everything else there, he felt comforting, somnolent. Nonetheless, he struggled to suppress his internal longing for those moments.

Every time Marco was returning from Pollachi, he experienced a period of strife and conflict within himself. It started as soon as Anasuya's hotel sign came into his view, the signboard illuminated by a naked bulb, inviting, promising. He tried to fight off his desire to spend a good night's rest at the inn, savor the hospitality of Anasu. Lillu, however, was awaiting him at home, she would not forgive him if he was a day late arriving home, she had very efficient means of expressing her pique and rancor and she could be at it for days. Lost in his discordant thoughts, Marco herded his cattle along the road. In the end, though, he invariably found himself walking towards the hotel, driving the animals by the characteristic shouted commands.

The craving for spending nights at Anasu's hotel grew on Marco as an insuperable part of his routines during his trips to Pollachi and back. Despite the inner dissension, he felt the allure of the hotel inescapable. As the months went by, it became increasingly easier for him to overcome the clashes in his mind, set aside Lillu's long face and anger.

At the hotel, Marco became more than a regular guest. Anasu expected him to show up every month, exactly at the middle quarter of the month. She knew his likes and dislikes. She kept everything ready to his satisfaction on the nights he was expected.

It was the peak of summer; the nights were insufferably hot and sultry. On one night, when Marco arrived at the footsteps of the hotel, Anasu hurriedly came with water in a brass vessel for him to wash his feet. As Marco sat on a bench fanning himself with a fan made of palm leaf, Anasu went in to set his dinner. On a wide stainless-steel plate, she served rice, much larger portion than normal, almost double the helping she usually served him, **Sambar**, the vegetable stew in a larger bowl, the mutton curry on a wider plate, again a bigger portion than normal. As Marco came and sat for his dinner, he apparently did not notice anything unusual, he was very hungry and thirsty, he started to have his dinner right away. As was her habit, Anasu sat cross-legged in front of Marco, watching him. Marco could not finish all that was served, a substantial part of the portions remained on the plates. He got up and went to the verandah to wash his hands. As he came back, he was surprised to see Anasu hastily consuming all that was left on his plates. She quickly finished her dinner, collected the empty plates, started walking to the kitchen. A shy smile on her face, her eyes downcast to the floor.

It did not take too long for Marco to figure out what he just witnessed. He was well acquainted with the customs and conventions of his neighboring state; his frequent travels to the province and interactions with its people had helped him to know their ways and traditions. There was an open secret among the folks of a particular ethnicity, discussed only in intimate and hushed up tones: if a woman stealthily consumes the partly eaten dinner left over by a man, it had only one singular meaning: that she is helplessly attracted to him, she is lusting for him. Marco was not unduly surprised or puzzled by the titillating message in Anasu's flirtatious ritual. He had already noticed her unusually genial demeanor ever since he arrived at the hotel that night, the sweetness in her voice, her coy and demure movements around him. He, however, did not imagine them all to be a portent for an amorous advance.

Until that night, Marco never knew Anasu had her bedroom tucked away beyond the kitchen and the storage room. It was a small room with a solitary window opening to the backyard of the hotel. Next morning, when he woke up on Anasu's bed, she had already left the room. Marco could hear her stirrings in the kitchen. Lazily lying on his back, he casually surveyed the room. The wall on the right had an assortment of glossy pictures of gods and goddesses: the flute playing Krishna, Kali in her ferocious self, Saraswati with a heavenly smile, at peace, standing in the middle of a lotus flower floating in a blue lagoon. On the wall on the left, a tiny wooden altar with the bronze statuette of Ganesh, the elephant god, tiny vases with stumps of burned out sandalwood sticks on both sides of the figurine. Slowly, Marco again glided back into his slumber. He woke up only when Anasu called him for lunch. He relished and savored the lethargic comfort of the hotel, the warmth of Anasu's loving care, her ceaseless efforts to please him. He was not in any hurry to resume his journey home.

At home in Manoor, Lillu was in turmoil. In her mind, Marco was to come back with animals three days ago; however, there was no news about him. Frightening scenarios emerged and disappeared in her head only to give rise to ones even more alarming, disconcerting. During the last three months, she recalled him coming home from the trips a day late than usual, invariably kindling skirmishes between them. She did not know whom to turn to for advice and help. At first, she thought about approaching the parish priest; then, suddenly, as by intuition, she decided to seek counsel and assistance from Sheemon upadesi, Simon. She had never met him before but had heard much about him.

"When your mother, Lillu, came and knocked at my door, it was late afternoon, I could hear the children bustling out of the school next door, their boisterous chatter on their way home. As I opened the door, I saw her standing nervous, her face tense and drawn. As soon as she came in, she started sobbing uncontrollably. Tell me what the matter is, there is a solution for everything, but you have to tell me what troubles you, I told her. Through her tears, she told me the story of her missing husband, her apprehension, her alarming conjectures about what might have happened to him. I consoled her as much as I could, assured her that her husband would certainly come back to her in a day or two, he cannot be away from someone as beautiful as she was. Blended with tears, I could see the semblance of a smile quivering behind a tress of hair dislodged and fallen on to her face. I asked her to let me know when her husband returns, I would visit them, make acquaintance with Marco"

As if to fulfill Simon's consoling prediction, Marco came home two days after Lillu met Simon. Lillu welcomed him with a burst of tears, closely questioned him about his whereabouts during the whole week. He met them all with a steely silence, only for a while, then exploded suddenly into a relentless tirade about what all unexpected events could occur during a trip, how one of the cows became sick, unable to walk, he had to spend days in the open, nursing her to health to be back on track. Lillu heard him silently, wiping her tears time to time. She was not convinced by any of Marco's explanations for being so late to return home. She was suspicious. The next morning, Lillu went to church; rather than hearing the mass, her intention was to meet Simon, inform him that Marco was home.

It was late afternoon when Simon arrived at Marco's house. The sun had slid down from the summit to the western horizon, still the air was hot and muggy. As he came up the masonry steps leading to the front yard of the house, he saw a herd of cattle tied up under a jackfruit tree, the massive trunk of the tree was crowded with baby jackfruits, green and just emerged out of their flowery pods. Further away, Marco was busy at the family well, with a pulley and rope he was drawing water from the well, collecting it into a large tin bucket. He carried the bucket all the way to where the animals were, poured it on one of the bulls; the bull stood motionless relishing the cascade of cool water flowing on its sides. At first, Marco did not notice the visitor, or rather he ignored him. He did not want his work interrupted in any way; he went back to the well. When he returned with the bucketful, he looked at Simon acknowledging him, they exchanged niceties, then Marco abruptly blurted out,

"Look at these animals, aren't they beautiful, I am going to haul a good bit of profit out of them".

Trying to share Marco's enthusiasm, Simon said,

"Indeed, these cows and bulls are looking very good; it must have been hard for you to bring them, all the way from Pollachi".

That was the moment Marco went totally silent, his face becoming taut. He turned his back abruptly and started walking towards the well. As he was leaving Simon behind, he murmured,

"I must get on with my work"

After that, Simon did not remain too long under the jackfruit tree. As he was about to leave, he tried to pat one of the handsome young bulls on its back, but, the animal was in no mood to be endeared. Shaking its head menacingly, the bull was ready to charge at Simon. He swiftly stepped back and was on his way home.

Marco slaughtered a few of the animals and sold the meat at his butchery, the rest of the herd were bought by his regular customers from the neighboring villages. As soon as his stock of animals were disposed, he was in a hurry for his next trip to Pollachi. He set off in the usual way, lunch packed by Lillu in his hand, the boat ride through the backwaters to catch the train to Pollachi. But he did not return home for two weeks, and in subsequent months, two weeks turned into two months, at the end, he was not seen at his house at Manoor for six months at a stretch. He was unaware or rather did not concern himself of what had happened at home. His butchery started by his grandfather was closed down permanently, Lillu stopped waiting anxiously for his return home. After being away for long periods, he used to make it home, once in a while. On those rare visits, Lillu ignored him meticulously. Meanwhile, a strong rumor had percolated among the prying villagers of Manoor that Marco was living in Pollachi with a woman of different community, speaking a different language. The gossip had reached Lillu's ears as well. For her, it was not just a gossip, she had no difficulty taking it as a reality.

Marco had succumbed to the seductive allure of Anasu. He found the befuddled enticement of life at the hotel irresistible. Like the scouts of Odysseus entangled in the hallucinogenic Island of Lotus Eaters, he did not have the desire to break free.

For Lillu, life at home was lonely and miserable. Wilted by humiliation of being practically abandoned by an unfaithful husband, she was desolate and tormented internally; nonetheless, she tried to put up a facade that she was facing everything bravely, unshaken. Her only source of solace and succor was Sheemon upadesi; it was only to him she opened her heart to unburden herself of her heartaches and anguish. He was a patient listener, his words comforted her, consoled her, she felt his utterances rang sincere, empathetic. She visited him frequently at his lodge behind the church. When she came to see him for the first time, she was very emotional, worried about Marco not having returned home. She was not sure how Simon was going to react to her concerns; being a foreigner, would he even be able to understand the mundane difficulties of a village woman like her. By the end of that visit, however, she was already feeling comfortable talking to him confidently about her angst and tensions, seeking his counsel and advise.

Every time Lillu felt perturbed and downcast, she found herself knocking at Simon's door. She knew he would somehow pep her up, have some suggestions to untangle the plight confronting her at that moment. She was, however, aware of the gossipmongers of Manoor. They are very adept at weaving harlequin fables out of nothing. It would be good yarn in their hands: a young woman recurrently visiting the bachelor cabin of a foreigner. She was particularly petrified by Mathooty. Though torpedoing marriage proposals was his forte, he also was deft at fabrication and propagation of hearsays. Though she did not prefer it, Lillu was compelled to visit Simon covertly after sundown. As her house was within a short distance from the church, it was not too difficult for her to slip through the dusk into the churchyard, stealthily.

As the weeks and months passed, Lillu's relationship with Simon grew more and more personal. Unbeknownst to them, they stepped out of the boundaries and norms of being a parishioner and upadesi; they were more on a friendlier term. Even when there was not a burning issue to be thrashed and settled, they enjoyed each other's company. Free and unrestrained, Lillu could joke with Simon, she even dared to tease him about his accented Malayalam. She rejoiced in their mutual affection.

One evening, when Lillu arrived at the building behind the church, the yard between the church and cemetery was dark and silent as always. The door to Simon's room was closed, but not locked. As she tapped on the door, he called out from the other end of the room asking her to come in. On entering, she could see him in the faint light of a kerosene lamp with a clear glass shade. He was sitting at a small desk close to his bed, on the table an open book and some papers he was working on. He beckoned her with a smile as she walked towards him; she settled down on a tripod. Lillu had come to talk to him about something flustering her that evening: she had picked up a quarrel with one of her thorny neighbors when the woman tried to pry about Marco, engage in smutty talk laced with double meanings. As Lillu was narrating her encounter, Simon, as always, appeared to pay close attention; nonetheless, he was not saying anything in response to her; he seemed to be fixated on Lillu's face, his eyes widened in amazed disbelief. He was trying to contain his excitement. At long last, something he had been searching for the last several years was at hand: the visage of a young woman he always wanted to paint, a model entirely conceived in his own mind. He was ecstatic to realize the product of his imagination has suddenly materialized, she is sitting face to face with him, only inches away from his easel. For a long time, he had an idealized image of a female face in the depths of his mind; a creation wholly by the elements of his artistic sensibilities. He also knew such an envisaged woman was unlikely to exist anywhere in reality. Nevertheless, the realization did not prevent him from exploring and seeking the woman and her face far and wide. He had searched for her in vain in the depths of Sub Saharan Africa, streets of Amsterdam, tropical jungles of Sri Lanka and during the years he spend in India. The exactitude of the young feminine face in his mind and the face of Lillu was almost uncanny, they seemed juxtaposed to each other, congruent by every centimeter. Indeed, that was not the first time he had met Lillu; however, none other times he could recognize her face identical with that of the elusive woman he had in his head. Why the striking similarity awaited this long to reveal itself to him until that particular evening? Was it the lighting: her luminous face outshining the subdued illumination in the room and accentuating her facial features? As he was pondering the mystery, Lillu got up from her stool saying that it was getting late and she had to leave. Simon stirred himself up as if from a reverie. He asked Lillu if she could visit him again the next day. Lillu was surprised a bit; he had never asked her a favor before.

In the following evening, when Lillu came to Simon's lodge, he was at the far end of his room, at his desk near the bed, the kerosene lamp dimly lighting up his papers on the table. He appeared as if he had not shifted or moved from where he was the previous day. Nonetheless, there was something new that caught Lillu's immediate attention: a tiny table bristling with brushes of many kind, tubes of paint, charcoal sticks, rags, a pallet and an easel with an empty canvas. When Lillu came near, even before she took a seat, Simon said,

"I am going to paint you; I am going to draw a picture of you on this canvas, if it is alright with you".

Lillu could not fully comprehend Simon, but she was visibly fascinated, she smiled in agreement, sat down on the tripod. Simon instructed her to sit still, asked her to tilt and turn her face until she assumed a pose he was seeking and satisfied with. Within no time, Lillu heard the scratching noises of Simon's charcoal stick moving around on the canvas. After a while the room was imbued with the smell of paints and solvents. Simon had just squeezed out some paint from a couple of tubes on to the pallet, he was mixing them up with a pallet knife. He worked on the painting assiduously for an hour, continuously and intermittently shifting his gaze between the canvas and Lillu's face. When they were finished for the day, Lillu was curious to see her picture; when she tried to have a peek at the canvas, Simon said,

"I am not done yet, it might be ready by the time your visit next time"

Nevertheless, Lillu was perplexed to see only a few intersecting lines, circles and a variety of other forms in blackish color on the canvas.

Lillu could not come see Simon for a few days. Her first-born, Varu, was with her; he had come to spend a few days with his mother. The four-year-old boy lived with Lillu's parents a few miles away. They were very fond of him. Lillu's dad, a retired school teacher, was the one most attached to the child, he enjoyed teaching his grandson alphabets and numbers, play soccer with him. When Varu was returned to his grandparents, Lillu was anxious to visit Simon, she longed to see him. She was surprised at herself realizing that she was missing him, in an inexplicable way. She was hurting when she was away from him.

That evening when Lillu knocked at Simon's door, he opened the door instantly, at the first knock, almost as if he was expecting her. As soon as she entered the room, Lillu's first pointed question was,

"Where is my picture"

Simon pointed to the canvas near his table, kept turned against the wall. Simon went and turned around the canvas so that Lillu could see his work. When she looked at the painting, she appeared utterly confused, as she came closer to view it, her expression grew more cofounded, disconcerted,

"This is not my face", she exclaimed.

"Where are my eyes, where is my mouth?" she demanded to know.

"I don't like it, I am not there in the picture at all"

She pouted, a petulant expression on her face. Simon could understand her piqued disappointment. Nevertheless, it was futile for him to explain to her that art was life transformed into something new, something that never existed before by an intimate and mysterious process. It was more than evident, Lillu was not a connoisseur of a painting with cubistic leanings tempered by surrealistic overtones. Inwardly, Simon knew he did the painting chiefly to satiate his own creative urges, not necessarily for Lillu nor for her appreciation. However, she had to be mollified somehow, he thought. She seemed to be visibly upset, disappointed.

"I am sorry, Lillu," he said.

"I would do a painting exactly looking like you, I promise".

Lillu looked at him not being convinced.

"When you come next time, sit for me, I would start the painting right away".

After a few days, it was exceptionally dark when Lillu got ready to go visit Simon. The sky was blanketed by monsoon clouds, distant rumbles of thunder; a cloudburst could happen any time. Lillu, however, was not discouraged, she locked the front door of her house, started to walk with a folded umbrella in her hand. No sooner than she walked a few yards on the road, heavy rain started to fall, she quickly unfurled the umbrella, but the raindrops were pelting on the umbrella like pebbles, they were so heavy and swift, they could have pierced the dome of the umbrella. Even with the torrents from above, Lillu braved on. Because of a strong wind, the rain some time appeared to fall horizontally, drenching Lillu and her white clothing. By the time she entered the church campus, she was dripping water. She was holding the umbrella against the wind and the spray of rainwater. Then, suddenly, she felt that she saw the shadow of the sexton on the outer verandah of the rectory; nevertheless, she thought that it was unlikely he could have recognized her through the blinding rain, she was effectively hidden behind the umbrella.

At Simon's front door, Lillu, soaking wet, dribbling water, her clothes clinging to her body, stood for a few minutes in a futile effort to dry herself. She had not realized the door was partly open, Simon watching her from the other end of his room. He called out to her to come in. She gingerly walked into the room. As she walked towards Simon, she left a string of small puddles of water along her path. As soon as she saw a towel on Simon's bed, she grabbed it to wipe her dry; but Simon quickly intervened to prevent her from what she was about to do.

"I want to paint you just as you are now, wet, drizzling water"

Simon said. Then only Lillu noticed that Simon was awaiting her, all set to paint; an empty canvas on the easel, strong organic smell of paint in the room. Lillu's face was gleaming in the sheen of water; a few locks of her wet hair had fallen on to her face, haphazardly, sticking to her skin; drops of water from her hair rolling down her face to drip on to her clothing. He asked her to sit on the tripod. With her soggy clothes, she sat on the stool uncomfortably. With a routine already familiar to her by now, Simon directed her to tilt and turn her head until he told her to remain stable and still. Simon started to work behind the easel, Lillu could hear the brushes and palette knife striding around the canvas, he was in a fervent rush, his movements feverish, he looked at Lillu frequently, then shifting his attention back again to the canvas. In a frenzy, he appeared to work against time; as if he was trying to snatch a dancing mirage before it vanished into the faraway horizon.

After a few hours of intense work in near silence, Simon decided to stop for the day. Lillu got down from the seat. Her clothes had dried, but still sticking to her body contours, she pulled and puffed them up until they acquired the appearance of normally worn attire. As she picked up her umbrella and ready to depart, Simon said,

"It would take another three more days to complete the picture, could you, please, come for the sitting, don't say no"

Lillu acquiesced to his request with a broad smile.

The rain had ceased, nonetheless, she opened the umbrella, held it over her to shield her. She was not certain if the sexton had retired for the night or he was still on his beat.

Modeling for Simon, sitting motionless and silent for hours together, Lillu found it back breaking. She, however, endured it all, not a word of complaint. She had a feeling that she was doing something worthwhile, she was doing it for Simon. On the last day of the marathon, Simon announced the painting was almost complete, he would do the final touches before Lillu returns the next day.

The following evening, when Lillu arrived at Simon's door, she could hear strange rumblings of Simon's baritone voice within. His door was unlocked. As she entered, his rendering hit her full blast, he was reciting something in a language entirely foreign to her; she, however, assumed it could have been English. Ascending and descending rhythmically, his recital was midway between prose and poetry. He did not stop even after seeing his visitor, he went on as if he was fulfilling a ceremonial obligation, he gestured her to come in as he was delivering strings of words, blaringly, full-throated. As Lillu came closer, he stopped his recital and in the same breath said,

"It is done"

Lillu saw the canvas on the easel, turned towards the wall. Simon turned it around so that Lillu could see the painting. Instantly, she recognized herself in the painting, she kept on staring at the picture in amazement. She never knew she was that beautiful. She was depicted as if she had a dip in the pond and just came out of the water. She was wet all over; a few tufts of wet hair had fallen to her face, drops of water on her face twinkled like crystals. Her customary dress of *mundu and chatta*[8] was replaced by a long gossamer gown accentuating and revealing the details of her physique. Looking at the painting, Lillu had a mischievous smile on her face. Whenever Lillu contemplated mischief, she had the peculiar habit of gravitating her entire smile to one corner of her lips leaving the rest of her mouth bare.

Simon was happy Lillu was not displeased with her painting. He did the painting mainly to appease her, calm her pique at her image having been distorted in the first painting. In the effort, he knew he had compromised his artistic style and preferences, rendering a work espousing realistic tech-

---

[8] *A loose fitting white top.*

niques. Nonetheless, Simon realized a few factors anew, that realism too presented opportunities for creative pang and pleasure, that the subject of the work, besides being the inspiration for the artist, could also influence his temperament. Simon felt Lillu had an expressive figure; in silence, her frame exuded emotions. He was stimulated to study those amorphous expressions in colors and brush strokes. He saw mystique in her large eyes, her playful smile, unruly hair, her long neck adorned by the single string of a gold chain.

During one of her evening visits, Lillu found Simon unusually serious and grave. She did not seek an explanation, but she knew he was under some undefined stress. She perched on her usual seat, the tripod. Simon kept on looking at her, making her ill at ease; however, at the next moment the stress and tension quickly abated as Simon said,

"I would very much like to paint you once again; it might take several days, you would sit for me, won't you"

Lillu was fascinated that Simon wants to place her once again in a picture. She was only glad to model for him.

After a few days, when Lillu came to Simon's lodge, he was busy giving the final touches to a jar of Trifle he was preparing. She was captivated by the colorful dessert, the layers of red, white and yellow and a few other hues in between. The room was imbued with a fruity scent, instead of the usual odor of paint and turpentine. Simon scooped out two large spoons of the dessert in a bowl, offered it to Lillu saying,

"This is called Trifle, see how you like it"

That was the first time Simon had ever offered her anything to eat or drink. Lillu settled on her stool to have the dessert. As she was enjoying the sweet, Simon got busy setting up everything needed for painting. He placed a large canvas on the easel, brought out and emptied a canvas bag on to his table, there were several tubes of paint, some of them squeezed to the last drops of paint, others half way, some others plump and full, untouched. Bristling among the tubes were charcoal sticks, dark and sinister. Simon picked up a couple of the sticks, two tubes of black and sienna colors, set them apart, returned the rest of the tube collection into the canvas bag.

Lillu finished the dessert and was waiting, as usual, for Simon's directions to settle her into one of his preferred poses; but Simon told her that he would like her to model standing this time. As he was adjusting the canvas on the easel and carefully selecting the charcoal sticks, Simon asked her, very casually, to take off her blouse, Lillu was shocked and taken aback. However, as if she came under an instant spell, as if she was following a mesmerist's overpowering command, she slowly removed her *chata,* the loose blouse, but held it against her chest. Simon, however, motioned her to get rid of it altogether, continued his compelling instructions even further. In a few minutes, following him spellbound and bewitched, Lillu found herself fully disrobed. Simon directed Lillu to stand next to the stool, supporting herself placing her right hand on the trivet. Simon hastily got busy in front of the canvas, restive and edgy as a possessed man. He was making the initial charcoal sketch of the model in front of him, he used his naked fingers and rags liberally to spread, shade and erase the dark lines taking shape on the canvas. Lillu heard only the scuffing noise of the charcoal stick scooting around the canvas, then, suddenly, she got the sharp smell of linseed oil and turpentine; Simon had squeezed out a small length of black and sienna paints on to his palette and was mixing them and the medium with a palette knife. He brushed the amalgam on to the canvas closely following the lines and forms he had already drawn in black.

Lillu was modelling in the buff for almost two hours, standing like a statue with minimal support, resting her right hand on the stool. She was exhausted, needed a break. When Simon announced that he was going to call it a day, she was glad and relieved, could not wait to put her cloths back on and head home. As she was exiting his room, Simon reminded her that the painting needed much more work, he expected her to come, model for him until it is completed. He knew she would be back for a sitting.

It was an exceptionally balmy day in Manoor. Simon's room with only a small window, placed way up, almost close to the ceiling, was very hot and humid. Since the last four days, Simon and Lillu had been working on the painting. Simon was busy at the easel, Lillu at the trivet, standing motionless, naked, sweating a trifle. Simon was pleased with his work so far; the painting was taking shape as he had intended. As the days went by, he was increasingly inspired to make it one of his finest creations. That day, Simon had been painting much longer than usual; he, nevertheless, was still relentless in his passion and fervor. Lillu, on other hand, was fatigued and weary. At the end of that day's session, she plumped to the bed nearby with sheer abandon. She laid there on the white sheet, exhausted; her head resting on her folded right arm, eyes closed, her loosened black hair spilled on to the sheet framing her head, the left arm languidly reposed over the left flank of her torso, the right leg extended, the left slightly flexed and resting on the other.

Simon looked at Lillu on his bed, listless and tranquil. Works by the masters of the past flashed through his head; Venus by Titian and Botticelli; Olympia by Manet and Maja by Goya. His instant impulse was to set up another canvas.

"That was the day you were conceived"

Simon told Muthoma, sitting attentively listening to Simon's chronicles. Initially, he could not fully comprehend Simon's startling revelation.

"Yes, in this room"

"On this bed"

Simon emphasized pointing to the dilapidated semblance of a bed, that once belonged to him. As Simon's disclosure sank into him, Muthoma could not believe it or fathom its implications. Overcame by a myriad of memories and emotions, Muthoma sat there stunned, his eyes transfixed on Simon. Noticing Muthoma in a quandary, Simon said,

"Muthoma, I am your father"

A declaration, sounding irrefutable and conclusive. In his life in the village, Muthoma never knew the person purported to be his father nor had seen him. Everyone, nevertheless, recognized him as Marco's son. Marco, however, was not there when Muthoma was born, while he was growing up in the village; he had disappeared from Manoor for long into the unknown. No one cared to enquire about him; for most, he was an outcast. Their sympathies were with Lillu, living alone, bringing up two boys all by herself.

Not having known a father's love or care, Muthoma did not miss those finer privileges while growing up. Muthoma had mixed feelings looking into Simon's eyes, sitting across from him, emphatically claiming to be his father. Until Simon's assertion, Muthoma was not aware of a void, a paternal presence, in his life. When an opportunity presented itself to fill in the lacuna, he did not know how to act upon it. Simon's disclosures about his mother bemused Muthoma; they opened a window on the intimate and personal life of his mother. He, however, could not imagine and place her in the nocturnal exploits of her as described by Simon; her stealthy visits to Simon's lodge under the cover of darkness, modelling for him in the nude, ultimately bearing his child.

"Vellana", white elephant, his peers at the school used to call young Muthoma, disparagingly. At the school, he stood out with his fair complexion and crimson lips. The insults and affronts grew sharper and sinister in his adulthood. His adversaries called him a bastard, often behind his back, many a time, right on his face. The name calling infrequently came to violent confrontations and blows. Thinking about those days, looking at Simon sitting in front of him, Muthoma felt that there might be some truth in the allegations concealed in the barbs having been thrown at him. May be, Simon, indeed, was his father. The dangling realization, nevertheless, did not cause any emotional convulsions in Muthoma.

He got up, started to pull out the rest of the paintings stuck between the headboard of the cot and the table, stacked them up along with the paintings of his mother. He searched and found a torn bed sheet in the room; wrapped it around the paintings. He told Simon,

"We should get out of here before someone finds us"

They exited the room through the front door, closing it tightly behind them. It was past midnight, pitch dark, very suitable for making away with the booty, not plundered or stolen, but recovered. Muthoma was walking carrying the stack of painting on his head. Simon did not know where he was leading him. As if he had read Simon's mind, Muthoma said,

"We should hide these for a couple of days; I know a perfect place where it would be safe and hidden"

After a few yards, they came in front of an abandoned house, in total disrepair, falling apart in places. That used to be the house of old Margi and her daughter Glidi. Glidi was mentally ill and deranged. Often, she used to wait for an imagined and prospective groom to visit her, make her acquaintance, lunch ready on the table. When nobody turned up, she threw all the dishes on the floor, stamped and stomped on them, shouting profanities. When Margi passed away, Glidi was institutionalized at an asylum before she too died, tragically.

Muthoma placed the paintings in one of the inner-most rooms in the house, concealed them under a heap of rubbish he could find on the floor. None would get to these here, Muthoma was confident. They were transferred from the parish premises to their rightful owner and perhaps, to his offspring. No sensible soul would dare to come, scour and comb this house about to crumble and collapse to the ground any time; especially with the hushed rumor circulating around the village that the house was haunted by the spirit of Glidi, still waiting for her suitor.

As Muthoma and Simon were walking to Varu's house, Simon continued his narrative; how he was abruptly banished from Manoor: It was past eleven, the night was moonlit; Lillu had stayed at Simon's lodge a little longer than usual. As she was exiting the front door she was startled to see someone moving around at the narrow gap between the other end of Simon's building and the cemetery wall. She walked hastily, almost ran towards the church gate, she had no other way except to pass by the person moving around at the gap. As she went past him she distinctly recognized him, it was the sexton. She was certain he identified her too in the moonlight. In the morning, Simon had to go and mediate between two feuding neighbors about the boundary of their individual properties; he was partly successful in his efforts. However, when he came back to his home, he was surprised to see his door locked up, an outsized padlock hanging from the bolt. He went around the church campus looking for someone to seek an explanation for the lock out. He could not see the sexton or the parish priest, the premises seemed to be deserted. Simon had only the cloths he was wearing with him, he was hungry as well. He decided to go to Lillu's house. She welcomed him. As he was having the breakfast Lillu offered him, she told him what had happened to her the previous night. Simon instantly realized why his front door was locked up.

Lillu invited Simon to stay in her house as long as he needed to. As the days went by, however, it became apparent that the people of Manoor were incensed by this living arrangement. They also had heard the stories of Lillu's clandestine rendezvous with Simon at night, most probably propagated by the sexton. They were disappointed by Simon's behavior and they did not hesitate to betray their displeasure to him. They turned their back on him whenever their paths crossed. Simon was saddened by the villager's reaction. These were the same folks always considered him as their friend and benefactor, their Sheemon upadesi. He experienced the entire village of Manoor turning hostile to him. He became an unwelcome foreigner in the village. He realized that it was time to leave the village. One early morning he found himself sitting on the wooden seat of the boat soon to leave for Thissur. The oarsman was waiting for one of his regular riders. As he finally came and took his seat, the boat started to move along the water surface, parting the carpet of **Kulavazha** as it glided forward.

The night was cool and windy, it was the third day since Muthoma and Simon had hidden the paintings at the abandoned house. Muthoma, as usual, was on the verandah of Varu's house, trying to sleep on a bench; but he found it difficult to fall asleep. He was mulling over the possibility that Simon could be his real father as he professed. He felt, the possibility giving him a vague sense of assurance and belonging. Without he being fully aware of it, his probable relationship with Simon was gradually being assimilated and taking hold in his mind. Twisting and turning on the narrow bench, Muthoma remained awake for another reason: Simon was returning to England on that day, they had to retrieve the paintings to be taken along with him. He wanted to do it before day break, without drawing anyone's attention. He also was afraid that he might oversleep and wake up to see the morning sun on him.

At the opportune time, Simon and Muthoma were on the road walking towards the deserted house. The air mildly windy and silent, there was no one around, it was still very dark. As they reached the crumbling front door of the house, Muthoma lit a candle he had brought along; they tiptoed to the room where they had hidden the paintings. They found the canvases as they had left them. Muthoma picked the entire stack of paintings, tried to carry under his right arm, but the stack was too large and a bit heavy; he placed it on his head, walked out of the house.

Simon and Muthoma started to walk towards the Emmau river; they needed to catch the rowboat to Thissur. As they moved along the road, it was very still and silent all around; they could hear only their own footsteps. As they reached the makeshift jetty, where the boat picked up passengers, the wooden boat had not arrived. Simon and Muthoma were the only riders waiting for the boat. Muthoma brought down the canvases, kept the stack slanting on a short stone embankment. He and Simon heaved themselves up to reach the top of the embankment, sat there dangling their feet above the ground, looking in the direction of the river where the boat was expected to come from. They were silent for a while, then Simon said,

"I came all the way from England to reclaim something very important in my life: these paintings and you"

"I don't know if you could imagine how happy and gratified I am"

"Without you and your help, I would have never been able to find and recover these works of mine, Muthoma."

After a moment of break, Simon continued,

"Well, after all you are my son, sons are expected to help their dads"

Neither of them could gauge the expressions on their faces, it was too dark at the riverbank; nevertheless, Muthoma heard Simon chuckle.

Before too long, the flickering light of the boat was seen far away on the river, it came closer and closer to the jetty. As it finally berthed, Simon and Muthoma boarded, Muthoma carefully placed the canvases in the boat leaning the stack on one side of the boat. There were tiny puddles of water in the boat, Muthoma took care the pictures did not get wet.

As Simon and Muthoma stepped into the boat, the oarsman strained his eyes to get a closer look at Simon. Thinking Simon was unlikely to know Malayalam, he asked Muthoma about the foreigner with him.

"This is my father" Muthoma replied.

"Yes, he is my son"

Simon intoned in Malayalam.

The oarsman had many further questions to ask; but he had a load of passengers to reach Thissur in time; he started to paddle. The boat started to move along the river. ***Kulavazha***, the water hyacinth was in full bloom, the boat parted them as it moved forward.

At the railway station, Simon bought a ticket for himself and a platform or visitor's ticket for Muthoma. They were waiting for the train to arrive. They were silent. Then, unexpectedly, Simon put his arm around Muthoma and hugged him. Not familiar with the western ways of showing affection openly, Muthoma was taken by surprise, embarrassed and, felt suffocated. Then he saw the Madras Express approaching from south, spewing black smoke and steam, slowing down to halt at the station.

# Thirteen

The ditch road from the west adjoined the main thoroughfare of Manoor at a point not too far from Bhanu's coffee house and the fabric store; from Aputty's grocery, however, it was about a ten minutes' walk. The junction was not much of a significance for the people of Manoor except that the limited number of stores were south of the junction, the customers from the north and west had to go past the intersection for shopping at these stores. On Sundays, the juncture could be thinly busy; that was the day beef was available at the butchery at embankment on the right side of the crossroads. Nevertheless, the intersection was a landmark in Manoor, solely because the one and only streetlight of the village was situated at the junction. Any point or location in the village always had reference to the streetlight, or that was how the villagers invariably utilized the landmark.

The streetlight of Manoor stood on a cement pedestal, not more than two feet in height. An inscription in front read "Manoor" in Malayalam; crudely lettered, the mason might had etched it on the wet cement during construction. A six feet iron pole rose from the base, on top of which was the four-sided lamp, each side with clear glass; a pointed finial in brass on the domed top, inside a kerosene lamp with the wick assembly. The pole, the outer framework and the dome of the lamp, all painted in dark green, blended with the verdant surroundings. During the day, the passersby did not pay much attention to the light as it stood melded into the air and environs of the junction; at night, the dark green colored light dissolved into the enveloping darkness; the oil lamp faintly flickered inside, it threw no light on to the surroundings.

Until a few years, Manoor did not have a street light; it came into being as the direct result of a democratic process the inhabitants of the village never knew before: the elections to the Panchayat. Championed and promulgated by Mahatma Gandhi, the idea of Panchayat was to decentralize government, entrust the governance of individual villages to the villagers themselves. The governing body was composed of a president and representatives elected from defined regions of the village.

Normally, the hamlet of Manoor was sleepy and docile; the village, however, stirred and woke up as the election was announced. They were elated by a vague excitement; most of them did not know what was involved, how the election would impact their lives. Two prominent citizens of the village, nevertheless, knew distinctly how they would be affected by the election and the Panchayat: Adhikari and Hyder. Adhikari feared his power and sway over Manoor would be curtailed or ended if Panchayat was established after the election. Hyder foresaw a rare political opportunity, a long-awaited opening for his party to establish itself in the village, perhaps, even capture the nascent governing body, Panchayat, for his own party.

Though he was known as Adhikari in the village and he demanded to be addressed as such, his real name was Gopala Kurrup. His official responsibilities were rather restricted and limited: collect land taxes, record births and deaths, arrange and make certain newborns are promptly vaccinated against smallpox. However, he considered himself representing the government in Manoor. He, somehow, had the strong conviction that he was imbued with powers and privileges far beyond he was officially afforded. He projected himself as authoritative and commanding. The villagers accepted him as the arm of the government. They always viewed anything related to government with awe and certain degree of fear.

Gopala Kurrup inherited the position of Adhikari from his father; he was the last to bear the rank in a long line of Adhikaris over the past few generations. It all started with Ayyappan. He belonged to a cast of untouchables; he was allowed only fourteen feet away from upper class homes, lest he makes the homes unclean. Nonetheless, everyone needed him and his services; he was a master of all trades, yesterday's version of today's handyman. He was a small-time carpenter; if one wanted some coconuts to be brought down, Ayyappan was the one to be called, he was a proficient climber of the tall trees; required to send someone on an urgent errand to one of the neighboring villages? everyone trusted him to do the run. He was not a mason but had enough skills to undertake small masonry jobs. He was everywhere for everybody. With a droopy mustache and a towel tied around his head, turban like, he was one of the most popular and visible characters in the village.

It was midsummer, there was a mild stirring and excitement in the village. The sub-collector, the regional administrator, was visiting the village. As his Jeep came and stopped at the village center, a number of villagers crowded around the vehicle, curious, awe stricken. Ayyappan too was among the onlookers, expectant and inquisitive as others. A clerk from the collector's team came out and pushed back the villagers, made a circular clearing around the Jeep. Soon, the sub-collector stepped out of his vehicle; a six feet tall man with a blond mustache, in a dark blue pants and a khaki safari jacket, a leather belt tied above his waist; in his hand, a three feet cane with silver casing at the ends. Ayyappan was overwhelmed looking at the official. He had never seen a white man before. He thought the skin color of the collector was as white as the tusk of an elephant. He knew it was an exaggeration, but he let it stand because that was the closest comparison he could come up with at that moment. He stared at the official as if he was someone unreal; never before, he had come across someone that imposing and commanding. The official looked at the villagers, as if he was scrutinizing them individually. As he was viewing them in a circular fashion, Ayyappan felt his eyes, for the fraction of a second, met the piercing eyes of the collector. Ayyappan overcame with an admixture of adulation and respectful dread. As if in a reverie, Ayyappan rushed to the collector, fell prostrate at his feet. It was an uncontrollable reaction to the way he perceived the white administrator. Puzzled, but clearly appreciating the reverence and the expression of willing servility by a subject of the Royal Kingdom, the official looked at Ayyappan as he was lifted and helped to his feet by a clerk.

"What is your name?"

The collector asked in halting Malayalam.

"Ayyappan"

"From today, you are the Adhikari of Manoor"

He turned to one of the officials accompanying him, ordered something in English. Ayyappan could not comprehend what was taking place. He, however, was to know subsequently, how his life took an abrupt turn at that moment.

Ayyappan did not find it easy to slide into the government position of an Adhikari. He continued to do the odd jobs for the villagers with one important difference: ever so gradually, the upper-class village folks began to respect him owing to his new position. When he visited their homes, he was offered a chair in the front yard, but, still keeping the safe distance of fourteen feet away from their homes.

As time went by, Ayyappan stopped accepting job calls from the villagers, devoted full time being an Adhikari. Loved and respected by the people of Manoor, he held on to the position until his death at the ripe age of ninety-two. His elder son inherited the job to keep it until he expired leaving the position for his offspring, Peethamber. The name "Peethamber" was normally in the reserve of higher-class members of the society, not to be taken by untouchable like himself. His given name was Aipu, he shed it when he was in his late twenties and took the name of Peethamber, much to the consternation of the upper class. As an Adhikari, Peethamber was disparate from his predecessors in many ways. He did not hesitate to throw his weight around; assumed that he had the authority to order, command anyone in the village. Above all, had a propensity to amass wealth and he was very successful in the effort; within three years in his position, he grew rich, acquired properties. The villagers did not stop wondering how he achieved all his opulence. Bribes, they suspected, but they also knew opportunities for bribery were very limited for an Adhikari. Unchecked and unexplained, he prospered. Nevertheless, the nosy and inquisitives of the village noticed something lacking in his otherwise enviable life: though nearing forty, he was still a bachelor. Peethamber, however, was not conscious of the deficiency. Then, on a hot summer evening, everything changed, abruptly.

It was the opening day of the yearly festival at the Manoor temple. The golden idol of the deity was about to emerge from the temple. Enshrined on a bedecked elephant, the image was held in place by a bearded priest precariously balancing himself on the tusker, a large umbrella, ornate and colorful, stood unfurled above him and the idol. Down on the temple ground, the drummers were lined up playing with verve; along with the horn players they seemed to have lost in themselves. Two columns of young women extended all the way from the steps of the temple to its gate several feet away. They were performing the *Thalappoli* ritual, invoking peace and prosperity for the village. Held in their hands were brass platters, gleaming, annular. Auspicious objects of rice, flowers, fruits and coconut halves arranged around the periphery of the trays. A lighted oil lamp sparkled at the center, illuminating everything on the brass plate, lighting up the visages of the young women.

Seated on a chair, Peethamber was observing and enjoying the religious pageant from a vantage point, a location slightly elevated from the ground, closer to the temple. He was rocking gently with the drumbeats. As he started to view the dual line up of women in the *Thalappoli,* he did not pay much attention to anyone particular in the group; however, he did look at them individually, first the women in the line on the right, then those on the left. Going down the column on the left, Peethamber's eyes abruptly froze on a woman midway in the row; he tried to go past her, but his eyes returned to her, almost instinctively. Never in his life he had this experience, being drawn to someone with such overpowering intensity. He saw her face aglow in the auburn light from the oil lamp on her brass platter. On the crown of her head, she had worn her hair in a chignon, festooned by a flower garland, her earrings flashed as her head moved. She wore the traditional attire of jerry laced *mundu* and a scarlet red blouse, leaving her midriff bare.

Peethamber went home that night with a ruffled mind, preoccupied by the woman in the left line of the *Thalappoli.* With the resources at his disposal, it did not take much time or effort for him to determine the identity of the woman: she was Meenu, hailing from a prominent family in Manoor, the niece of Paramu Kurrup, a landowner of the village. Her mother passed away during childbirth; she was brought up by Paramu Kurrup. For her, he was her father, protector and guide. In their matriarchal family system, he was only a caretaker of the household, the head of the family was Meenu's mother. When she passed away, the mantle was inherited by Meenu along with the family estates. Paramu Kurrup took care of it all meticulously until she attained adulthood. However, it was then, he started losing his mental sharpness, bedeviled by forgetfulness. Nevertheless, Meenu trusted his acumen, continued to seek his counsel in every decision she made. Her uncle, meanwhile, was constantly troubled that Meenu had not found a mate yet, though she is past her thirties. In the matriarchal system practiced by their society, there was no marriage, but only a living arrangement, instead. When a male was found suitable by the head of the family, he was welcomed into the household as her conjugal partner with only subdued and limited privileges, no right to the family assets.

For many days, Peethamber did not know what to do with Meenu, mirthfully stuck in his heart, making him uneasy, pensive. He thought deep and hard to find ways to get closer to her. Then he took a bold decision: make a proposal, offering himself as a male partner for Meenu. He was aware of the incompatibility of their individual positions in the caste system; he, in the lower rungs, she, in the unreachable heights. Their differences notwithstanding, emboldened by his past experiences in challenging conventional taboos, he determined to go ahead with his plan. His attraction and fascination for the woman in the left line was so irrepressibly strong and powerful.

Gopu was Peethamber's chain man. He was often seen around the village with a long metal measuring chain folded into a canvas bag. He was responsible for gauging individual land properties in the village for determining taxes; and on a personal level, he also was Peethamber's sole confidant. Peethamber sent Gopu on a mission to present the proposal to Paramu Kurrup and with an implausible instruction to meet Meenu if he could manage it, let her know his feelings for her.

Gopu was not very optimistic about the success of his assignment. As Peethamber and Meenu are mismatched in their castes, he was in serious doubts if the proposal would ever be accepted. Nevertheless, apart from the incongruity of their social ranking, he had no doubt his boss was more than a suitable match for Meenu.

It was past midday when Gopu arrived at Meenu's house. Paramu Kurrup was relaxing on an easy chair, cooling himself with a decorated fan made of palm leaves. He thought Gopu came to measure one of the family properties. As he came to know the actual purpose of Gopu's visit, he sat up in the chair to hear what Gopu had to say. As he was not too confident of the proposition he was to make, Gopu tried hard to make it as palatable as possible. He went on to elaborate Peethamber's personal attributes, his wealth, his power and authority as a government official. He thought a strong and appealing picture of Peethamber would help overshadow the stigma of him belonging to an inferior caste.

Paramu Kurrup continued to pay rapt attention to Gopu, saying nothing. Gopu finished talking, waited for a response from Paramu Kurrup; but Paramu Kurrup kept his pondering silence for a while more. Then he smiled heartily to say,

"I have known Peethamber for a long time; this is something we, certainly, could consider."

Gopu was overjoyed by the answer. His mission on behalf of his superior was successful, Peethamber, in all likelihood, would succeed in his plan. He was in a hurry to go and let Peethamber know the welcome outcome of his visit. As he was walking along the long verandah towards the exit of the house, he heard a stir and footsteps behind one of the doors. It was Meenu hiding from view, listening to his conversation with her uncle. Gopu thought it was an opportune moment for trying to accomplish the remaining part of his mission. In a hushed voice, as if addressed to no one in particular, he threw a sentence in the air,

"The Adhikari wants to come and meet you, tomorrow evening"

Gopu saw Meenu withdrawing to the interior of the room behind her, a shy smile on her face. By announcing the impending visitation by his boss, he had gone one step ahead of what Peethamber had asked him to do. He was certain, however, Peethamber would not be incensed by the minor transgression.

It was nearing ten at night. Peethamber was walking on the road leading to Meenu's house. With a silk shawl wrapped around his torso, carrying a lighted hurricane lamp in his hand, he cut a solitary figure on the vacant road. A dog from one of the road side houses barked at him. Undeterred by the barking, he proceeded, entered the front yard of Meenu's house. Instead of going to the front door, he walked around to the rear of the house, where the kitchen was. He located the kitchen door, knocked at it. There was no answer, by his second tap, however, the door opened. It was Meenu at the door, smiling, an oil lamp in her hand. She had her luxurious black hair untied and let loose behind her; her jerry-laced *mundu* tied above her chest leaving her shoulders and arms bare. She applied sandalwood paste on Peethamber's forehead, welcomed him in and closed the door behind them.

Before day break, Peethamber was back on the road returning home. He had extinguished the hurricane lamp as there was pre-dawn light to see around, a dog barked at him again, perhaps the same dog who protested his presence the night before. The road was still vacant except a milkman at a distance, carrying the milk vessel on his head.

Peethamber, on most days of the week, came to visit Meenu, spend the night with her. His routine was to come in well after nightfall and leave before daybreak. The practice went on uninterrupted for many days. However, one early morning, when Peethamber was leaving Meenu's house, walking towards the gate, he noticed a shadowy figure, unexpectedly, standing still a few feet away from his path. As Peethamber came closer, he recognized the person to be none other than Paramu Kurrup. Until then, Peethamber never thought Meenu's uncle was aware of his nocturnal visits to his niece's chamber. He was a little perturbed, thought Paramu Kurrup had planted himself in his way to confront him. But, soon he realized his concern and anxiety were misplaced. Paramu Kurrup smiled broadly and said,

"As affaires have gone this far, why don't we make it formal"

Peethamber was only glad to acquiesce, though he was rather surprised how he was being accepted to a higher-class family, so readily, willingly.

During the days followed, Paramu Kurrup made preparations for the ceremony, accepting Peethamber as the conjugal mate and partner for Meenu. He had invited friends and relatives of the family to witness the ritual and the celebration to follow. Most of them came for the occasion. A few, however, turned down the invitation. They were the stalwarts of orthodoxy, arching their brow, protesting the intermixing of the lower and upper castes.

Consulting an astrologer, Paramu Kurrup selected an auspicious day for the solemn ceremony of welcoming Peethamber as Meenu's male partner. It was a sunny morning. On the open porch of the house, traditional arrangements were set and kept ready: a large brass inlayed wooden measuring drum, filled to the brim with rice; fresh flowers, ripe bananas and other fruits on a shiny tray, a tall brass lamp with seven lighted wicks, a grass mat for the couple to sit. Peethamber was the first to come and sit facing the arrangement; Meenu came soon after, accompanied by Paramu Kurrup. Peethamber was elated to see her precisely as she appeared in the lineup of *Thalapoli*: her hair in a chignon on top of her head, a flower garland girdling it; the same red blouse and jerry bordered *mundu*, her midriff playfully exposed between the two. Gopu handed a *mundu,* new and neatly folded, to Peethamber. He solemnly offered it to Meenu; she accepted it ceremoniously, her eyes half closed. It was a short and simple rite, formalizing Peethamber as Meenu's mate; less of a husband with finite privileges, Meenu having the upper hand being the head of the household.

After being welcomed into the family, Peethamber began to spend more time at Meenu's house. Paramu Kurrup often sought his help in the day-to-day affairs of the household. Working closely with Meenu's uncle, Peethamber realized a disturbing fact: Paramu Kurrup was uncertain about what he was doing, most of the time. He could not remember the names of the farmers who had leased land from the family or other details. Often, he vacantly looked at the books for several minutes, finally pushing the books to Peethamber to take over. After a while, he withdrew, almost entirely, from dealing with the family accounts to relax in in his favorite easy chair, only to respond vaguely to Peethamber's occasional queries.

As a couple of years went by, Paramu Kurrup was a changed man. He would sit in his favored chair for hours at a time, looking at the sky, vacuously, emotionless. Meenu was exceedingly saddened and in tears as she realized to her horror that she was not being recognized by her beloved uncle. Repeated and concerted prompting and prodding did not make any difference. Paramu Kurrup had gone mad, a loud rumor went around Manoor.

Under the changed circumstances at Meenu's home, many responsibilities of the family were thrusted upon Peethamber. He, however, was only happy with the turn of events. He eased into the role effortlessly, Meenu approving him complacently. Before long, beyond being the less of a husband to Meenu, he became an integral part of her family, literally surrogating the living absence of Paramu Kurrup. He shrewdly assumed the power and authority of the elder man, complimented them to the sway and attributes of an Adhikari. Peethamber felt he was unquestionable in the village. To augment and consolidate his status further, he appended the suffix, "Kurrup" to his name, cleverly, stealthily. No one dared to question or challenge him usurping to the upper echelons of the society by adopting a higher cast designation. Nonetheless, in the caverns, there was rage and grinding of teeth among the old guards of conformity.

Over the years, Peethamber, to all intentions and purposes, became the head of Meenu's family, she, withdrawing into being a wife and mother. Peethamber fathered five children, four girls and a boy named Thambi. Thambi was ambitious, always in a hurry. When he was only thirty-two, by constant squabble and bickering, he wrested the position of Adhikari from his ninety-year-old father.

Gopala Kurrup was the only son of Thambi. He inherited the office of Adhikari and cast epithet, "Kurrup" from his father. No one was aware or cared to investigate how the highly-respected designation of "Kurrup" sneaked into the lineage of the lower cast Ayyappan. The transition was seamless and ever so gradual, though it took years to take root.

Gopala Kurrup was very perturbed by the impending election to the Panchayat, he was afraid, the office of Adhikari, bestowed upon his family for generations, would be stripped away. He went to the district headquarters a few times to plead his case but came back empty handed. As the date for the ballot came nearer, he spent many sleepless nights.

Hyder, on the other hand, was irrepressibly enthusiastic about the forthcoming election. He felt it presented a feasible opportunity to propel his party and its causes to political heights. He was a committed soldier of the party. He had been a resident of Manoor only for a few years, not making much headway with objectives for which he came to the village. Originally, he was from the coastal city of Kolazhi, far away in the North. Youngest son of a wealthy timber merchant, Abdutty Haji. Besides owning two lumber yards and three sawmills in the suburbs of the city, Abdutty also had year-round logging operations in the forests on the slopes and valleys of the Western Ghats. Abdutty, a tall and robust man with a carefully trimmed beard, tiny but sparkling slit like eyes, thick lips, brightly white teeth partially seen in between. He always wore a chequered *mundu* of taffeta like material, secured around his waist with a green belt, small leather wallets on either side of the buckle, his half sleeve shirt tucked in under the belt. Abdutty loved luxury, as he could afford it. He owned a Bentley, the only one in existence, not only in the entire city of Kolazhi, but also in the whole of the southern province. He had never driven the car; he preferred to sit next to the uniformed chauffeur, feeling that he not only owned the opulent automobile, but also the man at the wheel. His morning drives were, usually, to one of the lumber yards. Sitting in the tiny office there, he would watch the elephants lifting and stacking logs. Among the elephants, he was very fond of one in particular, a tusker named, Chief, a towering and imposing animal: long powerful tusks, the trunk grazing the ground, the expansive earlobes fanning gently, the massive body, dark as monsoon clouds. The Chief was the only animal that could respond to the mahout's command to salute Abdutty as his car entered the yard in the mornings. The tusker would raise his trunk way above his head, trumpet a few times before moving to the next log to hoist. Abdutty loved the gesture and the Chief. Nonetheless, he knew that he treasured the Bentley even more.

Abdutty was very proud of his youngest son, Hyder; especially, when he brought home prizes he won during the annual celebrations at his school; trophies for winning elocution competition, essay writing and debates. When he graduated from the school at the top of his class, Abdutty foresaw a very bright future for his son. He wanted to plan and provide everything needed for his ascension to stardom. Sending him to the right college, he thought, was of prime importance for Hyder to achieve his full potential.

It was late one morning when Abdutty knocked at Hyder's door upstairs at home. Seeing the door unlocked, he pushed open the door. Hyder was in his bed, sitting leaned against the headboard, reading. On a table next to his bed was a heap of magazines and newspapers haphazardly strewn around; against the wall close to a picture window was a book case laden with volumes, mostly in Malayalam with a sprinkling of books in English as well. Hyder raised his eyes for a moment to look at his father, and then went back to the book. Abdutty was enraged by his son's casual indifference to his presence in the room.

"Get up, you scoundrel; don't you know how to respect elders"

Abdutty raised his voice. It was considered highly impolite for youngsters to be seated in front of seniors. Hyder reluctantly alighted from the bed, stood leaning against the bed, a disparate expression of fear, dissent and dismay on his face.

"Have you completed the application for admission to the college?"

"No, I don't want to go to college"

"Why. Tell me" Abdutty was roaring,

"They are not going to teach me anything beyond what I could get from these books"

Pointing to the books on the bookcase, Hyder said under his breath. Abdutty was astounded by his son's impertinent response. However, decided not to have a dialogue with him; he was convinced it would have been futile with a juvenile like Hyder. An iron hand would bring forth much better results, he thought.

"Don't be an imbecile, start working on it right away, I want to see it done by the time I return from the yard in the evening"

It was an order, shouted, resolute. Hyder knew his father would be persistent and obstinate until he gets his way; there was no way he could have been dissuaded.

With much reluctance and total lack of enthusiasm, Hyder enrolled at the college of his father's choice. It was a college on a hilltop in the suburbs of Kolazhi, run by Carmelite fathers, a prestigious institution. Admission to the college was highly competitive. Nevertheless, Abdutty managed it for his son with his name recognition and the social standing in the city.

For Hyder, the first week at the college was uneventful. The mandatory classes he attended were mere drudgery, he felt. However, on Monday, the following week, there was an abrupt turn of events. When he came to his classroom, he found it difficult to find a seat for himself. The room as overflowing with students, he saw a few of them outside the windows, looking in. There was an air of anticipation in the room. Then, the whole class fell silent. The professor walked in: a slender man in his mid-forties, attired entirely in white. His *mundu* was of rough fabric woven on hand looms, so was his long tunic reaching all the way down to his knees. The hand-woven fabric was preferred by most followers of Gandhi. The Mahatma had advocated wearing clothing produced by village weavers to promote self-reliance, encourage rural industries. Hyder felt the professor was frail and weak. Nevertheless, when he started speaking, his voice was powerful and projectile, reverberating within the walls of the classroom. He was to lecture on a work by a well-known poet in Malayalam. He detailed the points one should look for in a poem to realize the aesthetic vision of the poet. Hyder was amazed at the ease with which he forayed into the Indian classics, Greek mythology, Shakespearian verses and Latin American literature to illustrate and illuminate his arguments.

As he was returning home after the day's classes, Hyder was preoccupied with the class he attended on Malayalam literature. The professor who taught the class had made an enormous impression on him. He had found out the name of the teacher: Vijay Kumar, popularly known among the students as ViKu. Socially, he was soft spoken and taciturn; once on the platform of the classroom, however, he transformed himself into an intellectual fountainhead, forcefully driving forth his ideas and arguments. In his talks, he restricted himself to literature and its ramifications, consciously trying not to slide into social or political themes. It was doubtful if all his students fully grasped the dimensions of the concepts he presented; they were, rather, enthralled by his torrential eloquence. They thronged to his classroom, often spilling into the hallways.

Hyder looked forward to the Monday lectures of ViKu. Indeed, he loved the professor's talks, but they also had generated many questions and comments in his mind. Nonetheless, he did not have the audacity to address them to the teacher. On one Monday, the students of ViKu' class were intrigued as he entered the class with a large reproduction of a post-impressionist painting by Paul Cezanne. He displayed the painting entitled, "Monte Sainte Victoire" on the chalkboard behind him, then he started to recite a new poem he was to present and deliberate in the class that day. As soon as he finished rendering the concluding stanza, he quickly went back to the painting, started to address the class:

"When you look at this work of art, you see the colors, lines and forms; nevertheless, in order to **experience** this painting, you have to go beyond the pigments, brush strokes and structural forms; a sensation, engendered by the material attributes of the painting, has to evolve in your inner self, the consciousness thus generated is unique and highly individualistic; it is true of poetry as well."

ViKu went on,

"So as to realize the aesthetic beauty of a poem, one should go beyond the written words and the imagery conjured up by the poet. However, these elements should be allowed to give rise to a perception in your responsive mind; then you might even be able ascend to the aesthetic heights of the poet himself. Though highly unlikely to be achieved, one could aspire for it without a shadow of guilt". ViKu had a playful smile on the corners of his lips as he finished the sentence.

Hyder was inspired as his teacher continued to talk, but ViKu's lecture, as usual, was spawning many questions and comments in his mind. At one point, he could not contain himself; he stood up, asked a question to the professor concerning the last few minutes of his talk. The whole class turned to Hyder, alarmed, amazed. It had never happened before; a student daring to ask a question to one of the most scholarly professors on the campus. They thought, Hyder was challenging ViKu. The teacher, however, spent the next ten minutes, expounding further the concepts he already talked about, enlightening, answering every aspect of Hider's query. For Hyder, it was a rite of passage in literary dialogue during every ViKu's classes that followed, Hyder stood up to ask questions, offer his comments. The overflowing class waited to witness the exchange between the professor and his favorite student. Outside the classroom, Vijay Kumar appeared aloof and austere to a degree. Whenever Hyder happened to meet him on the college corridors, their mutual recognition was restricted to a gentle nod of the head. One day, however, their formality and distance dissipated, seemingly unexpected. The life of Hyder also took a different turn that day. It was lunchtime at the college; Hyder was at the dining hall sitting at a table, alone. He had just opened the lunch his mother had packed for him. She had wrapped up everything first in heat-softened banana leaf, then again in a grey plastic wrap. In the pack was a whole flat fish fried in coconut oil, garnished with spices, *basmati* rice steamed in clarified butter, a teaspoonful of red hot mango pickle; the grains of rice at the periphery of the patch of pickle already having turned crimson red. The spicy aroma of Hyder's lunch had wafted in the air around. Even before he took the first morsel, Hyder saw ViKu emerging from the enclosure reserved for the faculty in the dining hall. He was puzzled as he saw the teacher walking towards his table. ViKu joined Hyder at his table, settling down on a chair across from Hyder.

"Your lunch smells very good, inviting"

ViKu said, a broad smile on his face, gone were the reticence, the diffidence. Without indulging in further niceties, ViKu asked his student,

"What are you usually busy with in the evenings?"

Caught unaware, Hyder was searching for an appropriate answer; but even before he could respond, not waiting for his reply, ViKu said with a trace of urgency,

"A few of us meet every night at a place near my home for discussions, explore new ideas; would you like to join us?"

Hyder was thrilled. He was being invited to join a group led by the teacher he admired most at the college, the one who never fails to inspires him by his depth of knowledge and oratory. Hyder did not have to ponder much to accept ViKu's invite.

When Hyder arrived at the address given him by ViKu, he saw a dilapidated building, no sign of light emanating from any of its openings. He had to grope in darkness to locate the entrance to the building. He entered a space he thought was a corridor, started to walk forward. In the darkness, he could hardly make out what was on either side of the passageway, but he moved on looking for the room ViKu had specified. Take a left after entering the hallway, turn right, then two turns again to the left, knock at the third door on the right, he had said. Hyder arrived at his destination in total darkness. He fumbled and felt the door, it was locked from inside. He knocked at the door. Someone opened the door. In the pale auburn light of a kerosene lamp, Hyder could see a group of six young men, their hair disheveled, cloths shabby. ViKu was talking, perched on a desk. Without interrupting his talk, he waved Hyder in. ViKu was not in the hand-woven white as Hyder had always seen him in. He wore only a multicolored *mundu* and a sleeveless undershirt. He was talking in a low voice; nonetheless, the eloquence and potency of his words were just the same as they were in the classroom. Before the day's session ended, Hyder realized ViKu was taking a class on Marxism-Leninism, an antithesis to Gandhian philosophy, the pacifist's non-violent approaches to struggle. Hyder attended every session that followed. He was, soon, beguiled by the Marxist ideology. He was convinced of the leftist credo, conceivably fostered by the powerful presentations by ViKu and Hyder's considerable admiration for his teacher. As the study class progressed, however, ViKu, started to talk about armed struggle to overthrow governments, he had enlivened his words with added vigor and urgency. That was a turning point for Hyder in his exploration of Marxism. By nature, he was averse to violence, perhaps influenced by the residual effects of his early exposure to the pacifist literature by Emerson, Thoreau and others. He challenged many of ViKu's assertions in the class, questioned the tenets he expounded on the exigency of violent conflicts. Their contentious arguments and counter arguments made the sessions tense, unpredictable. ViKu grew more and more uncomfortable, intolerant of Hyder's interjections. Sensing the snowballing discomfiture between the teacher and himself, Hyder became increasingly infrequent to the nightly study classes before finally exiting the sessions altogether.

Hyder continued to see Vijay Kumar during his classes at the college; the same hand woven white attire, the same cogent rhetoric. Hyder, however, could see through ViKu's pretentions: the rough ivory clothing, his occasional references to pacifist ideas in his lectures. They were all part of a concerted effort to conceal his membership in a wing of the Marxist party, advocating armed insurgency as a mean to capture political power. ViKu knew the college authorities would not tolerate him to be among the faculty with the genre of party affiliations he had. The police, if they get the scent of his political persuasions, would chase him to his hidden away night classes. Hyder wondered if ViKu felt exposed in his presence. ViKu's conduct in the class, however, did not betray any self-consciousness. The dialogues between Hyder and his teacher were unaffected by their falling apart at the study class. Hyder strongly disagreed with ViKu's advocacy for armed conflicts; nonetheless, admired his analytical competence, his incisive arguments when the subject matter was literature.

Even before attending the study classes by ViKu, Hyder was a sympathizer of leftist ideology, mainly resulted from his widespread reading. The compelling presentations by ViKu, however, consolidated the socialistic thoughts in his mind, helping him to embrace Marxism as an effective means for societal change, though he had rejected the view that armed struggle is indispensable component of the transformation.

On a Friday afternoon, as he was returning from college, Hyder decided to visit the local communist party office. At the mouth of a narrow pathway between two buildings, a hoard of small signboards hung together haphazardly. They seemed to be jostling for dominance, but helplessly clung to each other, swinging gently in the wind. Among them were a sign for a tailoring shop, a document writer, a teashop, a used bookseller and stuck amongst the cache was a deep red sign heralding the Communist Party of India. All the businesses were strung along the two sides of the constricted alleyway; the party office was at the very end of the lane. As Hyder entered the office, it had a deserted look; no one at the solitary front desk, but he heard footsteps in an adjacent room. Soon, someone came to the front office, the person did not say much in a way of greeting but looked at the visitor askance. Hyder, instantly, recognized the face; he recollected him as one of the six young men at ViKu's night classes; the one who, from time to time, nodded his head in agreement when Hyder put forward some of his views contradicting ViKu's arguments. His name was Pratap, the local secretary of the party. Pratap, cautious and guarded, took some time before admitting his association with the night classes. Hyder spent a few hours with Pratap discussing Marxism, politics and ViKu's extremist thinking.

Hyder had a feeling he had found an ally in Pratap. In a number of conceptual areas, he recognized, their views were congruent. One can strive for workers' rights, remedy their grievances through democratic means, they both believed. Pratap had been active in the party for a few years. The long discussions with him prompted Hyder to be more involved in the party ventures. After the college classes every day, Hyder found himself at the party office, before returning home late at night. Motivated by Pratap, he visited small businesses in town, talking to the workers trying to make them aware of their rights, draw them to the party fold. He even participated in a few demonstrations in front of factories.

Abdutty and his wife had not missed noticing Hyder coming home very late at night, frequently missing at the family dinner. Hyder, however, had a convincing alibi: group study with classmates. Nevertheless, on a Monday morning, everything he had been striving to conceal from his father laid bare right in front of Abdutty. His Bentley was about to reach the front gate of one of his saw mills. He saw a group of men in a perfectly disciplined line, ferociously throwing their clenched fists into the air, shouting slogans. As he drove along the line of demonstrators, he could recognize many of them as his own workers, their slogans targeted at him and the managerial staff, admonishing, demanding pay hikes, benefits. As his car reached the head of the march, he could not believe what he saw, he was out of himself at the sight: Hyder abreast with two others in front of the rally, holding aloft a red flag, the insignia of sickle and hammer on the flag playing hide and seek in the wind.

That night when Hyder came home, it was very late; when he went up to his room to rest, he found the bedroom locked from outside. His collection of books thrown in a heap in one corner of the passage, his cloths and other possessions in another heap next to the books. He was very tired and exhausted, he did not try to figure out what might have happened; he badly needed to sleep. He laid himself on a long wooden bench in the passage, untied his *mundu*, with it covered himself head to toe. He fell asleep, almost instantly.

It was nearing eight in the morning. Hyder felt someone pushing his left shoulder harshly, shouting,

"Get up, you, scoundrel"

Hyder opened his eyes; his father was staring down at him, his face aflame with rage, his eyes reddened,

"How could you do this to your own father, to your own family"

Abdutty was roaring at the top of his voice; Hyder sat up, collected and tied up his *mundu*, he silently looked at his father, not even trying to answer him.

"Someone trying to undermine his own family has no place under my roof, I don't want to see you in this house by the time I return in the evening,"

Abdutty bellowed his judgement.

"If I do" he continued, "I would finish you up, mark my word"

Abdutty stormed down the stairs, stomping down on every step.

Hyder took a bath, had breakfast served by his mother. By midday he left the front door of his house, a plastic bag of books in his right hand, a bag of cloths in the left. He did not look at his mother at one of the windows, watching him moving away, tears in her eyes.

Hyder had no place except the party office to go for a shelter. Pratap was disturbed to hear what had taken place at Hyder's home, but was not surprised, as if it was already anticipated. He offered the small room behind the front office for Hyder to occupy.

Hyder had to quit the college; he did not have the money for paying the fees. Living at the party office, he participated in every activity of the party with fervor and total dedication. He was always at the forefront of demonstrations, very active in fieldwork, talking to workers propagating the party, organizing strikes to wrestle workers' rights from factory management. Once he was sent to his former college to mobilize the students to form a union under the aegis of the party. He did not succeed in the effort; the students were totally refractive to him, the college administration barred him from setting foot again in the campus. Hyder, however, knew he was going to be back. When pursuing a goal, he was always doggedly persistent, almost to the point of obstinacy. This desirable quality in him had not escaped the notice of the higher ups in the party. They also knew of his total dedication to the party and his organizational skills. The party quickly recognized a role Hyder could effectively fill in. It was a time when the party was making efforts to foray into the remote areas of the state. The party had identified Manoor and the neighboring villages as a virtual political vacuum, a fertile ground for new concepts to take root. Hyder was sent on a mission to awaken the populace of these villages to the leftist ideology. Hyder arrived at Manoor with pent up energy, verve.

On a warm cloudy morning, Manoor woke up hearing loud drumbeats. It was a skinny man with a *chenda*, a large drum, hanging on the left side of his waist. He was striking the drum as he walked; after a few steps, he halted to read aloud a note in his hand. Villagers could hardly discern what he was reading, they rushed to the roadside to hear a little better. It was an announcement about the forthcoming Panchayat election: there are five members in the Panchayat council, the villagers are invited to nominate members to the council, the nominations should be submitted within a specified time period: fifteen days before the election. The drummer concluded the reading, resumed beating his drum. He moved along the road, repeating the announcement intermittently, limping a bit balancing the heavy drum.

Adhikari was the first to rush and submit his nomination papers; but he was rejected for a technical reason: disqualified as he was already on government payroll. One of the candidates was Manu, the elder son of the Nambi Vaidya; the entire village knew he was standing in for the Vaidya, widely respected and needed by everyone. Manu was unopposed; so was the three other candidates. No one wanted to challenge them, they too were liked and well regarded in the village for various reasons. The fifth candidate drawing everyone's attention and curiosity was Hyder. He was the only one representing a political party, a party most in the village did not particularly like or knew about. Hyder, however, was very enthusiastic, energetic. He campaigned hard as he had an opponent: the parish sexton's second son, Andrew. It was ideology that drove Andrew to oppose Hyder, he had had stood up to him in every way he could ever since Hyder appeared on the village scene. He wanted to prevent the imported ideology of Marxism contaminating Manoor.

Hyder held campaign rallies and meetings almost every day. The locations were those already familiar to him: the vacant space with a rundown masonry wall across from Aputty's grocery and the open meadow next to the temple pond. He did not have an overflowing audience, nevertheless, a few people did come in to listen, mostly drawn in by his gravel voice. They were mesmerized by the fire in his words, his interlinked sentences flowing effortlessly, concluding in a crescendo. Many of them hardly grasped fully the ideas he presented, his admonitions, invectives and war cries. They, however, relished the dramatics of his speeches.

Andrew was challenged by the frequent campaign speeches by Hyder. He, however, was not adept at public speaking. Shy and introverted, he dreaded the exercise. But it became a necessity, he had to plunge into it to make an impression upon the voters. His friends and supporters encouraged him, prompted him. The first gathering he addressed was at the open space adjacent to the temple pond. He sounded inspired, he had passion, had strings of anti-Marxist arguments. Nevertheless, he stumbled upon them, stammered as he expressed them uncontrolled, gushing. A few among the listeners, in the back of the assembly, jeered. It did not take too long before the audience to disperse and go home, leaving Andrew mortified on the podium, closeted by his ardent supporters.

Not cowed down by his first experience with public speaking, Andrew and his cadre of backers held a campaign rally, again at the meadow next to the temple pond. This time, he was better prepared, well-practiced. His sentences were unhampered, flowing effortlessly with a certain degree of rhythm. Andrew seemed to engage his audience. Suddenly, there was commotion at the far-left periphery of the gathering. A dog, medium sized, brown body mottled with white blotches, rushed into the crowd, sprinted through the throng. Two or three men pursued the dog, throwing stones at it shouting, "Mad Dog! Mad Dog!". The stones hit someone among the spectators. The people panicked, scattered, running away from the scene as quickly as they could. Andrew was left again at the rostrum dismayed, viewing the meadow in front of him devoid of a single living soul. His followers huddled around him. It was a crude election devilry played on them by Hyder and his comrades, they quickly concluded.

The election results were as predicted by many. The one who generated the loudest din and stir prevailed. Hyder won the contest with a slight edge over the number of votes Andrew garnered. Though he was vanquished, Andrew found a reason to be gratified: the number of votes he received was very close to the number his socialist opponent netted; it was also a clear indication that a substantial segment of the Manoor villagers held anti-Marxist views.

The newly constituted Panchayat did not have a space to assemble. In the evenings, when classes were over, they made use of the village elementary school for the purpose. During the first meeting, most of the time was spent selecting the president of the Panchayat. The majority of the council, nominated Manu for the position. Hyder, however, bitterly opposed the proposal, claiming the presidency for himself. He was the only one truly elected by the people of the village, he argued. Nonetheless, the rest of the council did not relent; they proposed a vote among themselves: Manu verses Hyder. Manu received the majority of the votes. Hyder had no other recourse than to accept the majority decision.

During the next few meetings of the Panchayat, the members discussed the various developmental projects to be undertaken in Manoor. However, they stumbled and woke up to a disturbing reality: The Panchayat has no funds to carry out the planned projects. The body had not started collecting taxes; they were yet to formulate a framework for the purpose. However, there was someone who had been collecting taxes year after year: Adhikari. The Panchayat, Manu suggested, could demand the taxes collected so far that year, to be transferred to the new governing body of the village, the Panchayat. Everyone knew it was a difficult proposition to put into practice. Adhikari angrily refused to comply. The nascent village body wrangled with him for many days without making any headway. Finally, the Revenue Officer from the district headquarters had to intervene. Adhikari relented, handed over the funds to the Panchayat.

The money extracted from Adhikari was not anything substantial; not enough to finance a major project like the road repair. The members of the Panchayat discussed at length, how the finite amount of money could be utilized, but could not come to an agreement. Then, Manu got up and gave a short pep talk,

"We established a Panchayat; but, how many in the village know about this body that sprang up among them in the village, do they know we are here for their benefit, we are working in isolation. We have to do something to make our presence felt in the village, however symbolic it might be, everyone in the village should recognize we are here for the village"

He concluded his speech inviting suggestions from the five-member council. Everyone put forward their individual ideas including one from Hyder to provide free lunch for school children. Nevertheless, none could secure unanimous approval. Varkey was a member nominated from the eastern region of Manoor, an unassuming middle-aged man sitting uncomfortably on a short bench originally meant for tiny tots. Silent most of the time, but he closely followed the proceedings of the Panchayat. He got up, proffered his suggestion: install a street light at the junction of the main road and the ditch road at Manoor; the name of the Manoor Panchayat could be inscribed at the pedestal of the light; no one could miss the streetlight and the etching at the base, he added. The proposal gained universal acceptance among the Panchayat members, especially Manu, the president.

Before long, the solitary streetlight of Manoor came into existence at the junction where the ditch road met the main road.

# Fourteen

More than the streetlight itself, there was a character the villagers invariably associated with the light: Velai. Along with the installation of the streetlight, came his appointment as the lightman, the one and only employee of the Panchayat. He was the one who kept the light lit at night, doused it at dawn. Every day at dusk, he could be seen walking towards the streetlight, a short ladder in his right hand, a can of kerosene in the other. As he walked with a gentle swinging of his right hand, the ladder creaked rhythmically. At the green streetlight, he leaned the ladder on the pole, climbed to reach the light, opened the glass door, ascertained there was enough fuel in the reservoir, lit the wick and dismounted the ladder. He repeated the exercise in the morning, this time, however, to extinguish the kerosene lamp.

It was an unusually hot and sweltering morning. Velai found it uncomfortable to be lazy in the bed and daydream, as he usually does. He got himself ready, reached the streetlight earlier than usual. Pre-dawn darkness was still lingering around the village. The kerosene lamp in the streetlight remained lit, throwing its weak rays on to the immediate periphery. As Velai tried to rest his ladder against the light post, he was taken aback noticing someone sitting at the base of the streetlight, leaning against the cement pedestal. On a second look, he realized it was Muthoma. Ignoring Muthoma for a while, Velai rested his ladder a bit away from Muthoma, got busy with his routine of putting off the oil lamp, cleaning the glass case around it. At daybreak, as the slanting sun rays illuminated the streetlight and the surroundings, Velai tried to wake up Muthoma, but to no avail. He appeared to be in a deep slumber; his eyes close shut, a short ***mundu*** tied around his waist, Muthoma's hairless torso, plumb and fair, appeared exposed and bare.

Velai hung around Muthoma some more time; he did not feel it right to leave someone he knew for many years in the state he found him in. Added to that altruistic feeling was a degree of curiosity as well. He was walking around, keeping an eye on Muthoma. After a while, suddenly, he saw Muthoma's lips moving. Eyes still closed, he was saying something Velai could not understand, it was a language foreign to him. Then he saw Mathai coming along the ditch road. He wondered for a moment why Mathai was going to his cloth store at this early hour, but he quickly squashed that thought as irrelevant. He waited for Mathai to come closer, he wanted Mathai's help to understand what Muthoma was whispering. Hearing Muthoma for an instant,

Mathai said with a eureka expression,

"It is English!"

"We should get Devassy here, only he could understand this"

Even before he finished his sentence, he ran to Devassy's house, nearby. Devassy, excited and curious, came to the scene in haste, listened to Muthoma, now reciting a little louder,

All the world's a stage,

And all the men and women merely players:

They have their exits and their entrances;

And one man in his time plays many parts,
His acts being seven ages. At first the infant,
Mewling and puking in the nurse's arms.
And then the whining schoolboy, with his satchel,
And shining morning face, creeping like snail
Unwillingly to school. And then the lover,
Sighing like furnace, with a woful ballad
Made to his mistress' eyebrow. Then a soldier,
Full of strange oaths, and bearded like the pard,
"Shakespeare"

Devassy exclaimed. The language, the rhythm, the form, unmistakably Shakespearian; nonetheless, he could not place the verse in the Bard's voluminous oeuvre. Muthoma was vocalizing Shakespeare with a peculiar accent, it was neither British nor Indian. Perhaps, it was the archaic intonation of Shakespeare himself, Devassy fancied. All the more exhilarated and puzzled, he hurried home, came back with an anthology of Shakespeare's works. He had located the verse in "As you Like It", he had marked the page. He wanted to compare Muthoma's recital with the printed verse. Muthoma, however, had moved on; he had started rendering something else in a mysterious language Devassy could not comprehend. He waited almost two hours hoping Muthoma would recite Shakespeare again; but it did not happen. Disappointed, nevertheless, deeply interested in the phenomenon he witnessed in Muthoma, he went home.

When Velai came to tend the streetlight next morning, he found Muthoma in the same position he saw him the day before. In front of him was a brass tray with banana peels, an empty silver tumbler with traces of milk. Velai gently touched his shoulder, in an effort to wake him, but no response. Muthoma started to murmur again, his eyes still shut. Velai was puzzled beyond words. Then he heard footsteps approaching, it was Devassy with a small stool in his hand. Settling down on the seat placed close to Muthoma, Devassy intently strained to hear Muthoma's utterances, but, was again confronted with a language exiting Muthoma's mouth, even more bizarre than the one he heard the previous day. Notwithstanding the incomprehension, he persisted with patience. All of a sudden, Devassy recognized Muthoma switching the stream of words to a language, he thought, was Latin. He had only a smattering of the classical lingo, utterly inadequate to understand the contents of Muthoma's recital. However, he knew someone, eminently qualified, he thought, to decipher Muthoma's Latin stream of words. He was Fr. Roland, a Benedictine monk living a few miles away from Manoor. A Latin scholar, an expert on church history; he was living alone on a hillock, a hermit.

As Devassy climbed up to the top of the hill, he could see the surrounding landscape spread out below, extending to the valley and beyond, merging with the Emmau River in a verdant haze. As he walked up the narrow pathway to the hut, the hermitage, Fr. Roland was hard at work in his vegetable garden. A tall man in a slightly soiled cassock, appearing to be in his sixties; flowing beard, grey and grazing his chest; salt and pepper hair, long and unkempt. He greeted the visitor as he continued to pull out a head of cassava root from loosened earth. Devassy had met him once before, hoped the father remembered him. He welcomed Devassy to his retreat, an unassuming Spartan space: a cot at the far end, a wooden desk laden with books nearby. The most compelling presence in the room, however, was a large window opening to a farmstead. In the small piece of land, Devassy saw, a variety of plants and fruit trees growing densely brushing with each other. Right under the window a papaya plant bearing a cluster of fruits crowding around the stem. The yield from the little farm, Fr. Roland gave away to the villagers from far below; they came up regularly. They have gotten used to the freshness and purity of the vegetables from Fr. Roland's farm.

At the window, Devassy was admiring the green beauty of the farm, the plants swaying in the breeze. Fr. Roland came with a glass of vegetable juice,

"This is the elixir of nature, you would like it"

He said handing the drink to his visitor. While sipping the acrid juice, Devassy was trying to hide the scowl creeping on to his face, in spite of himself. While gulping the gluey extract, Devassy talked about Muthoma under the streetlight, his recital of passages from lofty works of literature in different languages; the languages came in a continuous stream, some known, others entirely outlandish. Devassy requested the father's help in comprehending one of his recent whispers in Latin. Initially, Fr. Roland was hardly enthusiastic about Devassy's request, his interest in the affair lukewarm; nonetheless, acquiescing to Devassy's persistent pleading, he agreed to come down to Manoor.

When Velai came early next morning, he found Muthoma remaining motionless, transfixed, his eyes closed shut, appearing to be in a deep meditation. In front of him was the brass platter with a few banana peels, an empty glass, a few fruits, uneaten. As Velai was on the ladder attending the kerosene lamp, Devassy came with two stools in his hand; he was expecting Fr. Ronald to walk up any time, as he had promised.

Devassy saw Fr. Ronald coming along the main road, a cleaner cassock, the hair and beard fluttering in the morning breeze. The priest was carrying a basket on his shoulder held in place by his right hand. The basket, fresh vegetables and fruits from his farm, was a gift for Devassy. Devassy placed the tripods in front of Muthoma, he settled on one of the seats, the priest on the other next to him. They were on a vigil to observe Muthoma from close, waiting to hear the Latin utterances to escape his mouth. Muthoma, nevertheless, was silent, still as a statue. Minutes went by, then abruptly they saw his lips moving, heard him saying something unintelligible to either of them. Stupefied, they looked at each other. Was he verbalizing the stream of his conscience, Devassy wondered, but why on earth in such inexplicable languages. Muthoma, in a low voice, was speaking in a steady stream, shifting from one peculiar language to other at unpredictable intervals. Unexpectedly, as Devassy and Fr. Ronald were on the verge of being weary, in the clutter of the tongues from Muthoma, a strand of words stood out, the father instantly recognized it as Sanskrit. Devassy too, did not have difficulty identifying it. Nonetheless, neither of them could understand the ancient classical language. Fr. Ronald came up with a quick suggestion: they should seek the help of Narayana Bhattathiri, an authority on Indian classical languages, particularly, Sanskrit; nevertheless, a recluse, unapproachable. Fr. Ronald, however, was confident he could meet him, request his help. He had met him a few times in the past. He left for Bhattathiri house in a haste.

Narayana Bhattathiri lived in a large antiquated house close to the village temple. Ordinarily, he hardly came out of the house. The villagers do not see him for weeks and months at a time. For many, he was non-existent. Nevertheless, he was well known among the scholastic circles specializing in ancient languages. He was recognized for his seminal treatise on the subject, exclusively brought out by an obscure publisher, perhaps once in several years. His entire life was devoted to the study of the origins of Sanskrit; its influence on other Indian languages. He spent his entire waking hours confined to his large study in the right-hand corner of his house. Even his immediate family, his wife and three children, did not see him for days.

As Father Roland entered through the gate totally assembled in bamboo, he saw Bhattathiri house at the end of a sandy walkway. A large structure, dilapidated in some parts. He could not see anyone or anything moving around the house, an eerie silence pervaded. As he was searching for a door to knock at, a figure appeared at the courtyard next to one side of the house, shriveled and hunched with old age, a wrinkled face, large protruding eyes.

"What do you need? There is no one in the house"

The priest immediately knew, it was an instructed lie.

"I am here to see Bhattathiri; I am a friend of him"

"He does not see anyone"

The lie was partially unraveled. Fr. Ronald scribbled his name on a piece of paper, requested the old man to take it to his master. The man reluctantly took the piece of paper, disappeared into the house. Within a few minutes, the elderly man returned, smiling toothlessly, a trace of guilt on his face

"Thirumeni would see you, he is waiting for you," he said.

He opened the door wider, welcomed Fr. Ronald in. The old man led him through a stuffy, long corridor to a closed door; wide and ornate, intricate wood carvings on both shutters of the door. The man pushed open the door to a spacious room, the musty air was more intense in the room than in the corridor. Fr. Ronald was amazed looking around the room. The walls were covered with shelves stacked with volumes of books, reaching up to the ceiling. One of the smaller bookcases was set apart for manuscripts handwritten on palm leaves, tied and bundled together in volumes. A long bookcase right in the middle of the room, practically divided the room into two. He could see a few volumes on the floor, some of them left wide open. Fr. Ronald could not see or hear Bhattathiri anywhere in the room. The old man, then, led him to the other side of the dividing bookshelf. The scholar was sitting on a grass mat leaning on an overstuffed cushion, barrel shaped and faded. Small stacks of books around him, a legal pad and pen next to him. He was in a *mundu*, his hairy upper body exposed; short, partially grey beard bristled on his chin. Bhattathiri looked at the father through his thick-lensed glasses,

"I have not seen you for a long time,"

Bhattathiri said pointing to a chair, asking the priest to sit down.

After a few pleasantries, Bhattathiri pointedly asked the father,

"What brings you here today?"

Fr. Ronald briefed him of what was happening at the foot of the streetlight at the junction; multilingual utterings of Muthoma, especially his mutterings in Sanskrit. He requested him to come and decipher them. Bhattathiri was intrigued, nevertheless not overtly excited.

"I shall be there in time"

Encouraged, Fr. Ronald hurried back to the junction where Devassy was awaiting him. As he was walking back, he pondered about Bhattathiri last words – what did he mean by "in time"? Devassy, sitting close to Muthoma, was intently listening to him; so far, he could hear, as before, only a jumble of esoteric mumblings. Fr. Ronald joined him in the vigil. It was only a few minutes since the father had returned, he was surprised to see Bhattathiri at a distance, walking towards them. He was attired entirely in black, a charcoal black *mundu*, a shawl of the same color cloaking him from head to toe. Bhattathiri joined Devassy and the priest listening to Muthoma. Not too many minutes elapsed, Muthoma broke into the Sanskrit verse they were waiting for. Is this what Bhattathiri meant by "in time"? Was he able to break into Muthoma's malfunctioning subconscious, overtaken by an avalanche of world languages and quotes from each? Fr. Ronald thought to himself. As soon as he heard Muthoma speaking the words softly, but with utmost precision and clarity, Bhattathiri cried out,

"It is a passage from "Bhagavad Gita", the cream of Mahabharata"; the stanzas 11 to 16 to be precise".

Then he went on reciting the whole verse, in the original Sanskrit; he, then, translated them into English,

"Thy tears are for those beyond tears; and are thy words, words of wisdom?

The wise grieve not for those who die – for life and death shall pass away.

Because we all have been for all time: I, and thou, and those kings of men.

And we all shall be for all time, we all for ever and ever.

As the spirit of our mortal body wanders on in childhood, and youth and

old age, the spirit wanders on to a new body: of this the sage has no doubts.

From the world of senses, Arjuna, comes heat and comes cold, and

pleasure and pain.

They come and they go: they are transient. Arise above them, strong soul.

The man whom these cannot move, whose soul is one, beyond pleasure and

pain, is worthy of life in Eternity."

"Where did he get this prowess, this flawless diction, this unfailing memory of each line?"

Bhattathiri wondered aloud.

"Some would have sought an explanation in terms of the occult; certainly, I am not going to indulge in that"

"Maybe he is possessed by a benevolent ghost, I am ready to give you that."

Bhattathiri said good humoredly, laughing.

By this time, a small crowd had gathered around, wondering what was taking place at the streetlight; they were drawn by Bhattathiri shrouded in completely black clothing. He had joined Devassy and Fr. Ronald carefully listening to Muthoma, eagerly awaiting a discernible passage to drop out of his mouth. Unexpectedly, to everyone's surprise, Muthoma started to declaim, this time in chaste English, little lauder than usual,

"The seeker after truth should be humbler than the dust. The world crushes the dust under its feet, but the seeker after truth should so humble himself that even the dust could crush him. Only then, and not till then, will he have a glimpse of truth."

"These are Mahatma Gandhi's words"

Someone among the small group of spectators shouted. The one who yelled, dashed towards Muthoma, folded his hands together in a prayerful disposition, remained there motionless, overcome with emotion. Everyone knew Kesu Nambeeshan; he was an ardent follower of Mahatma Gandhi. He had taken part in the "Salt March", the historical civil disobedience movement led by the Great Soul, protesting British rule in India. When Gandhi was assassinated, Nambeeshan fasted for many days, keeping an oath of silence. He led a near ascetic life, strictly adhering to the Gandhian principles. He wore only coarse homespun clothing, practiced stringent vegetarianism. Every morning he spent an hour at Charkha, the wheel, spinning yarn from natural cotton, a Gandhian practice to nurture self-reliance and discipline, foster inner peace and tranquility.

Hearing the exalted words of his idol and guru coming out of Muthoma's mouth, baffled Nambeeshan, inciting him at the same time to a meditative mood. Meanwhile, Bhattathiri had returned home, without drawing particular attention from anyone. Devassy and Fr. Ronald continued their vigil, paying close attention to every word and sound emerging Muthoma's mouth. Nevertheless, whatever they heard were beyond their comprehension, weird words and passages, sometimes long and tortuous. Initially, Fr. Ronald had only tepid interest in what was taking place at the base of the streetlight. After spending a few hours at the site, however, he got deeply involved in the phenomenon of Muthoma. He wanted to explore the linguistic aspects of Muthoma's whispers as deeply as he could. Having spent many hours as he had at the feet of Muthoma, without seeing any encouraging results, he could have slipped into disappointment, but he was persistent. Along with Devassy, he was attentive to every word Muthoma spoke, every sound and syllable came out of him. Then, utterly unexpectedly, Fr. Ronald heard a stream of words ringing from Muthoma, in a rhythm all too familiar to him. Muthoma was murmuring softly, but distinctly,

Beati pauperes spiritu, quoniam ipsorum est regnum caelorum.

Beati, qui lugent, quoniam ipsi consolabuntur.

Beati mites, quoniam ipsi possidebunt terram.

Beati, qui esuriunt et sitiunt iustitiam, quoniam ipsi saturabuntur.

Beati misericordes, quia ipsi misericordiam consequentur.

Beati mundo corde, quoniam ipsi Deum videbunt.

Beati pacifici, quoniam filii Dei vocabuntur.

Beati, qui persecutionem patiuntur propter iustitiam, quoniam

ipsorum est regnum caelorum

Beati estis cum maledixerint vobis et persecuti vos fuerint et

dixerint omne malum adversum vos, mentientes, propter me

"It is The Sermon on The Mount!"

Fr. Ronald called out to Devassy, his voice grave with reverence, his amazement tempered with disbelief. It was sundown; in the auburn rays of the setting sun, Fr. Ronald's white hair and beard took up a copper glow.

"Listen"

He said to Devassy, then he started to translate the Biblical passage he heard from Muthoma, verbatim,

"Blessed are the poor in spirit, for theirs is the kingdom of heaven.

Blessed are those who mourn, for they shall be comforted.

Blessed are the gentle, they shall inherit the earth. Blessed are those who hunger and thirst for righteousness, for they shall be satisfied................."

Muthoma continued to remain in the same position they saw him in the morning, eyes closed, his face serene, murmuring incessantly. Devassy and Fr. Ronald did not try to listen into what he was whispering, they knew none would be intelligible to them. Nevertheless, they were dumbfounded, could not stop wonder and speculate about Muthoma, his unexplainable exploits, his ability to handle multitude of languages, his phenomenal memory.

As dusk set in Manoor, Devassy picked up the two stools, started to walk home; Fr. Ronald promised Devassy that he would return the next morning. The happenings at the foot of the streetlight had intrigued him, they have captured his imagination, they have already become more than a curiosity for him.

The singular streetlight of Manoor should remain lit until six in the morning, every day; that was the edict of the Panchayat. However, Velai usually arrived at the streetlight junction by half past five, on most days. The road was desolate and dusky as he walked, carrying his short ladder and the can of kerosene. At the junction, he would sit on the cement pedestal of the streetlight, lit a **beedi**, smoking peacefully, keeping his mind vacant, waiting for 6 o'clock to strike. He, however, did not have a watch or a clock tower near around to look up. However, when the eastern horizon brightened up, when the slivers of morning cloud shimmered, he knew it was nearing six. Still, he waited for a flock of birds in the sky, five or six in number; they flew from east to west every day. When they appeared dipped in the optic gold of the rising sun, when they swished just above his head, Velai was certain it was 6 o'clock. This ingenious system never had failed him. He, then climbed up the ladder, went on with his routine, extinguishing the light, cleaning up the glass casing.

On that day, as he was walking towards the streetlight junction, Velai remembered Muthoma sitting at the base of the light, whispering in a language he never understood. He wondered if he was still there at the light as he was the previous day.

When Velai arrived at the streetlight junction, it was still dark; however, the immediate environs of the streetlight were dimly lit. The light, certainly, was not emanating from the feeble kerosene lamp on top of the pole, he knew. As he came closer, Velai saw Muthoma in the same position as he saw him the day before. In front of him were six candles, partly burned out, but still lit. The ground in front of him swept clean, the marks of the broom still visible in the sand. Next to the candles, a wicker basket brimful of fruits: a hand of bananas, guava fruits, mangos, a long slice of golden yellow jackfruit. The foreground of Muthoma was strewn with flowers and flower petals, a few coins glistening among them. A bunch of rice panicles heavy with ripened grains at the tip, rustled in the breeze. Away from the flowers and candles, a rooster, its legs tied together, noisily struggling to free itself. Muthoma was motionless and silent, his face placid and equable. He had ceased to mumble and mutter. His eyes closed shut; nonetheless, his eyelids were parted ever so slightly, almost to the breadth of a hair, exposing the white of his eyes as a thin line. On his thick lips, hint of a smile. The light from the candles played on Muthoma's face.

# Acknowledgements

During my early youth, I learned about the English language and literature more from my father than I did at my school. My father was an English teacher at a Catholic high school. Many an evening he used to review and teach me the works being followed at my school. Once, while discussing Perl S. Bucks' "Good Earth", he was very uncomfortable trying to explain to me the meaning of the word, 'concubine'; however, he achieved the objective without overstepping the confines of his perceived modesty. When I went to college at a distant city, my father insisted that I write home only in English which I did. Invariably, however, my letters came back with his corrections in red ink. I gratefully and affectionately remember his helping hands in my early forays into the English literature.

This novel would not have been completed without the help and cooperation of Sanjeewani my love, my wife. She was my critic and ardent promotor at the same time. Her encouragements sustained me during the long process of writing this novel. Her well-thought-out criticism and appreciation of each chapter when it was completed, prompted me to proceed to the next one with verve and enthusiasm. Her patience and assistance in myriad ways is thankfully acknowledged.

"A Village Under the Streetlight" was diligently edited by the Cambridge Editors of Boston. I thank for their professionalism, precision and time-bound execution of the assignment.

# About the Author

**Thomas Palayoor** is a cancer researcher and molecular geneticist by profession. In the United States, he has worked at the medical schools of the Ohio State and Yale universities. He has written short stories in the Indian language, Malayalam and received awards for his radio plays. Besides his active interest in creative writing, he also has a zeal for painting. His works are mostly abstractions in oil. He has held a one-man exhibition of his graphics in Belgium, a commercial success. He continues to pursue his passion to write and paint alternatively. "A Village Under the Streetlight" is his first novel. He lives with his wife in the Boston area.

www.ingramcontent.com/pod-product-compliance
Lightning Source LLC
Chambersburg PA
CBHW031420020726
47499CB00005B/1528